THE SMALL BOOK

Zina Rohan

Visit us online at www.authorsonline.co.uk

A Bright Pen Book

Copyright © 2010 Zina Rohan

Cover photograph by Frank Hurley:
Four Australian troops walking over duckboards, Flanders October 1917,
nla.pic-an23998557 (National Library of Australia)

British Library Cataloguing in Publication Data.
A catalogue record for this book is available from the British Library.

ISBN 978-07552-1230-9

Authors OnLine Ltd
19 The Cinques
Gamlingay, Sandy
Bedfordshire SG19 3NU
England

This book is also available in e-book format, details of which are available at www.authorsonline.co.uk

THE SMALL BOOK

By the same author

THE BOOK OF WISHES AND COMPLAINTS

THE SANDBEETLE

THE OFFICER'S DAUGHTER

For Darius with love – and thanks
for the best advice of all

From reviews of THE OFFICER'S DAUGHTER (Portobello, 2008)

'What a story, and what a heroine! Passion and pride, bravery and foolishness – it's all here.' *Isabel Allende*

'This is a huge book in every sense of the word: it is a tour de force, a wonderful novel which will stay with you for years. Very highly recommended.' *Historical Novels Review*

'*The Officer's Daughter* is a gem . . . a haunting quality saturates the story, a rawness reminiscent of *A Thousand Splendid Suns*, and like Khaled Hosseini's novel, it leaves you with a deeply felt sense of the powerlessness and arbitrariness of life adrift on the detritus of war. Part of this is due no doubt to the fact that at its core is a story wrapped around real people, which lends it a rare power and authenticity that lingers after the last page.' *Bookseller*

'This good, old-fashioned tale cries out for a screen adaptation.' *The Tablet*

'Rohan's work is quite simply fascinating, wholly gripping and a delight to read . . . We award Zina ten Bookmunch points.' *Bookmunch*

From reviews of THE SANDBEETLE (Flamingo, 1994)

'With her debut, *The Book of Wishes and Complaints*, Zina Rohan climbed so high that it seemed the only place for her writing to go was down. It is a tribute to her talents and nerve that her second novel, *The Sandbeetle*, floats even higher. Rohan is a teller of tales able to span years with one sharply etched scene, to hold a reader to events even while she is lifting them across the arc of a fable.' *Independent on Sunday*

'There is humour as well as pathos in Leo's sharply observant account. Rohan deploys powerful metaphors of assimilation: the chameleon merging instinctively with its background; the sandbeetle making its home in the most inhospitable of habitats.' *Times Literary Supplement*

'Rohan's clear, clean prose packs a cumulative punch. The beauty of her writing lies in her mastery of understatement. *The Sandbeetle* is a good story well told.' *Guardian*

'There is a quiet, trenchant elegance to Zina Rohan's prose which, together with a lurking sense of irony, strikes a rich, dynamic balance between coolness and warmth, darkness and light, comedy and outrage. *The Sandbeetle* is an engrossing, densely-textured narrative fabric, crafted from robust, affectionately acerbic characterisation, sharp-eyed attention to fine human detail – comic or poignant or both – and Rohan's understated but sure formal control over her lively, argumentative cast. Her astute compassion, her refusal either to judge or offer pat solutions, combine with this consummate story-telling skill to produce a novel which rewards you more the further you read.' *Scotsman*

From reviews of THE BOOK OF WISHES AND COMPLAINTS (Flamingo, 1992)

'*The Book of Wishes and Complaints* is such an accomplished novel it disdains the description of debut. In it Zina Rohan unwraps the pain of Czechoslovakia with delicate fingers of irony.' *Sunday Times*

'Zina Rohan shuns the grand gestures of much writing about Stalin's Europe to concentrate on regular low-level doses of irony, insight and charm. That may sound like faint praise, but many novels with twice the pretensions of this one will fail to deliver half as much.' *Observer*

'Rohan shares Kundera's piercing sense of irony but adds her own brand of warmth and humanity. From start to finish *The Book of Wishes and Complaints* is a novel of admirable wit and clarity.' *Times Literary Supplement*

'A sympathetic and unusually mature first novel which owes its life and realism to its author's ability to be both astute observer and compassionate insider, availing of some of the best elements of two literary traditions.' *Irish Times*

'Zina Rohan has a wonderful, often comic instinct for the everyday, the kind of domestic detail that tells us everything.' *Independent on Sunday*

'Emotions are described with unnerving clarity and you become totally involved with Hana's dilemmas. Cleverly, Rohan denies us the Hollywood happy ending, offering us a question mark instead. A compelling first novel.' *Time Out*

'A fine and darkly humorous first novel.' *Sunday Telegraph*

Part 1

1915

From the diary of Dr F. S. Mason (RMO)

... and they have told me to stand by for an early duty tomorrow. Unlike the ranks who have been told to prepare, I know what it is to be, and I quail.

15 July 1915

This has been a wretched business. They have made a murderer out of me and all of us who were present. If that unfortunate man, Private Miller, was innocent of the charge, and indeed even if he was not, I fear I may never again sleep easily in my bed, unsullied by what I witnessed and by what I have been party to. For all that I fell out to one side and crouched behind some shrubs, with, I have to say, the chaplain shaking beside me, I could neither block the sounds from my closed ears nor clear the image from my closed eyes. As we were marching to the designated spot, I tried to distract my mind by casting us as members of some amateur theatricals, each carrying the props suitable for his rôle. There were the ten men shouldering their rifles, a sergeant shouldering a pair of shovels for filling in the grave; there was the chaplain with his cross, the APM with his maps and pencils, the officer with his revolver, and I with a bandage and a scrap of white cloth in my pocket. Only the charged man walked unencumbered, slipping occasionally, as we all were, because the path was muddy under a gentle drizzle that has persisted these recent days, and the light still dim.

Not a man spoke, as there was nothing to be said, nor was there birdsong, since by this time of year nestlings have flown and the dawn chorus is stilled. The fine rain fell directly, no breeze or wind to disturb it, or shake the leaves on the branches. We heard our own footsteps and beyond, at some distance away, the ordinary sounds of a waking camp, shouts and whistling, and a part of a song.

Someone, I do not know who, had gone ahead, perhaps yesterday, and driven a post into the ground. When we rounded a bend and saw it there, we all faltered, every man of us, I am

3

certain, filled with dread. Had there been a lone tree or a sapling to which the accused man might have been tied it would not have struck us so horribly as did this stake, erected for the purpose, the site chosen at a distance someone had measured out from a strip of ground, more or less even, some twenty paces away.

The officer tied Private Miller's hands behind his back, led him across the ground to the post and instructed me to follow. I'm told that they often give a man a hefty drink or two beforehand so that his senses are dulled, but this fellow, so some of them said afterwards, was a teetotaller. What that meant to me was two things: that his mind would have been clear and his perceptions sharp, and that the men in the firing party came from among his own unit, else how should they have known he was not a drinker?

He was a small man – one of those many that I have seen who are undersized because they are undernourished, and who should not, in my opinion, have been found fit for service. The volunteers who are so proud to be on the King's business with a rifle in their hand have unfortunately among them eager runts, lacking in height, in teeth – and it would seem in wits. The charge was 'deserting while on active service', which he may indeed have done. But if he had intended to leave the field he ought at the least to have tried, as others have done with success as I should know, to create the impression that he was unfit for it. Egg white added to the urine, for instance, has induced me to believe a soldier was suffering from diseased kidneys and to have him discharged. And it was many months and some hundred Rankers declared unfitted for the corps and repatriated before I realised that an irregular heartbeat did not come from any failure in the organ but from ingested cordite. This man apparently did not have the intelligence to resort to such ruses, even though I think he did once come to see me complaining of dizziness and headache, for which I probably gave him some of the new Aspro. He now stood before me, grey in complexion, as well he might be, dry in the mouth and unable to swallow.

The officer asked him if he was ready and, although he can not possibly have been, the poor fellow nodded, which set his helmet wobbling so that without thinking he tried to put his hands up to straighten it again, but could not because they were tied. Then the officer nodded to me to do my part and I bent to pin against Private Miller's heart the piece of white cloth to act as target. After this I removed his helmet and wound round his eyes the blindfold that would shield him from the sight of what was to come, and also shield his executioners from any expression they might see in his eyes. Ultimately, all true expression is in the eyes. My duty done, I made my retreat as swiftly as I could with any dignity, and my place was taken by the chaplain whose murmurings could only be heard by the condemned man. When I turned again, there were the chaplain's lips opening and closing, and all that could be seen of Private Miller's face was his small chin, jutting somewhat as he listened. Rather too soon, I thought, the officer pulled him backwards until his body came to rest against the post, and a rope was passed through his bound arms and around the post several times.

A minute later the chaplain was beside me again, now mumbling to himself, although I could not say if it was still prayers, or curses for the situation in which he found himself. And indeed, in which I found myself. It could be argued that a chaplain can at least assure himself that he has helped a man's soul to be at peace and ushered him into everlasting life, perhaps even reasoning that, if this man's terror was such that he was prepared to bring his company into disrepute and himself be remembered only as a degenerate coward, then he was best out of this life and into the next one, and the sooner the better. But my concern is with the living, and it is a vile contravention of my professional oath to bring certain death to a healthy man, or at least to one not diseased, before his time. And while the chaplain's business is to care for the well-being of a human soul, and the commanding officer's to care for the well-being of his platoon, it is mine to give thought not only to the patient before me, but to his dependants as well.

Yet I have been given no information regarding this man, whether he has a wife and children, or aged parents, or siblings who rely on him, as so many have. What becomes of them now? No one knows nor considers it their concern for, after all, what becomes of those millions whose sons or husbands or fathers have fallen in the field of battle? But they, at least, may have campaign medals to display, and unsullied reputations to boast of, although in fact the man they grieve for may have died in some accident on the battlefield, or drowned, or drunk himself to death. So long as there is no document accusing a man of cowardice, then assuredly he was a hero.

I may not have been asked to take aim or pull a trigger, but it was I who pinned the patch of white over Private Miller's heart to direct the bullets, and then had to stand by in order afterwards to pronounce him dead, which as a matter of fact he was not, but was slumped over his holding ropes, his legs twitching, like a hare that has been run over by a motorcar. The officer then had to stride up and finish him off with a single shot from his revolver into the back of Miller's drooping head. I suspect this must be the case too often when a man is condemned to be shot and the firing party are detailed from his own company.

I imagine how they must rail at their sergeant when they are told; how they must plead to be excused. How they must offer to exchange their rations of rum if only he will let them off! But when their pleading comes to nothing, and the ten men are forced to tramp behind their comrade to the execution ground, is it any wonder then that, no matter how much it is explained to them that to be merciful they should aim for the heart and shoot true, they cannot. If they themselves rebel and cast away their rifles, in all likelihood they too would face Court Martial and stand condemned. So they fire wildly, some no doubt up into the air, and their target is then wounded like a renegade fox, but not killed until the officer delivers the *coup de grâce*. Then all of them return to their bivouacs, vomiting.

And to which of them is it any comfort that they handed their rifles over to the officer so that, behind their turned backs, one of them might be loaded with blanks? There is not a trained serviceman who cannot tell the difference as the shot is fired, because the recoil of a blank is softer. What is more, in order to know, that shot has to be fired, the trigger pulled. Even if a man knows that his weapon carried the blanks, he knows it only after he has fired, so that in his intent, in his obedience – that quality so necessary in a soldier, especially of the ordinary ranks – in his own estimation he is as much a culprit as are his colleagues who fired the real bullets.

Now they may think their company is twice disgraced: first

by the man's cowardly desertion which has left a gap in the ranks and jeopardised the safety of the men around him, something which of course cannot be tolerated, for as it is said, if a private soldier were shown toleration for declining to face danger, then all the qualities which we would desire in a fighting man would be debased and degraded; but they are also disgraced, I believe, by being made into executioners.

I understand that these things should be done, but let those in command who hand down the sentence of death also carry it out. For a commander-in-chief who is accustomed to sending large numbers of men to their deaths, as it is his duty to do and theirs to obey, it may be no great burden to add another name to his list. How different it is for a soldier to have to take aim at one of his own in cold blood. I fear these men will be plagued by nightmares in the weeks ahead, and for myself, as I look at the clock in the light of my candle, I dread giving myself up to sleep.

When it was all over and they had rolled the corpse into the grave they had made ready, the APM noted down the map reference so that, as he put it, there'd be no more scuttling away. Then he turned to me and remarked, with unwonted cheerfulness it seemed, that I should prepare to do this again as there would undoubtedly be the need. 'I thought,' I retorted, 'that these things are done in the interests of discipline and as an example.' 'Did you indeed?' he said, bestowing on me a pitying smile. 'But when a man's in such a funk, do you think he gives a d*** about another man's example?'

Part 2

1946

Pam

I knew they had to be inside because there was that much rain out, so when they didn't answer I kept on banging at the door, then waiting, then banging again. Called through the letterbox a couple of times. A woman across the landing must have heard me because she opened her door just when I was bent over with my nose in the letterbox. 'You won't get anything from them,' she said. 'There's something not right in there. Ever since –' 'I know,' I said. 'They're family.' 'Oh,' she said, recognising me when I stood up. She waited a moment, but when I shut my mouth she made a face, annoyed and disappointed, and closed her door again, sharpish.

I gave the shouting another go. 'Come on, then, our Roy. It's your Aunty Pam. Come along and open up the door.' I had this feeling he was right there, listening, and thinking, the way he does, when you never know if he's going to do what you want or the opposite. Then suddenly I heard him having a struggle with the key, him being only a little lad, small for his age, and small anyway. We're built small, our side of the family.

When Roy opened the door the smell nearly knocked me down and I thought, what's their mother doing? But I had a fair idea and just said, 'I expect the two of you could do with a good scrub', and walked past him to look for his sister, young Margaret that they all call Mig, because it's what she called herself when she wasn't able to say her own name the first days she tried. Spitting image of her brother, she is. You'd think they were twins except for the age difference. They've both got this mousy hair that stands up like a wire brush, and scratchy voices the kiddies on the street mostly have. He's ten and she should turn eight in a few months, poor lass, too young to understand – properly, I mean, what was going on when their mother woke up and found her husband dead in the bed beside her.

Only thirty-one was our Bill, but his heart must've been older. Worn out, the doctor said, before its time. I thought it was worn out with too much loving, and all of it for his wife. I've said to

Mr Pollitt, more than once, 'Those two, my brother and Annie, they love each other so much they don't even notice they've got children at all. They might as well be orphans, Roy and Margaret, for the attention they get from their mother and father.' I don't know why I bothered saying it because Mr Pollitt had been able to see the truth of that as well as anyone, better than most in fact, but all he said was, 'I should have liked to love my wife as much as that.'

When they sent round from the school to say Roy and Margaret hadn't been seen in two weeks and there was no answer from Mrs Hoskins, even though the teacher had written *and* gone round and tried to get in, I told Mr Pollitt and he said of course I should get over there straightaway. 'You do what you have to, Pam,' he said. 'Whatever it is. Find out what's going on and set it right, and if we have to manage without you for a while, well, we will. After all, it won't be the first time, will it? And don't worry about your wage. If the Party can't look after its own when they hit bad times, it has no business being in business.' That's one of his sayings, and it tickles him. The theorists like Mr Dutt hate it, of course. But then, he's not English, I suppose, so he's not pragmatic. He hasn't got the English common sense Mr Pollitt always says we need so much.

It's all ideas with Mr Dutt – and only ideas. When Mr Pollitt said we should have racing tips in the *Daily Worker*, years ago this is, you should have heard Mr Dutt going on about taking things seriously and the importance of the purity of belief, as if he was a church minister who had people wanting to dance in the aisles! He can be a hard man, and there've been many times when they've come head to head. But that's by the by.

After Roy let me in I found Margaret under the kitchen table with her little legs up round her ears, playing at being invisible like a tortoise in its shell or, since it was Margaret, like a hedgehog rolled up to show its prickles. She stank as bad as her brother. 'Come on out, love,' I said. 'It's your Aunty Pam.' But she didn't move. She might just as well have been deaf. 'I'll get you your tea,' I said. 'You'd like your tea, wouldn't you?' Nothing. Roy was standing next to me, breathing hard, not a word from him, and I had this feeling he was enjoying watching me not getting the little one out of her hidey hole. So I thought to myself, it can't carry on like this. They're all sad and upset, we're all of us sad and upset, but it can't carry on like this. They've got to be told what's what and who's who. So I got down on my knees, bent under that table, grabbed hold of Margaret round her legs and dragged her out. I'll say that for her, she didn't change her position but stayed stiff and rolled up like she was glued up in a little ball.

'All right,' I said. 'That's step one. Step two next.' Although for the life of me I wasn't sure what that was to be. I could heat the copper for the water to give them both a bath or take a look in the cupboards to see what food there was. Or go into the bedroom to take a look at Annie. There's folk who'll say I should have done that first of all, but I thought my first duty was to those children, never mind that their mother has always made me feel uncomfortable.

There's things should be known about Annie. From what I heard, she used to hang about whenever the branch in Openshaw had Party meetings and gatherings, looking out of place – like a visitor come to gawk, which is what she was, I suppose. Only showed up to make eyes at our Bill, it was said. Her folk aren't like ours. She grew up in a big house on the edge of town with her own bedroom. She went to one of the private schools for girls where they wore uniforms. And it's always been my belief that she went with Bill to spite her parents, to shock them, really. Well, it did shock them and it was talked around that they didn't speak to her for three months. Bill was just twenty-one at the time, but Annie wasn't yet twenty so her parents could've put a stop to it. But you got the feeling they didn't dare. They'd spoiled her so much they didn't dare. I always thought that was their weakness. If they were so much against it they could have put their expensive feet down and saved us all a lot of trouble. They could have made the lass wait a year or two and who knows, she might have changed her tastes in the time. Or our Bill might – though I don't think so.

In the end I expect they gave in because she told them she wasn't going to give up her 'one true love', not now and not ever. But even though they came to the wedding, they hadn't put a penny towards it, or a thought into it, no matter it should be the bride's family's do. No matter they were rolling in it. So my mother said, 'Let them be sour if that's what they're like. We don't need their money anyway. I'm only sorry for our Annie,' she said, 'growing up with folk like that.' And she started setting money aside for the wedding breakfast, little bit by little bit. But when they rolled through the door, Mr and Mrs Delahaye (the only Delahayes north of Nottingham), you could see they thought it was a poor do. They probably had the spread Mother and Father had put on every day, and thought it was ordinary.

After that I said to Bill he should come down to London with his wife, and leave those folk behind. I'd ask Mr Pollitt, I said. He gave me my first job here as stenographer in King Street, so he might do something for Bill. And he did, on the *Daily Worker*, because our Bill had already made a bit of a name for himself as a union activist in the locomotive works at Gorton Tank in Openshaw, just like Mr Pollitt before him.

But about Annie. Now I'm not saying she didn't sincerely love our Bill. She did. That's the trouble. She loved him too much, and he loved her too much so that he forgot everything else. All through the hard times when there was enough to be doing and no time and no money, the trouble he'd go to, to get her the tasty little things she craved was like nobody's business. When she was expecting, and wanted cherries too early in the year, he got them for her. Never said how or who from, but he got them. I said, an apple would have done her just as well, but he said, an apple's not good enough, doesn't taste the same, and anyway this is Annie.

And then after they were born what he did was always for her, not for those two kiddies. You'd see them in the afternoon, Bill and Annie walking out with their arms round each other, and the children trailing behind. I used to wonder, if the kiddies took it into their heads to run off, how long would it be before their parents noticed? Maybe Bill and Annie had got so used to being on their own when Roy and Margaret were out of London because of the bombing they couldn't get it into their heads that they had their children home again. But I don't think that's it. I think Annie had turned our Bill's head from the first day, and he'd lost sight of what mattered most.

When the Blitz started, it was Mr Pollitt – as if he didn't have enough of other things on his mind – who suggested our Roy and little Margaret should be evacuated. He had sharp eyes for how folk go on, and he knew that expecting Annie to leave town with her children like any ordinary mother would be a waste of time. So he came to me and he said, 'We need to get those little ones out of harm's way, Pam. If Marjorie and I have evacuated our own two kiddies, why don't you take Roy and Margaret back to Openshaw to your mother's? I'm sure Ken and Edie will fit the three of you in.' Ken and Edie – that's Father and my mother.

You can tell from how he speaks that Mr Pollitt is close to our family, and as a matter of fact he always has been. Part of it is that we come originally from the same place, Droylsden in Lancashire – a lot of the types I meet say they've heard of it. Mother grew up like a younger sister with Mr Pollitt, and used to spend all the time she could in their house. So, when his family moved to Openshaw, well, so did my mother and her father, who were the only ones left at home by then, because all the older sisters had married and moved on. Mr Pollitt's mother, Mary Louisa, as good as took my mother in, and kept an eye on her, first when she was a small child and later when she went to work at the mill. Mary Louisa was the best, is what Mother always told me, and I know Mr Pollitt loved his mother to bits. I never saw a man so upset by a death as he was when she died only a couple of months after the start of the war that's just gone.

But it wasn't only the growing up with our mother. A lot of things Mr Pollitt did for us were for Father's sake, because he said he'd learned so much from him. People should be told that when the war in Spain started, ten years ago now, and the British Battalion went off to it, Mr Pollitt tried to stop them having execution for deserters. They wouldn't listen, but he really made an effort, since he felt so strongly about it. And *that* was all down to Father, who'd signed up to the Party as soon as it was launched because of the way they'd executed the deserters – well, that's what they called them – in the First War. First he had the nightmares from having had to do it, then he joined the Party. Better to be doing things than having nightmares is what Father always used to say.

It wasn't only the actual firing squad that made him so angry, it was this feeling he had that there'd been an injustice, and that there wasn't any way he could find out. What he kept telling us, Mother and Bill and me, was, 'How do we know they were deserters? They tried them and convicted them in ten minutes, and sentenced them in five. And those bigwigs in the courts, them with their law books and their whiskies, did they ever go where the ranks had to go? Did they heck! Did they see what those others had to see? And if they did, and then couldn't do it any more, or fallen asleep, or dropped their rifle in the mud, would we have been executing them? Would we heck! It was one rule for them and another for the likes of us, and don't you ever forget that, because it never changes. Class never changes.'

Well, we grew up with that and we never did forget. Apparently Mr Pollitt was very affected when he first heard Father talking about it, and asked him how many executions like that there'd been. But Father said he didn't know. He said, how could you know when these things were kept secret? So then Mr Pollitt tried to find out for himself and discovered that the details were all locked up, and were meant to be so for a hundred years. They didn't want the public knowing what had been done, and how it had been done. They were frightened of the people's opinion, so it must have been because they knew that what they had done was wrong. But actually the public *did* begin to hear about those firing squads, and started making a fuss about it, some of them, so the secrecy didn't do all its job, in spite of everything. Anyway, that's what Mr Pollitt always said. And he said those executions, one working man being made to kill another in the bosses' war, was like a microcosm of the war itself, people being turned against each other who'd've had no quarrel otherwise. So in a way it was because of Father and the firing squads that Mr Pollitt got me away from the dye works in Openshaw to my job at Party headquarters in King Street. That was in 1929 when I was seventeen, half my life ago, which I can hardly believe, and as near as you like to the very day they made him General Secretary of the Communist Party of Great Britain. What a ring to it that's got!

But there we were, eleven years on, German bombers over London every night, and Mr Pollitt was all for sending Roy and Margaret – and me – back up to my parents in Openshaw. All three of us? Me too? 'It's a small place,' I said. It was a tight enough fit when we were growing up, my brother Bill and me.

'God knows where they'd put one extra. And what about my work here?' 'Things are different in wartime,' he said. 'They'll just have to manage without you.' They, not we. There's so much, isn't there, in one tiny word. But it can have such a big story inside it.

I suppose the best way to tell it is to come back to our Bill and his beloved Annie. When war was declared that September, right at the very beginning, Bill announced he was going to be a conscientious objector. I remember how he came in with the pamphlet Mr Dutt had just written, waving it, shaking it at us and so excited. 'It says it here,' he said, and I said, 'You don't need to shout, Bill, we can all hear you', but he wasn't going to stop for me. 'Listen to this,' he said, and he started reading out of it like those Jehovah's Witnesses do with the Bible to prove things to you. All about how this was just like 1914 all over again, another imperialist war run by the capitalists using the workers as their pawns in their struggle for world domination.

Bill said Mr Dutt said the Communist Party was calling on every section of the working-class movement to end the war which the criminal ruling classes wanted to keep going so they could make money out of it. It was the wrong war, said Mr Dutt, and we should all be fighting for the success of the Party. 'So you see,' said Bill, 'if I get called up I won't go. I'll drive the ambulance if they want, but I won't fight this wicked war. And they can send me to prison if they have to.' Now I don't think my brother cared one way or the other about the imperialist war or the anti-Fascist war. Not truly. Really all it was, was that he wanted to be able to stay home by his wife, especially since our Margaret had only just been born, and Mr Dutt's pamphlet was as good as giving him permission to do it.

Anyway, I already knew what Mr Dutt had written. I should. They'd had me type it. But I thought, yes, and we just had that other pamphlet six weeks ago from Mr Pollitt saying everyone should join the war against fascism. I'd typed that one too, which was my real job to do, because Mr Pollitt had made me his secretary once he saw the value of me, and I can remember it by heart, word for word. He said: 'To stand aside from this conflict, to contribute only revolutionary-sounding phrases while the fascist beasts ride roughshod over Europe, would be a betrayal of everything our forebears have fought to achieve in the course of long years of struggle against capitalism.' I thought that was very fine, and I still think so, but it led to trouble, of course, for Mr Pollitt – because Moscow went with Mr Dutt and they said Mr Pollitt was trying to get the British Communists to defy the Communist International.

There was such an argument between the two of them, Mr Dutt with his face all nose and cheekbones, banging his bony finger on the table with every syllable, saying there could only be one view, which was Moscow's, and that was to oppose the war. And on the other side Mr Pollitt was making a speech to them all against the rise of fascism in Europe, so passionately – the way he gets when things are dear to his heart. Mr Pollitt had got really agitated when we found out that Moscow had made that pact with Germany, and in secret too. He felt so let down, but it didn't seem to trouble Mr Dutt at all, except that he was never one to let you see his feelings. In the end, it was put to a vote in the Central Committee and all of them went along with Moscow and Mr Dutt, except for Johnny Campbell from the *Worker* and Mr Pollitt. And since Mr Pollitt stood by what he'd said he had to step down from leading the Party. They pushed Johnny Campbell to one side too.

It was a bad, bad time. But it got worse. As people weren't supposed to know there'd been disagreement, they made Mr Pollitt write statements he didn't believe in, and for the sake of Party unity he had to pretend he'd made a basic error. And then Mr Dutt said he hadn't recanted enough and made him do it all over again, but more fervently. It really pained me to see it when I had to type that horrible thing too, and, believe me, if I could get it out of my head I would – but I can't: 'After the most serious consideration of the whole situation, I unreservedly accept the policy of the Communist Party and the Communist International, and pledge myself to support it, in explaining, popularising and helping to carry it forward to victory.'

Mr Pollitt had to say that his resistance to the Party line was an impermissible infraction of Party discipline which played into the hands of the class enemy. And then, like a bad kid at school, after he'd been made to say sorry, he had to promise to behave better in the future and beg to be allowed to prove it by taking his place in the front ranks of our Party in fighting to win the masses for support of the policy of the CPGB and the Communist International.

Well, I knew what he really believed, and went on believing, since he told me. And anyone with eyes to see or ears to hear should have been able to tell, because they sent him all over the country making speeches – they had to, because the masses weren't interested in listening to anyone else – and when he was talking about the air-raid shelters in Stepney for the workers, how flimsy they were, and the filth and disease because there were thousands of people and no latrines, while the boss class had deep safe clean shelters to protect them, you knew he was speaking from the heart. Like he was when he talked about the mass graves in London with the quicklime, and how he coughed up his guts to see the women going round picking up pieces of people's bodies, trying to find out if it was anyone belonging to them, and priests and rabbis saying a few words over the pieces because no one knew what denomination they'd been. He'd be speaking in Birmingham or Glasgow, where it hadn't been so bad yet, and he was telling the crowds to get ready because it could be their turn to have that bombing next, and they should be thinking about air-raid precautions and push for the best for their families.

But if someone spoke up out of the audience asking about Russia, where was Russia, and why wasn't she helping us, he'd say, well, Russia has to look after the interests of her own people, doesn't she, two hundred million of them, but when the time comes and something happens to put them in jeopardy, then you'll see they will act, and when they act they will do the job. When he said that, I could feel that underneath it all he was really agreeing with the questioner, but he couldn't say so. Instead, he'd tell the audience that when the Russians had gone into Poland they'd been welcomed by the people with flowers, which you don't usually get when an invading army comes in, and they'd set all the political prisoners free but put the bankers and landlords in jail in their place; and then he'd remind people that the workers had control in the USSR, which they didn't here, not at all, and how their lives over there were sublime, while all we had was cardboard coffins and quicklime. And all of that was true, of course. But sometimes it sounded a bit as though Mr Dutt had written his speech, like when he said this war wasn't any concern of the working class, and that Mr Churchill himself had said it was simply a continuation of the 1914–1918 one.

So, as I say, it was a bad time, but then you had to laugh sometimes too because there were always plain clothes policemen in the hall, always thinking they were merged with the public but sticking out like the King visiting the shop floor, scribbling away into their notebooks, waiting for Mr Pollitt to slip up and say something against the law so they could arrest him. And he knew it, of course, so he'd make remarks like, oh, what a lot of shorthand writers we have in today, well, gentlemen, let me tell you this – are you getting it down? – and they wouldn't know where to look.

But there was something truly precious that I learned from that time, all the awful eighteen months of it. I learned that Mr Pollitt was the most loyal human being I've ever known. He could have left the Party, couldn't he, when it was treating him badly – especially since they were wrong and he was right. But he didn't. So when he said, 'Take those kiddies up to Openshaw and your mother's, they'll just have to manage without you down here', my feelings must have shown on my face because I remember how he put his hand on my shoulder and said, 'Eh, don't worry, lass. I can stick this out, so you should be able to as well. Think where you come from. The very best stock there is, in my opinion. Don't forget, I've known your mother longer than you have, since I was a lad. Did she ever tell you we went to Sunday school together, like a proper little pair of brother and sister? And my mother was as like a mother to Edie as she was to the rest of us after your nana died so young. Edie was in our house all the hours she could be, so I know her as well as I know myself, and I know, I *know* she'll want her grandchildren by her in safety. Take them up to Openshaw, Pam.'

As far as I'm concerned, it may be the Party that employs me but I work for Mr Pollitt. In the end, if he tells me to do something, that's what I'll do. But I couldn't just snatch the kiddies up and disappear with them, as if I'd know how anyway. I'd never had much to do with children and hardly anything more with that pair. I went to our Bill's in Somers Town round the corner from my room in King's Cross and got there just as he and Annie were settling young Margaret into her cot. She was only just over a year old and Roy was four, lying on the floor in the living room making out a matchbox was a lorry. 'We've been thinking,' I said, 'Mr Pollitt and me. We've been thinking that maybe Roy and Margaret would be safer out of London. He thought Mother's would be the place, but of course nobody's asked her.'

You should've seen how quickly Bill and Annie spun round and grabbed hold of each other by the hand so fast you'd think they'd been preparing for this. 'I won't have Annie go anywhere without me,' said Bill, as defiant as if we'd been arguing over it where I hadn't even begun. Annie was already clinging onto him like somebody who's just been rescued from drowning. 'I can't . . .' she started, but I put my hand up to stop her. I knew what she couldn't. 'You don't need to tell me,' I said. 'The idea is the children would go up with me, if Mother thinks they can squeeze us in.' I noticed our Roy had stopped vroom-vrooming his matchbox and was looking at me from under the table, not upset, not concerned exactly. Just interested.

I pretended I wasn't surprised but it's not the truth. I was shocked. Not a squeak of protest from my brother and his wife, not even a make-believe that they didn't want to be parted from their little ones. You wonder why they went through the business of having babies at all. But what do I know? I had Bill write to our parents to ask if it would be all right and started getting my things together. I didn't need to wait for an answer.

Mother's letter back was short. She'd always found trouble in reading and never was one for writing pages for the sake of it. She said, 'Tell our Pam we are expecting her and the children. I will be glad to see how Roy has grown and to meet little Margaret. Father is very pleased that we can help.' Mother's only managed to get down to London once since Bill and Annie married, and those two have never left since they moved here. So this was going to be Father's first ever sight of his grandchildren.

We all went to the station, Annie carrying Margaret like a parcel, our Bill with a case for me and another for the kiddies, and me holding Roy's hand. What a small hand it was. It just sat in mine, not pulling away, not gripping, just sitting where it had been put. The station was packed with families. Some children were being sent out on their own with labels hung round their necks (like cattle, I thought, going off to auction). There were mothers and their children, fathers kissing everyone goodbye, and nobody wanting to think if it was going to be for the last time. I took a guess that I was the only aunt in charge when it should have been a mother.

When we got into our compartment and Annie handed Margaret over, the baby set up such a wailing I thought, well, this is a fine start if we're going to have hours of it. But Roy, who'd managed to get himself a corner right up against the window, pulled at my skirt and said, 'Put her on me.' So I did. I sat her on his little lap, and he held her round her middle as if she was his teddy bear. She shut up, just like that, so I said to myself, she must've spent a good bit of her short life on that lap already.

They dozed off soon enough, the two of them, and when she looked properly asleep I slid Margaret over to me because I was afraid our Roy's grip on her might loosen and we'd have her slipping down and hitting her head. I looked out of the window and wondered what was happening back in King Street, and what Mr Pollitt would be doing with himself now that he was demoted. Deposed, more like. It felt to me that I was the one running away, that I should have stayed back with the work and the action, and that the kiddies were simply an excuse – not of my making – but an excuse all the same. My temper was up against Annie then. *She* was the shirker, ducking her duty and taking me away from mine. It's not good to brood on things like that, I know, but sometimes a person can't help it and you can end up, as I did, with your heart beating in your head from a fury you don't know where to put.

It was early evening by the time we arrived and what with Margaret needing her nappy changing, Roy jiggling about because he was bored, I suppose, and me with two suitcases to haul out of the luggage compartment, I was in a high old temper for reasons of my own. It was such a blessing to see Mother and Father on the platform, ready to take charge.

Father reached out for Roy and lifted him down, and Mother took our Margaret while I pushed the two cases out. So there we all were, with Mother rocking the baby, who'd stopped her caterwauling as soon as she knew she was in the hands of an expert. I turned to Father and thought he looked a bit pale, and wondered if he wasn't feeling poorly. He'd bent down to have a good look at Roy, since he'd not set eyes on the lad in the flesh before, though I think they'd had photos sent them. 'My word,' he said, looking up at me for a moment. 'My word, our Pam.' Then he got up and took Margaret out of Mother's arms and cradled her, and the kiddie stared up at him and he stared down at her. 'My word,' he kept saying, shaking his head as if it was being troubled by flies.

'That's enough, Ken,' Mother said. 'We'd best be getting them back. This littl'un needs her bottom washing.' So it was nearly the same as when we left – me holding Roy's hand, the man lugging the cases, and our Margaret being carried, but this time by someone who wanted to do it. 'You'll have to make do with the settee, love,' Mother said. 'But you'll do all right there, won't you?'

As it turned out, I didn't stay up in Openshaw more than a week. That first evening, after Mother had the children fed and washed and bedded down, and Father had helped me clear up after our meal, we sat round the table over the teapot and they wanted to know the details about what was really going on in King Street, although of course, like everybody, they already knew the gist. If Mr Pollitt had told me he knew Mother as well as he knew himself, she could return the compliment. She got so agitated over it all when I described the row with Mr Dutt and how the Central Committee had voted. She said, 'Poor Harry. He must be in pain, Pam. He's a Party man through and through, but if he thinks Moscow's got this one wrong, well, I didn't know the ins and outs of it before, but I'd go along with what he says any day, don't you think, our Ken?' And Father said, 'Aye, I do.' Then he said, 'I'm almost glad Mary Louisa isn't with us to see this. It broke her heart, poor old soul, when she heard they'd pushed him out. In fact, I think it were that that saw her off.'

We all sat in silence then for a few minutes and Father piped up again. 'I don't know about you, Edie,' he said, 'but I think our Pam's place is back in London. I think Harry needs every bit of support he can get wherever he can get it from.' 'But what about the children?' I said. And Mother laughed. 'Do you think I can't manage to see to a couple of kiddies on my own? It's been

23

a long time, love, and I'll be sorry to see you go, but Ken's right. You should be where you're needed most. I were over the moon when our Bill wrote to say you'd be coming, but first things first.'

They asked after Bill and some about Annie, but not overmuch. I know Mother. She doesn't like to say hard things about a person and if those things come to mind she'd rather keep quiet than air them. So after a few days I went back down to London and wasn't sorry. How was I to know I'd be sorry soon enough? How was I to know I'd not be seeing Father again, that he'd be dead by VE Day, hardly weeks after the kiddies had come back to London? At the time, though, I thought, good: Roy and Margaret were in the best of hands, I'd had a spell with Mother and Father, but what I wanted most was to be back at my job in King Street.

What I hadn't realised was that Mr Pollitt wouldn't be there, that he'd be spending months back in Lancashire speaking at various public meetings and writing his autobiography. And because he wasn't General Secretary he wasn't being paid by the Party any more, so he had to go back on the tools, though he said he didn't mind that as it brought him closer to the workers again. Good to keep your hand in, he said. A man shouldn't forget his skills. Stupid as I was, I didn't stop to think that without Mr Pollitt, but with the war on, I was going to have to leave King Street too. I ended up on the ambulances, just the same as our Bill, and though I came to enjoy the driving I saw more than I ever wanted to see while I was doing it.

But then not a year later came the turnaround: Hitler went into the Soviet Union, Moscow instructed King Street to support the war, King Street changed the Party's official position, and Mr Pollitt was brought back as General Secretary. You'd have thought he'd have gloated, but he didn't. And, since Russia was Britain's ally now, Mr Pollitt was let off war work because now the government needed him for propaganda, to pep up the communist-minded workers. And, once *he* was needed again, well then, so was I. The irony of it all was that now our Bill didn't have an excuse not to enlist any more! So off he had to go. And then, would you believe, the military turned him down because they said he had a heart murmur. Who could credit it – a man as young as that with a weak heart! It was the first we'd heard of it, any of us, and poor Bill didn't know which way to face. But at least he could still stay home with Annie. So he kept on with the ambulances, though they went on calling him a Jerry-lover in the street.

Oh dear. Poor Annie. There she was, thinking she'd kept her husband, all through the war – and then she woke up next to his corpse. So there you are. I've come right round to where I started, in their flat in Somers Town, Roy stinking to high heaven when he opened the door to me, Margaret hiding under the table, and Annie in her bed with her head under the pillow.

After a bit I did go in to see her, and it gives me the shivers just talking about it. Her own mother wouldn't have recognised her. Her own mother *definitely* wouldn't have recognised her. She couldn't have been out of that bed since the day Bill died, except for the funeral – and she was hardly there for that either. Not in her head she wasn't. She couldn't have combed her hair or washed or changed her clothes or her sheets. She looked as if she hadn't eaten either, her face was that grey and thin.

The curtains were closed, and the windows, and I couldn't breathe in there. I drew the curtains back and had a bit of a fight with the window to let some air in. 'There,' I said, 'that's better, isn't it?' And I could hear my voice high and false, like when people are talking to little children or very old folk who're deaf or daft. Annie wasn't listening anyway, so who was I doing it for? 'Now then, Annie. Let's get you some . . .' but I didn't know what to say next because she was a mad woman. Mad with grief, mad for letting her children go weeks without food, for all she knew, without going to school, without everything.

People say that when you've got children it puts things in perspective, and you have to rein in your grief because you have to think of them. But not Annie. As far as she was concerned, the world was over. If she hadn't taken notice of her two children when everything was as she wanted it, she wasn't going to start now. Oh Lord, I thought. What do I do now? I turned round, and there was Roy standing in the doorway watching me in that silent way of his, looking and looking. I never saw anyone who looks so much. It puts the wind up me sometimes, and him so young.

Roy

What did she have to come for? She didn't have to come. We don't need her here. I can look after Mig, like always, like Nana Hoskins showed me. I know how to do everything, how to get food and everything. We pick stuff up off the street in the market, and people give us stuff. I looked in Mummy's purse and found the ration cards and she's got some money there too. And Mig's best at nicking milk bottles, and apples sometimes. Nobody notices her 'cos she looks so small, and people think what she's got is what she's meant to have. Mrs Barker give me all their sweets because of Daddy dying, so then Mrs Green give us each a banana. That was funny 'cos we didn't know what you do with it till Mrs Green showed us. She laughed when she did and said, 'Look how time passes, and things happen and children don't know a banana when they see one!'

Getting things is easy because when you look sad people give them to you. And we did look sad, 'cos we were sad. They say, 'How's your mother, dear?', and I say, 'She's ill. She's in bed.' And they pat my head and say, 'Well, you be a good boy and look after her', and I say I do. But I don't look after her 'cos she don't want to be looked after. She wants to die. Mig don't look after her neither, but that's because she's only seven, and Mummy frightens her.

When Daddy woke up dead, Mummy started screaming. We didn't know what it was 'cos it didn't sound like a person, it was like a run-over dog, so instead of getting out of bed we hid under the blanket, and I held Mig's hand. But then she said, 'Is it Mummy, that noise?' So I said I'd go and look, and Mummy was sitting up in bed and her mouth was open in this big black square. I could see her teeth and the wiggly thing in her throat. And I thought she was like a baby crying. She took a big breath in but instead of breathing out there was a scream, then another one, and all the screams was the same. Then I saw Daddy next to her and I thought, why don't he tell her to shut up? So I went to his side of the bed and pulled him and said, 'Daddy, Daddy.' But he sort of rocked, all in one piece when I pulled him, stiff like. So I went back to bed and got in next to Mig and said, 'Daddy's dead.' But she didn't know what I meant. I don't think I did. Not completely.

Then there was people banging on the door. And shouting through the letterbox, 'Mrs Hoskins! Mrs Hoskins! Are you all right? What's happened? Open up, Mrs Hoskins.' So I said to Mig that I was going to open the door, and I did. And she come with me. And all the neighbours was there, Mrs Barker and Mr Barker, and Mrs Green (there isn't a Mr Green now, he didn't come back), and Mrs Stewart and her big son Daniel and her daughter Sally, what's going to get married, and Mr Finch who lives all by himself and always has. And they were in their night things with their coats on top so it must've been early. They hadn't combed their hair and Mrs Barker and Mrs Green had them rollers in, what made their heads a funny shape. They all pushed by me and Mig and rushed into Mummy and Daddy's room and stood round the bed watching Mummy screaming and then they was all shouting at her to stop.

Mrs Green said, 'Fetch the doctor, somebody!' And somebody done it but I don't know who, but before he come Mrs Barker had this bottle of stuff, and she tried to pour it into Mummy's mouth, but it just bubbled back out, like it was pushed out by the next scream. Then she started coughing like she was being sick. But then she went all quiet and flopped down on her pillow so I think she must've swallowed some. Me and Mig, we was by the door together, and I could see how everyone was glad that Mummy'd gone quiet, and everything was quiet until someone shouted, 'But what if she's died too?' So they all started patting her cheeks and shouting her name and yelling at her to wake up.

Then the doctor come and he was fat as a pig, and he pushed all the people away and bent over Mummy in the bed so we couldn't see her no more. Then he bent over Daddy and said he was dead and they'd have to get in the undertaker. But then someone noticed us and shouted, 'My God! The children!' So I grabbed Mig's hand and tugged it and yelled, 'Run!' Grown-ups shove you around when they decide things for you, but I do the deciding now.

They was much slower than us, the neighbours. We're used

to running up and down the stairs, but grown-ups always hold the rail and walk, so they couldn't catch us. They go down step by step, looking down to see where to put their feet. But we've chased up and down them stairs every day like all the kids, ever since we come back from Nana and Granddad's, and what you do is you look ahead, not down, and you let your feet just run, and follow them, 'cos it's a game and it makes the doors open like them cuckoo clocks. You run past a door and the person pops out and you run down past the next door and a person pops out, and they yell at you, and it's always the same way, but nobody's really angry I don't think because they never come and knock, not on our door anyway.

By the time the neighbours got down the bottom and started to look and see where we'd gone, they couldn't find us. We ran through the arches and the gate and out the Chalton Street side, where they was putting the market up. So then it was easy 'cos we could dodge under the barrows and hide there. Nobody asked us nothing or looked at us 'cos we was always in the market, so they was used to us. They didn't say things like: And where's your parents? They was too busy unpacking their boxes and shouting at each other like they always do, and though it was very early there was already lots of people on the street, hoping to get things before anyone else.

There was that man with the striped shoes what's always selling things from inside his coat, watches and things. And cigarettes. And there was the one what always has eggs, but under his barrow not on top. We was going to take some but I told Mig we shouldn't, not then, because eggs break and we couldn't go straight home with all the neighbours there. But we did nick a milk bottle from a doorstep and some bread from a woman's basket when she put it down. We took it up the street and sat on a bench and had our breakfast there, which would've been all right except a copper come and sat down right there next to us and said, 'Roy and Margaret?' And Mig was surprised that he knew her name proper. He said, 'Your mother's very upset. She's looking for you everywhere.' I thought, no she ain't. She never looks for us. Mig said, 'Where's my daddy?' But the copper didn't say nothing. He said, 'I think you two nippers better come home with me now, don't you?' I didn't think so, but he was big and people was staring at us because of him. People always stare when there's a copper. They think it must be something interesting if there's a copper. So we said, all right, and he got up and grabbed our hands, not on our hands but round the wrists, like it was handcuffs, so that I knew we wasn't going to be able to run off again, not just then anyway.

When we got brought in home the neighbours was all still there. 'Poor lambs. Just look at them!' It was Mrs Green, bending down with her arms out. They all looked at us. They had these huge faces and their eyes was wet and moony. It was all crammed and crowded but they stepped back like we was the King and Queen and made a sort of path between them for us, and the copper led us up this path to Mummy's side of the bed and we passed men in pyjamas and ladies in coats and nighties, all the way to the end where Mummy was, not in the bed no more but on the chair where she brushes her hair. Her face was all white. Her skin looked like you could see through it, but there wasn't nothing on the other side. There's a mirror there and I saw them things, you know, blobs on it, places what didn't reflect. I hadn't noticed them before. Daddy wasn't in the bed no more. But they'd closed the door to the living room so I thought they must've got him in there, the women and that. I thought I'd go and look, and then thought I wouldn't.

Mummy held out her arms for us and when she did that there was this reflection of one of her arms in the mirror, like you could see the front of her arm and the back of it at the same time. She pulled us to her, though we didn't want to go, but she didn't make no noise 'cos she'd probably used it all up. But while she was pressing us on her chest I wished it was Nana and not her, and I knew Mig was thinking the same. Anyway, Mummy wasn't thinking about us but about Daddy. 'How could you do this to me?' she kept saying. 'How could you leave me like that?' But she wasn't asking us.

Mrs Green said, 'We'd better find their aunt, whatsername?' And Mrs Barker said, 'Pam, isn't it? Miss Hoskins. She's not married, that one.' And Mrs Green said, 'Don't she work for the Communists?' So Mrs Barker said, 'They're all Communists.' Then she asked Mr Finch to go and find Aunty Pam at the Communists' and he said he didn't mind, and he went. Mrs

Stewart come in with a tray. She'd made some tea, really sweet she said, because you need sugar when you're in shock, she'd put in four spoons, she said, and they all said, Oh! Then she sat down on the edge of the bed nearest Mummy's chair and put the tray on the bedside table. And she sort of undid Mummy's arms to make her let us go and put a cup in her hand and told her to drink it up, dear, it'll do you good. But Mummy couldn't drink it, I could see that. She couldn't drink nothing. She just sat there with the cup in her hand, staring and staring.

Then Mig said, 'Where've they taken Daddy?' That made Mummy start crying so much that the teacup was shaking and the tea was spilling. So Mrs Stewart took the cup away from her, and she drunk the tea.

When Mr Finch come back he was still alone. He said our Aunty Pam wasn't at the Communists', she was somewhere else at a meeting out of town but the Communists had said she'd be coming back in a few days. Mrs Green told the other neighbours that she'd stay over, because she knew what it was like to lose your husband. That way she'd be able to keep an eye on the children *and* on poor Annie Hoskins. Look, she's going to get some rest now. It was true that Mummy was lying down again, probably 'cos of the stuff Mrs Barker poured in her mouth, and she'd closed her eyes. Mrs Green took our hands – it's like everyone wants to hold our hands just now – and said, 'Let's go into the living room, shall we, and let your mother sleep it off.' All the neighbours went out first and then Mig said to Mrs Green, 'You're wrong. Daddy hasn't got lost. He's dead, you know.'

Pam

The first I heard of our Bill dying was when Mr Pollitt and I got back into town from Leicester. We'd had some exceptional meetings, as he said himself, with folk queuing to sign up after his speeches the way they always do. He does thrill people so when he speaks, to make you think he was born to be on a platform. But he doesn't speak just any old how. He prepares and rehearses, and I know because there are times I'm there. 'What d'you think, Pam? How did that passage sound to you?' he asks me, though as it's not really a question I don't put my bit in. Well, I wouldn't. I haven't the knowledge or the expertise. But after the meetings people had wanted to stay on, talking to Mr Pollitt, because he's got that special touch. He's very direct. It's the way he talks, the way he uses language so that what he says makes sense straightaway, and folk realise he's lived a life as hard as theirs.

Mind you, some of them do get a mite twitchy when he says it's right that the Party is co-operating with the Labour government for the moment. We get the odd person heckling, saying we shouldn't believe the government because in the end it's all the same, all part of the capitalist system, and what they're offering is only to keep us quiet. And Mr Pollitt hears them out, and nods, and says he understands how they feel, but just for now we need to go along with the government. And it can go on a long time, the argy-bargy, but he's always patient. I've heard one or two back in King Street say he shouldn't waste his energies on all the chat when meetings are over, but he thinks the chat is as important as the meetings. More, sometimes. And he always likes to start as early as people can manage after their work, so that they have time to go on to the pub after. Some of them back in King Street don't approve of that either. Some of them think if you're committed you should leave off going to the pub. But Mr Pollitt says a man's a man whatever his politics, and why should people give up their small pleasures? He's not a religious teetotaller like a few I could name, and likes the odd glass of beer

31

just the same as many. Even a whisky from time to time. And you should see him smoking!

I always try to be in the hall before he arrives, especially when it's a place where they haven't had him come and speak before. I like to see their faces. There's always this surprise, this shock because he's wearing a suit and tie, all properly done. But he says it's a matter of self-respect and it shows people that you respect them too, and you shouldn't ever turn out looking slovenly and expect to be taken seriously. I think that's right. Appearances are important – not only being clean, but looking as if you've made an effort and not just popped out of the house for a bit of a chinwag. He's a stickler for being on time too. Never be late, he tells people, and do your job not just the best you can, but the best it can be done. Then if anyone tries to sack you, you'll know it's victimisation. Sometimes, when we're travelling in other cities, he'll make a point of popping into the local cathedral if there is one, and has me come along with him. It isn't for the religion, of course, but the craftsmanship. 'Look at that, Pam,' he'll say, and tip his head back to point up to some special detail in the vaults. 'Think of what went into the making of that. Those men must have been proud of themselves, and we can be proud of them too, don't you think? Even though we don't know their names.'

Back in London we got off the train so late that there wasn't any point going to Headquarters, so we all went to our homes. That's why I didn't hear of it till next morning. One of the neighbours, a Mr Finch, had been by King Street and left me a note, and by the time I got round to our Bill's flat they'd taken him to the mortuary, and boxed him up. You don't believe a person's gone if you can't see the body. You look at the coffin, lid down and all closed up, and you think to yourself, it could be anybody in there, or no one at all. They could have put whatever they want in there. Silly things go through your head, and when you look back on them you realise they were silly. Why would anyone pretend our Bill was in his coffin if he wasn't? But I suppose, at the time, those ideas come into your head to help you keep the reality out. You don't want to have to think, I'm never going to see my little brother again.

What I *did* have to think out was how I was going to tell Mother. She'd had to bury Father only last year, poor soul, which was bad enough. I went up for it, and made Bill come with me, but we left Annie and the kiddies behind. Mother said to, and it was for her to decide. She looked dreadful. Half dead herself, to tell the truth, and half her weight had come off her, I thought. But when I asked her what had happened, if Father had suddenly sickened with something, she wouldn't say. Only shook her head and put her face in her hands. That wasn't like her, and I have to say I didn't know what to do, or what to make of it. But given all that, how was she going to take the news that the next one to go was her son? People say that's the worst of all, losing a child. I've never had a child nor don't expect to, but even I can see that having your child go before you isn't right. When Father went at least she had the support of the Openshaw Party, who are a good crowd and all she's got left up there now, but she'd be coming down on the train on her own, hours on her own with her memories. I had to write a letter because everybody's afraid of a telegram, and of course she doesn't have a telephone any more than I do.

Worrying about all that it didn't cross my mind they'd go and put on a church funeral. They knew perfectly well, all those neighbours, what our Bill's beliefs were. (Some of them had made a bit of a song and dance about it, he told me after he and Annie first moved in. Ooh, you must be spies from Moscow, and the rest of it. Stupid! But now, with the war over, half the country recognises what we owe to Uncle Joe.) But that funeral – I couldn't undo what they'd already arranged. They'd been good enough to get the whole thing going, after all – the undertaker, the vicar, the cemetery. You don't complain to the one who washed up that he broke a cup, do you, since at least he was washing up. But I suppose I didn't look so grateful that first few minutes at our Bill's, with him gone and all the neighbours on the chairs and on the bed, Annie still in it.

Young Roy was sitting close by his sister, like he always is, and the pair of them weren't saying a word. You couldn't have told what they were thinking. They were on the one chair together which they can do easily enough, both being so slight, and Roy had hold of Margaret by the hand the whole time. I had this sudden feeling, that little girl's not going to go anywhere without her brother at her side. Maybe not for the rest of her life. It came out of nowhere. But, like I say, silly things do go through your head sometimes.

Mrs Green, I think it was – the one who'd moved in to do the cooking and minding the children – she came up to me and she whispered in my ear, 'Funerals is for the living, Miss Hoskins. Don't you think so?' And she looked over to Annie in the bed. And I thought, was Annie a churchgoer, then, who only dropped it because of our Bill? And is she one again now, so soon? And for a moment I thought – and it wasn't a kind thing to think, I know – there's not much to you, is there, lass, if you chop and change so quickly. Lucky I didn't say it out loud! Maybe, if Annie's one of those that thinks she'll spend eternity with her husband in the life hereafter, then who am I to disappoint her? Especially not the day of the funeral.

Now here's a funny thing. They sang 'The Lord is my Shepherd' in the church before the burial, but the tune wasn't the one they'd had us sing all those years ago when I was still at school. I remember the tune because we once had a to-do about the whole business one evening at home, over tea. Father used to say school prayers were brainwashing, putting superstition into little heads before they could work things out for themselves, because what you learn when you're youngest is what sticks with you most. He said we weren't to sing the words. But Mother said we'd likely get in trouble if we didn't sing the words, the teachers would be on the lookout for it, and maybe punish us. Then he said if that happened he'd go down to the school and have it out with them, but she didn't agree.

'No, Ken,' she said. 'You're putting too much on them. They're too young for it. You can't have the children fighting your battles for you in public like that. Let them do it when they've decided for themselves.' 'Like as not, it'll be too late by then,' he said. And she said, 'Well, you weren't raised by a Party family, were you? You had to come to it by your own thinking and your own experience, and you'll have had enough hymns before that, without anyone telling you it were superstition. And I were sent to Sunday school every week, along with Harry – and it didn't make a nun out of me, did it? Or a vicar out of him!' That shut him up and they decided that if we wanted we could mouth the words, but not put voice into them. The trouble was, 'The Lord is my Shepherd' was my favourite – for the tune not the words, so I used to hum it, but, because the teachers were on the lookout like Mother'd said they would be, we were supposed to mouth the words, and if you hum while you mouth, well you're singing, aren't you.

At our Bill's funeral, when the organ played its first chord and they struck up singing, my first thought was, they've got the wrong tune! Just think, we're in a church I don't believe in, singing a hymn I don't believe in, and I'm complaining to myself that they're not doing it right. Why should it matter? It shouldn't have mattered to me. But it was like opening your mouth for a piece of carrot and getting cabbage instead. Then I pulled myself together, because the kiddies were next to me, between me and Mother, in the front pew the way they do for the family of the deceased.

Mother was like a ghost, white and thin as one, and the black of her coat and dress made her look all the whiter. Roy and Margaret had made a beeline for her when I brought her through the door, but before she remembered, and before anyone could stop her, Margaret sang out, 'Where's Granddad, Nana, where's Granddad?' Then of course the silly child remembered, and burst into tears. I have to say that as far as I know she hadn't shed a single one for our Bill. Roy didn't say a word. He just stood there looking really shocked. Sick, you'd have said. I wasn't surprised. When I'd gone up to Openshaw to fetch the kiddies back down to London once it was safe enough, I could see how Father had taken to Roy and Roy to him. Never apart for a moment once Father was home, Mother said.

So, there we were, the six of us – Mother, Margaret, Roy and me, and then Annie and that Mrs Green, who's a good woman and her husband killed in the last days. She was standing with Annie and more or less holding her up. I can't say I'm sure that Annie knew what was going on at all. She wasn't looking like herself, not like the girl who had tried to do the new jitterbug in the parlour, where there's not the space for it, and nearly knocked the cups and saucers onto the floor. But us apart, that front pew was empty. Not much of a family in numbers, us Hoskins.

The vicar said the things they do, looking all the while at Annie and sometimes at Roy and Margaret. Of course, he didn't know Bill to be able to come up with anything personal about him, and I think someone must have said something to him about Bill's beliefs because at one point he pipes up, 'But keep in your minds that Our Saviour said my Father's house has many mansions. So I think we may safely understand this to mean that there is room in Heaven even for those who have strayed, or lost their way, or been deluded, or diverted from the path of righteousness.' That brought me back to myself smart as anything. How dare they! When a man's in his coffin and can't defend himself! Mother and I gave each other a look over the kiddies' heads, then I took a sideways peek at Annie to see how she might be taking it, since this to-do was all got up for her sake, but she might as well not have heard a word of it for all the reaction on her face. Haven't they bothered to ask themselves what this sort of nonsense is going to do to the kiddies? I thought. The vicar in his black gown saying things like that about their father. Unless they were too young to understand the words. No, they weren't. They'd have had all that rubbish shoved down them at school.

As the service went on I began to get the feeling that the church behind me had more than just us and the neighbours in it, but it wasn't the moment to turn right round and see. Then all the singing and the praying was over, and as it's usual for the family to leave first, that's what we did. Mrs Green leading Annie, whose face was sunk so low on her chest you couldn't see it, then Roy, then me, then little Margaret, then Mother.

The place was packed out! They must have closed King Street up for the day. I couldn't believe it. I didn't know what to think. There was Mr Pollitt, well turned out as ever, and it warmed my heart to see him. But when he put his arms round my mother, his childhood friend, I could see he had tears in his eyes. I didn't know if they were from sympathy for a mother who's lost her son or from the sorrow of a son remembering the mother he loved and saw into the ground a few years back. Either way, it wrung my heart as nothing else had. He knew about Father dying and had written her the most wonderful letter of commiseration about it. He'd remembered everything, all the things Father had said and done, and you'd have thought, reading it, that Mr Pollitt owed half his beliefs and convictions to Father, even though that couldn't have been so. That letter was better than any obituary you get in the papers.

They stood there for a long time, Mother and Mr Pollitt, as if there weren't folk hanging round them waiting to say their piece. And I thought, she's got no one up there now, no family. What's to stop her coming down and staying with me? We could share a bed, no trouble. She'd told me we used to do that when I was just a mite in the first war before our Bill was born. And after!

I drew Roy and Margaret to one side so people could file by and shake Mother's hand – there was no point them trying to speak to Annie, as they could all plainly see. Everyone came up, even Mr Dutt, who you'd never think would put himself out for anything personal. And of course young Paul Cooke from the *Worker*, with his beard all over the place, looking just like what the public think a Communist should look like. I didn't actually stand there and count them, but it was more a question of who *wasn't* there than who was. I did so wish Bill could have seen that. How proud he would have been. So don't talk to me about the path of righteousness.

I put it to Mother that evening, when it was all over. 'No, love,' she said. 'I don't belong down here. I don't feel easy. You've your work to do, and I've mine at home where I know everybody and everybody knows me. And I've got too old and slow to change the view from my window. But it were good of you to ask, and right.' I tried saying she was younger than Mr Pollitt, but she said it wasn't the same for men, and everybody lived their lives in different ways.

Roy

Mrs Stewart said she was going to do the tea. I like Mrs Stewart, and I like her big son Daniel. 'Why don't you and Margaret come home with me, dear,' she said, 'while the grown-ups is talking, and help me set the things out? You'd like to do that, wouldn't you?' Actually, she wasn't really asking me 'cos she'd already got hold of my hand – again – and Mig's, and she was pulling us with her while she was talking and walking out the churchyard. But then I twigged she was taking us away so we wouldn't see Daddy's coffin going down, and I'm cross about that 'cos I think they should've let me see it. Not Mig, though. She's too young.

Mrs Stewart went on talking all the way home, over the Euston Road, up Chalton Street, across the courtyard with the bench round the tree and up the stairs, not to our flat on the fourth floor but to hers on the third floor. She must've done a lot of the getting ready before we all went out in the morning 'cos the table had a cloth on it and all the chairs was sort of round the walls, more chairs than she's got so some of them must've come from Mrs Green's flat, or Mrs Barker's or even Mr Finch's, though since he lives alone perhaps he's only got one chair. None of them come from our flat. I know because we went out early and Aunty Pam had closed the door behind her and locked it, so they couldn't've come in and got more chairs.

Everything's in the kitchen, Mrs Stewart said, all ready and waiting. So we went in there and she'd done sandwiches, corned beef ones and fish paste ones, and she'd baked a cake with real jam in the middle and sugar on the top, done special, she said, for me and Margaret, and all the plates with the food had tea towels over them, washed and ironed. I've never seen a tea towel ironed but maybe Mrs Stewart ironed them ones because of the funeral.

Their flat's the same as ours. The same rooms in the same shape as ours, but they have to use the rooms different 'cos Daniel and Sally is grown up, which means they can't share a room, Mrs Stewart said. So Daniel has to sleep on the settee and put it away every day. He keeps his things in Sally's room and has to keep them all tidy 'cos as he is big his things is big and there isn't enough space for them. I think it would be much easier for Daniel if he and Sally did share their room. Mig and I do and I can't see why we'd ever need to stop. But Mrs Stewart says that, since Sally is getting married soon, she'll be moving out 'cos Sally's young man's people have a whole house somewhere and Sally can live in that. Then Daniel will get his room back. I wondered if that would make Daniel happy he could have a room again or sad that Sally wasn't going to be living with them no more. Then I remembered Daddy isn't going to be living with us no more, and we wasn't going to see Granddad no more neither.

Mrs Stewart said there, there, darling, and give me a hug, which was nice. Then she give one to Mig too, and we both stayed there with Mrs Stewart for a bit. 'Now let's get those things out, shall we?' she said, and she give us each some empty plates to carry – four for me, for starters, and two for Mig. Mig carried them real careful and Mrs Stewart told her she was a clever girl, but Mig is always careful.

There was this stain under the window in the living room, what looked like it was an elephant with its trunk in the air. We've got a picture of an elephant with its trunk in the air in our geography book at school on the page about Africa. The book elephant's mouth is open, pink inside, and its trunk is sort of curled back over itself like it's a letter S. It's got enormous tusks, all pointy at the ends. Mrs Stewart's elephant didn't have no tusks. But Mig liked it. She traced it all the way round with her finger. 'What's it called?' she asked. 'Bumbo,' I said, and she agreed.

We put the plates on the table with its white cloth and Mrs Stewart stacked them up. Then we brought in the teaspoons and I had the knives. But Mrs Stewart said, 'I don't know why I put knives out. We won't be needing them, will we, since it's sandwiches and they're already cut.' 'What about the cake?' said Mig. Then Mrs Stewart looked at her and said, 'You're a sharp one, aren't you. Sharp as a knife! But I tell you what. I'll cut it into slices in the kitchen when everyone's ready for it and bring it in all cut up. Should we have forks for it, what do you think, just for today?' Mig and I thought we should have forks for it because that would be special, so I took the knives back and brought out forks instead. Mig counted them because she's good at counting, and likes it. Then Mrs Stewart brought out all the cups and saucers and asked Mig to count and see if there was the same number cups as there was saucers.

Then everybody else come, making a lot of noise, though not the Communists who'd been in the church. Aunty Pam had asked one of them, this tidy-looking geezer, if they were coming back, and he'd said, 'No, love. There'll be little enough space in a small flat as it is. And I'm sure the lady wasn't expecting a crowd like us.' Then he looked at her so sad and it nearly made Aunty Pam cry. The tidy man'd been with Nana, hugging her. P'raps 'cos Granddad wasn't there. I dunno. But he didn't come to Mrs Stewart's flat. So it was us and Nana and Aunty Pam and just all the neighbours really, and Daniel and Sally of course, and Sally's young man who's called William. Daddy's proper name was William but no one ever called him that.

They all smiled a lot, especially when they was looking at us, and I thought it was a strange thing to do, to keep on smiling like that after a person's dead. Then I thought maybe they was smiling 'cos otherwise they'd be crying and most people don't like crying, do they. I do cry sometimes, but not when people see, except Mig, of course. But that's different. Mummy was the only one who was crying, and her face was white and patchy and swollen, which frightened us 'cos she didn't look like herself. Aunty Pam's face was white too, and her lips looked very thin, like somebody drawn them with a pencil. Mig kept holding Nana's hand. Nana let her but it was like her hand was just a lump, Nana's hand, not holding Mig's. But then you could see she sort of shook herself, and sat down and pulled Mig onto her lap. I was jealous.

Nana went away next day. She left and went back home to Openshaw.

Pam

'You've been very good to our Annie,' I said to Mrs Green, when we were all done and the rest of them had gone. We'd taken Annie back to theirs and seen that Roy and Margaret had had a wash and gone to bed. Annie was sleeping too, having swallowed down a big glass of brandy which they'd asked Mr Finch to fetch her from the pub. 'That's all right, dear,' said Mrs Green. 'Don't you worry about her. I know you've your job to go to, and we can see to her here for a bit. I'm sure she'll come round in the end. It's the shock, you know. But she'll come out of it when she remembers she's got the kiddies to see to. I know what it's like. You have to see to the kiddies, don't you. And it's what keeps you going. But you'll see. She'll be all right in the end. We all are.'

I wasn't so sure, but I kept my mind to myself. What do I know, I said to myself. I've not had a husband to lose or children to see to. And I thought, that Mrs Green is a decent woman and she knows what she's doing. Actually, I don't like to say this just now but it's a fact and you should never be afraid of the facts: Mrs Green used to be one of those who called our Bill a Jerry-lover. And then, what with her husband being at the front, in Africa I think it was, and then not coming back at all, it's my belief she thought Bill had put up a show of having a weak heart in order to stay home by Annie. But now that he'd died like this, so suddenly, she felt badly about what she'd thought and was making amends, in her own way. So I let it go that she made a bit of a face when she said that about my having a job to go to, seeing as she knows where I work, seeing as she 'doesn't hold with it' or something of the sort. She might be making a judgement but she's not taking it out on Annie, and there's a lot who would. And maybe she was right. Maybe, for the first time in her life, Annie would see that she had children, really see it, and it would bring her back to herself. You tell yourself things because you want to believe them.

So I went home. Next day I saw Mother to the station, though not to her train because she told me to save the penny on the platform ticket. So we said goodbye in the ticket office and she told me to keep an eye out for Roy and Margaret. 'They've grown so much,' she said. 'It's hardly been any time but they've grown so, our Pam. And they don't sound the same either. Roy, he's like a little lad who's been all his life down here in London. You wouldn't think, would you? And there was me, silly old fool, thinking he were ours!' I said I supposed children try to fit in. 'Why?' she said. 'Have the other kiddies been teasing them, then, for the way they spoke?' But I said I didn't know. Then I went to work. I'd made her some sandwiches for the journey.

They were all so solicitous in King Street, especially Mr Pollitt. They kept telling me what a good comrade they'd lost in Bill so they could understand my grief. I'd never have thought having people talk about Bill so much, and so much in the open would be a help, but it was. Young Paul Cooke was the best. He's on the *Worker* too, started there just this year, taking the photographs. I remember our Bill telling me that Paul had a real talent, that he was always in the right place at the right moment, and that he had integrity. And I thought, well what else do you need? He'd been on the *Yorkshire Post*, along with Peter Fryer, Bill said, but when the *Post* had sacked Peter Fryer for refusing to leave the Party, Paul Cooke had walked out too, without a job to go to as far as he knew – so there's proof of integrity! Good thing for him there was the *Worker* to join, and good thing for the *Worker* too, by all accounts. Bill was his good friend, Paul said. And didn't look down on him for being so much younger, didn't push him about. He was going to miss him. In fact he said he didn't know how he was going to get along without him. It was hard to hear, but a good thing to know.

And there was work to be done. We were organising the housing squats to take over all those posh buildings some of the councils were keeping empty, even though Mr Bevan said empty properties should be requisitioned. There weren't enough places for living in, what with the bombing and the fires, and it was like Mr Pollitt said, nobody had built any houses during the war of course, and the only building there'd been before it was for the rich, so where did they think people were supposed to go? The thing is, not as many people got killed as they thought would be, but more houses were damaged beyond repair, and nobody had planned what to do about all the homeless.

Hundreds we got, squatters, all at one time, moving into these mansion blocks and the like, so quickly and so quietly the authorities hadn't got out of their beds by the time we'd done it. I was getting all the organisation of that on paper so people would know where to go and when to meet, and it kept me busy. It kept my mind on important things and when you're busy you don't brood. I was up and out early, out all day, too tired to think come evening time, but I felt – we all felt – it was a good job and well done.

It made me remember how exhausted but how – what's the word? – strung up Mother always said Father had been in 1920 when he went full tilt into the Hands Off Russia campaign. There was the government thinking to send people out to help Poland fight the Bolsheviks, and the people they were sending had only just come back from fighting in France! Father was down at the docks day in and day out to persuade the dockers they shouldn't load any ships with munitions bound for Poland, and in the end there was a strike, and they didn't. I might have been only a little lass at the time, but I could feel the excitement of it. Now I'm not saying our squatting campaign was the same – there are many reasons why it wasn't – but while it was going I'd say the satisfaction wasn't much different, the sense that we were doing the right thing, and that we were doing it together! You don't know, if you've never done anything like it, how that feels: the comradeship of it. You even get to feel warmly about some folk you wouldn't care for otherwise. Maybe that's how soldiers feel after a while. But there was trouble in it too.

I was so taken up with what I had to do, and the tougher it gets the more it does take you up, that I clear forgot about Annie and her difficulties. I suppose I let myself think Mrs Green would do what she had to and that Annie would come round, like she'd said. More and more I was away from my little room because I was out with the squatters in a luxury block in Kensington, even at night, because we had to have pickets round the clock to watch the place to stop the owners turning off our power supplies. So the weeks went by.

And then the summer was over – only three months ago

though it feels like three years – and through the windows we could see the children all going back to their new school term, and someone from King Street came out to me at the squat. She'd a letter, she said, that had been left for me at the office. Seems some woman had been trying to put notes through my door at home more than once and of course I wasn't there to read them, and one of the neighbours had told her to try King Street.

It was from the school in Argyle Street, where Roy and Margaret started after they came back from Openshaw. It was the headmistress writing. She'd not seen the children since school started again this term, she said, and hadn't been able to get an answer from Mrs Hoskins, but that there was talk of some family tragedy. As their nearest other relative, did I know what was going on? Well. If I'm honest my first thought was an annoyed one: what's Mrs Green been doing all this time? Then I had to remind myself that it wasn't really for Mrs Green to have to be doing anything. But at the same time I had my duty to the squatting because if you don't stick these things out, nothing gets done.

I can't say what I would have done if the decision hadn't been made for me. The squat collapsed, just like that. You'd have thought the government, the *Labour* government, would have supported the people trying to find ways to live when there were empty houses and barracks and the like. But oh no. What they did was put it about that if the squatters left quietly they wouldn't lose their places on the housing queue or be prosecuted, but if they sat on they'd end up in court *and* they'd go to the back of the queue, or get kicked right off it. So folk got scared. They lost heart. And they started leaving. And the Party gave in, even though we had the newspapers behind us – even the capitalist press!

I can't tell you how much it disappointed me, the Party caving in like that. Mr Pollitt knew it too. He couldn't look me in the eye for a good while. Apparently it was all down to five of our people having been arrested because of the campaign. They'd had a special meeting of the Executive Committee in King Street and decided the Party shouldn't associate itself with any more large-scale squatting operations until our five had come up in front of the magistrate in Bow Street. It was all going to depend on the evidence the police produced, or something like that. The

Central Committee were running around organising a collection to pay for the defence, but it hadn't to look as if the funds were connected to the Party, so they were getting the TUC and some Labour MPs to help out. They had some big-name barrister in mind, Sir Walter somebody somebody. I didn't think that was quite right – putting our five ahead of all those homeless – but it wasn't my place to say so.

Anyway, in a couple of days it was all over, and I went round to Annie's to see what was going on. And that's when I found her gone mad in her bed, Roy stinking to high heaven barring the door and little Margaret rolled up like a hedgehog under the table. Seems Mrs Green got short shrift. Annie told her to clear off, stop interfering, she could manage. So Mrs Green cleared off and Annie went back to being mad. Well, I did what you do. I got the kiddies scrubbed, teeth too – their teeth were coated, really horrible – and fed them, and next day marched them off to school. We had a bit of a meeting, the headmistress and me, and I said to her to keep an eye on Roy as I had the feeling he'd got used to running wild ever since he came home, and to keep an eye on young Margaret too as she was used to being wherever Roy was. Their mother's not in this world, I told her. And something's going to have to be done about that, though for the life of me I didn't know what.

Then, thank the Lord, the woman came up with the best idea I'd heard in a long time. She said, 'Doesn't Mrs Hoskins have parents still alive who could help?' I'd put the Delahayes right out of my mind, which wasn't that hard to do since they'd never really been in it. Soonest met, best forgotten is what I thought of them. Well, of course, I don't have a telephone, but that school did, so the headmistress and me, we spent the morning trying to find the number for Annie's folk, and in the end we managed it.

I was hoping she'd do the telephoning. I didn't want to have dealings with the Delahayes, but I'm family and she's not, so she dialled and I held the receiver. It was Mrs who answered. I said who I was, louder than I should, I think, because she said there was no need to shout, and I told her that our Bill had died of a weak heart. There was one of those pauses when you know the person doesn't know what to say, then she said, 'Oh, I am sorry to hear that.' Then there was another pause and she said, 'How is Anne taking it?' So then I told her that was the reason for my ringing, that Annie wasn't well at all, that she couldn't look after the children because she needed caring for herself. So it might be best all round if Annie and the children went back home to her mother and father to be cared for there.

This time the pause was a whole lot longer. Then she said, and her voice had gone high and tight, 'Oh, I don't think that would do at all. I mean, Anne of course. But we can't accommodate children. You have to understand, we haven't the space. This house is not set up for children. Not at all.'

Don't make me laugh, 'haven't the space'. What does she know about space and not having it? Annie told us often enough what her parents' place was like, and she made it sound like some sort of mansion. A mansion without space! Well, there's a new one. And what was that 'not set up for children'? Annie was a child once, wasn't she?

Mrs Delahaye said, 'There must be some organisation that can take care of the children while Anne is recuperating, so that they can go on going to school. There is no suitable school for young children in our vicinity, you see. So it would be better all round, don't you think, if the children were to remain in London. Can't you think of some organisation that might step in? I feel sure with your . . . connections . . . you should be able to think of one.'

'Oh yes,' I said, in a high old temper by now. 'I can think of an organisation that might step in. It's called family. But maybe you haven't heard of that one where you live.' And I banged the receiver down. Stupid, but there you go. The minute I said it I knew there'd be no going back. I couldn't send Roy and Margaret back up to Openshaw – for all I had the feeling that was where they really wanted to be. It wouldn't have been fair on Mother, she'd looked so tired. But what was I supposed to do with a couple of kiddies, when I never wanted them and didn't know what goes on in their heads?

But I thought it'll only be for the while, until Annie's got herself together again, though I'd have to try and get their points moved over to my ration book. Maybe it wouldn't be long enough to be worth the effort. I'll move in with the children, I thought, and move out when she comes home. I never imagined, not for a moment, that she never would come home.

Part 3

1998

Margaret

It was probably inevitable that it's all panned out like this. And yet I feel I should have taken greater care, been more alert to the likely outcome. But, I mean. Really. There is only so much guff a person can take.

When Peter's Information Group was absorbed by the Gardnor McKinley conglomerate late last year, we knew there were bound to be changes. We suspected their nature, but not the degree. And certainly not the manner. Now you may say we were sheltered, or complacent – and both those accusations would be fair – but it didn't cross our minds, locked in our cubby-holes with our books and journals and screens, that the virus to which so many businesses and companies had succumbed would finally turn its attention to us. Why should it? We were not like other companies, competing in the open market. We were a one-off, and indispensable.

The first indication that something was amiss popped up in our small works canteen. I remember going down for a coffee early one Monday morning and running into Paul Derides, of Small Arms, by the lifts. He was standing there with his capped cappuccino and looking more depressed than I'd seen in a long time – and this is a man known to us all as Eeyore. 'They're wearing straw boaters,' he said. 'I think I'll take the stairs.'

The minute I went through the swing doors I knew exactly what he meant. The canteen staff had been, to a man and woman, made jaunty in straw hats with stripy bands round the crown, and aprons striped to match. They were all so embarrassed they could barely look one another in the eye, let alone me. At the till Mohammad from Mauritius held out his hand for my 75p (and yes I know that's nothing for a coffee these days but the canteen is subsidised to make up for the lousy wages), and then tapped his head with one finger. His boater was evidently too large because it slipped down over his eyebrows. He swore something at it under his breath, took it off and laid it crown down on the counter, like a busker's hat. So I put the 75p in there.

At this point, of course, the manageress came by and he had to whisk the ridiculous thing onto his head again. 'Don't you think you've got them all up to look like jolly butchers,' I suggested, 'from a children's picture book?' 'Gardnor McKinley thinks them very smart,' she replied crisply, which was not strictly speaking an answer to my question. I should have understood that, where boaters begin, worse is bound to follow.

The second indication was the away-day. Journal by journal. The *Intelligence Review* publishes on the second Thursday of the month, so the Friday after was 'calendared' (their word) to leave the office empty, all phones switched to voicemail, *Hello, you've reached Margaret Hoskins at Peter's Intelligence Review. I'll be away from my desk until Monday, but do leave a message . . .* *International Defence* (a nasty suspicion that it was henceforth to be spelled with an 's') had to wait a week, *Peter's Fighting Planes* or 'the sky-divers', as we call them, a further week.

The away-day was out of town just beyond Aylesbury, in a minor manor fallen on hard times, made over into a conference centre, and they'd sent a bus round for us, for our convenience. For our convenience, and to make sure none of us escaped! A stranger with a clipboard stood by the driver to check our names against her list. If one had been missing, she'd call up an operative bloodhound to snuffle them to earth. Nelson Barkworth, Gardnor McKinley's placeman, who had swiftly dethroned our previous Director, the mild-mannered and academically inclined John Bates, dithered at the bus door. (We're all now convinced it was precisely his dithering skills that got him the directorship – that or the beetling of his eyebrows, so tangled and luxuriant that someone, his wife perhaps, should be encouraged to bring out the secateurs.) His irresolution was visible: should he be the first to plunge in and select a seat, and should it be at the back or the front, or indeterminately in the middle? Does the first man in display leadership qualities, or ought the Director step aside and usher his staff in ahead of him? Was his behaviour, his demeanour already being scrutinised by the woman with the clipboard, who was scribbling her impressions into a PDA for onward reporting?

We piled in like children, giggly, noisier than usual, clutching nonchalance like a packed lunch, but secretly wary of being asked to do something undignified. Kiss one another, perhaps, in a burst of sudden bonding or pit ourselves against a 200-foot chasm armed only with a 50-foot rope-ladder. People who have known one another for a long time, but only at work (corridor relationships, as I dub them), have reason to fear variety when it's thrust upon them.

We drove through the suburbs and into the outback of the Home Counties, where each dwelling with a drive and a hedge implied a safe house for the debriefing of sheltering agents. It was immediately evident that this countryside was short on chasms, so phobias of rope-ladders were put aside. The landscape was thoroughly English, gently rural in that domesticated way, but because of the circumstances faintly menacing. Why, after all, assemble the entire department of a respected outfit and convey them, willy-nilly, some distance to a specialised venue unless the intention is to remake them in the image of the venue?

Morning coffee and biscuits had been laid out for us on a long table covered in Persil whiteness. The sun poured in through smudge-free french windows. Young men and women in white shirts and black trousers beamed Antipodean welcomes and guarded the doors. The Americano coffee (weak, therefore) had been brewing on the hot plates too long; the biscuits were the institutional variety – split creams and bourbons. People surely know the sort of thing, and if they don't I can only say they're fortunate. We stood about with our cups and our biscuits, dropping crumbs, trying to chat with nothing to say. We were waiting for teacher, for someone to ring the bell. Beyond the french windows a careful garden rolled down towards a small wood. The lawn wasn't flat enough for croquet so the manor hadn't made it into the ranks of country hotel.

After about ten minutes one of the young men stepped forward, leaving his door unmanned. 'Hello there?' he said. 'My name's Jason? I'm your senior facilitator for this morning's session? But before we begin, perhaps you might like to freshen up. The restrooms are that way?' He indicated with his hand, looking the opposite way, out of delicacy. What has become of us, I thought. And whatever has become of full stops?

Obediently, we traipsed off, boys and girls, to piddle and splash water on our hands. Sidled back to where Jason and his junior facilitators had formed a gauntlet to funnel us into a room of elegant proportions, stripped of period, where functional but slightly padded chairs had been set out in rows describing two shallow semicircles: semicircles are less forbidding than straight lines and facilitators like to be fluffy, while we at Peter's are by nature sceptical and, we prefer to think, hard-nosed. The sash windows shone, and were locked. An extra, internal, pane of plain glass had been added to each window. Air from elsewhere hummed.

The semicircles were facing a screen, in front of which stood a small bentwood table with a PowerPoint projector. A brochure lay on every chair. One by one we approached a chair, picked up the brochure, seated ourselves, and began flicking through – the Pavlovian response of the literate. I'm certainly one of those sad creatures who cannot ignore the written word, initially. Fifty pages of bullet points fall into the category of printed matter that I would normally reject on sight, but the double glazing and upholstered chairs 'impacted' on me, as they say, as effectively as if they had been a pair of sweat-stubbled Hollywood heavies, so I kept to my seat. I scanned the introduction twice before noticing that to my right Greg Mitchell, whose patch is everywhere between Jordan and Pakistan, a man who runs to work in all weathers and then showers even when the boiler has packed up, was breathing heavily.

> This document is intended to serve as the plan to secure the delivery of the contract Key Performance Indicators and as a means of monitoring the delivery and status of the contract over time.

I read the sentence twice, then moved onto the next one, thinking to find clarity there.

> The monitoring methodology will of necessity be made up of a combination of the subjective judgement and the objective status of key outputs.

I read this one twice as well and was about to try again when Greg Mitchell tapped my forearm. 'Don't bother,' he whispered in a voice that hit the silence like a rasp. 'It doesn't get any better.'

'In that case,' I said, and prepared to get to my feet. But a representative of Gardnor McKinley plc was already on his, behind the bentwood table. His grey suit was very well cut. The microphone and overhead projector were his to command. Behind him on the screen were the words

THE FUTURE

and beneath them, in smaller type,

SYNERGIES AND PARTNERSHIP

'Ladies and gentlemen,' he began. 'Colleagues! You all know this is our first meeting since Gardnor McKinley were invited to take part in the modernisation process of Peter's Information Group, so I'm sure you'll all be wanting to be brought up to date on what future management initiatives will be initiated between the company and yourselves. Since we are committed to the consultative process do feel free to put any questions you want to myself as we go along and let me just say that we are all immensely privileged to be invited to work with you in these challenging days and be a part of the process of taking Peter's forward – '

Even though I was in the middle of my row, I felt a sudden need to freshen up again, so I picked up my bag and, muttering my apologies like a senior citizen caught short in the cinema, clambered out, and away. At the door some concerned junior facilitators clustered round me: was I not feeling well? I put a fraudulent hand to my brow and gasped a goldfish anguish. Some fresh air? I nodded. A pair of them, one at each elbow, escorted me out to the ante-room where the coffee cups had been cleared away and the biscuit crumbs vacuumed from the carpet. The french windows were unlocked with a key that one of the facilitators must have had secreted inside a sleeve, and I was ushered out into the open. It was quite delightful. Gentle rural twittering; bright sun on clipped lawns, more of it – dappled – under some large specimen trees; a climbing plant festooning the rear brickwork with clusters of gaudy lilac flowers. Wisteria, if

I'm not mistaken. If there had been dew earlier it had evaporated. A walk was called for. I flexed my wrists, shook out my ankles and headed towards the small wood.

'Oh, I wouldn't go down there if I were you?' One had spoken but all the facilitators smiled at me beadily.

'Why not? Is it dangerous?'

'You might get lost?'

'I doubt that very much,' I said. 'Since the garden slopes away from the house, all I have to do is look up and retrace my steps. Hardly taxing, wouldn't you think.' I noticed that I had put my question without a question mark. A rhetorical question, then, or perhaps a form of mockery. No worries, as they'd say. It had passed them by.

'You'll be missing the key session.' The tone was changing. I had detected, definitely, a full stop.

'Well, you know, I think I can live with that. And my colleagues are used to processing information, when there is some. I'm sure they'll give me a précis.'

'You wouldn't want to go without the question and answers.'

'I wouldn't?' They shook their heads. 'You'd be surprised how good I am at self-denial,' I said, feeling in my bag for a cigarette. They frowned and wrinkled their little noses. 'I've been known to go without questions and answers for weeks at a time.' A sad untruth, of course, for what was my job after all but questions seeking answers, but this was not, strictly speaking, the point at issue.

'It's very important that everyone is there. And seen to be there.'

'Why?' I was getting cross and may have made to stamp a foot.

'Company cohesion? We feel it's best if people all pull together? It's good for team spirit?' They were losing confidence.

'Well,' I said, 'for what it's worth, I didn't ask Gardnor McKinley to buy us out. And if you knew anything at all about research and analysis you'd know that team spirit isn't top of the agenda. We may pull side by side in an outfit like Peter's, but never together. If anyone asks, I absolve you of all responsibility for my actions.' Then I inhaled deeply and puffed a lungful of smoke at them. Childish, I know, but worth it at the time.

Bristling with dignity I stomped down the grassy slope and lost myself from their view by darting into the trees. From behind a fat trunk I peered back and saw they had returned into the house, perhaps to report an absconding.

Beyond the wood the land sloped up again to a hedge, bushy above, scrawny below. For one such as myself, thin and tending to be ill-kempt, crawling between the lower stems of a hedge is always an option. So then I was standing on a narrow country road in a place between somewhere and somewhere else, not a turning or a signpost in sight. I could wait for a passing tractor or walk in search of one. Being the impatient sort, I licked a finger, held it up to the wind, turned my back on its mild breath, and set off.

I was in town before lunchtime. A car travelling towards me at speed forced me to leap up onto the high grassy verge to avoid being hit. The driver unaccountably slowed to apologise, told me the station lay in his direction not mine, advised me to hop in, and bore me to the London train in a matter of minutes. I could have gone straight back to my flat but since it was still Friday I wasn't certain what I would do there, so I went to Peter's instead. The *Intelligence Review* offices were shrouded in silence; everyone at the away-day, by now replete with questions and answers, must be having their lunch, which chief facilitator Jason had talked up. *Three humungous courses, and if you're vegetarians, well, aren't you the lucky ones! No wine, though, folks, sorry. Don't want you all nodding off before the day's business is over?*

Through closed doors I could hear *Defence* being put to bed, but that distanced hum only increased the Christmas Day feel of our two-man cubby-holes, destined soon to become open plan. I sat at my desk thinking I might as well begin working on the recently arrived article by General Sir Reginald Eddington on the preparedness of NATO's most enthusiastic aspiring members to fulfil their obligations – were they to be admitted. I had asked for three thousand words and received nearer eight thousand, written, it seemed, in no particular order. I sighed comfortably and reached for my pen.

One week later: Margaret and Douglas

'Aunty?'

'Douglas!'

'Have you been given the boot? Dad says they've given you the boot.'

'Douglas, dear! They would do nothing so crude. I've been de-hired.'

'Why? What did you do wrong?'

'Oh, you know. Dug my heels in, usual thing, insisting on accuracy.'

'But that's your job! I thought that's what you were supposed to do.'

'Well, indeed. But not . . . Douglas, what's that noise?'

'Road works. Hang on a tick till I get past. I can't hear a thing . . . that's better.'

'You're driving!'

'It's OK, Aunty. Hands free, both of them on the steering wheel. No risk to anyone.'

'And in which of your horrible cars, may I ask?'

'You may not.'

'The guzzler, that means.'

'All my cars are guzzlers.'

'Only some are more guzzler than others.'

'Are you coming to the private view?'

'Douglas, dear. I never go to those things. You know that.'

'But this one's different, Aunty. Dad really wants you there for this one.'

'Why? What's so special? We know what's in it. It's a retrospective. Old, by definition – exhibits *and* artist, come to think of it.'

'No. That's the point. He says there's some stuff in it that he hasn't shown before, and only you will get it.'

'Well, I'll go later, and skulk around under cover, as I always do. Roy knows that. I just don't feel –'

'I know, Aunty. But this time's really different. Dad wants to be with you when you see it. He said.'

'Did he? Can't we go together later? Or earlier, perhaps? Oh no. I can't make earlier. Not yet. Not this week. It would have been all right next week, of course. I'll be a free woman by then, won't I?'

'Yeah, I know. It's crap and I'm sorry.'

'No one to blame but –'

'Sure, sure. I know. Sure. All the same. But look, if you won't come to the private view, will you come over to The Pile for the prog on Friday? You do know they're doing it on the box?'

'Of course I know! But I can watch it just as easily here.'

'Aunty! You haven't been listening. Dad wants to be with you to see it. The thought of it made him go all giggly, the way he gets.'

'Did it?'

'So Mum got huffy.'

'Did she? Oh. Well, maybe . . .'

'Knew that would get you going.'

'Yes, but Douglas, I –'

'So I'll stop by and pick you up. Sevenish?'

'No, Douglas. The programme's not till eleven, so there's no need to be at your parents' much before that.'

'Yes, there is. What about supper?'

'I don't need supper.'

'But I do, Aunty. If you're not prepared to come earlier, how do I pick you up without missing my supper?'

'You're being difficult. Don't pick me up.'

'You're being difficult. I want to pick you up.'

'We can't always have what we want, dear.'

'But I've been brought up to have everything, on demand, as you keep going on about. Started with the breast and then . . .'

'Yes. Well, now you're going to have the novel experience of something being denied you.'

'But you wouldn't deny Dad going through the catalogue with you before they get going on the box. Would you? Would you? Aunty? Hello? Hello? Are you there?'

'Yes, I'm here.'

'And?'

'Douglas, MI6 should have you on their books. Drip drip drip. More effective than water torture. I give in, I give in.'

'Course you do. But actually, Aunty. Are you all right? Are you going to be all right?'

'Financially?'

'I wasn't thinking of that.'

'I haven't the faintest idea.'

Margaret

By the Monday morning after the away-day I'd been feeling less bullish, wondering how to justify my skedaddling to my colleagues. Fortunately, there were still many hours to devote to General Eddington's overview of NATO. He would be getting his draft back accompanied by a full two pages of questions seeking clarifications, proofs, dates and explanations of acronyms. I would have pointed out to him the four occasions on which he appeared to have contradicted himself, his variable spelling of the name of a Polish general, and his confusion of a town in the north-west of the Czech Republic with another of the same name in the south-east, in Moravia. In other words, I could keep my head down with a clear conscience, and my person largely out of sight. Nelson Barkworth, however, didn't wish it so.

At about five o'clock, the hour he can usually be seen gathering his effects together to go home – he keeps industrial hours – he put his head round the door and asked me if I wouldn't mind popping by his office for a moment. So I popped. Nelson closed his door behind me and stood with his back to it, less by way of threat, I thought, than indecision: where should he situate himself for the showdown? Behind his desk: but that might appear cowardly. On his desk then: more comradely but less authoritative. Or on the sofa: but then he would have to pat the seat beside him and it is a small sofa. Too intimate for what he had to say. At the best of times Nelson doesn't look his interlocutor in the eye, and this wasn't shaping up to be the best of times. His gaze swam upwards but was thwarted by the overhang of his brows, so slid instead to the hydraulic hinge on the newly installed fire door of his redecorated office. (Gardnor McKinley, masters of the value of symbolism, had set about rebranding Peter's within months of the buy-out, see further under straw boaters. When governments change, the police keep their uniforms. But when regimes change, the tailors are called in.)

New carpet had replaced the old lino in a deep pile of what

I believe is called in the trade 'mushroom'. The walls had been painted in cream and burgundy; the woodwork in darker cream. The colours will have been recommended by specialists whose job it was to assure Gardnor McKinley that cream and burgundy were both classy and mentally soothing, and would not interfere with the feng shui. Three pot plants, one I recognised quite by chance as a ficus – the other two being from my point of view simply green – had been billeted at strategic points on the mushrooms. The soil round the plants was overlaid with a mantle of small burnished beige pebbles. Nelson's directorial desk, twice the size of its predecessor was, also following professional advice, placed at an angle away from the door and the ingress of marauding multicultural spirits. It had nothing on it but a hands-free telephone, a Mac, and a photograph of his wife smiling broadly despite being, so it appeared, strangled by the entwining arms of their gummy twin sons, who were identically missing their top front teeth.

To begin with Nelson merely shook his head over what he called my little tantrum and offered me a gin and tonic. I thought, they must have had a workshop on this after the Antipodean lunch I'd skipped: horse whispering for directors. Some of us, however, flinch when our line managers try breathing into our nostrils. Gin and tonic has never been my drink and Nelson administered it tentatively, like a student nurse scared of getting the proportions wrong. He padded through the mushrooms to his newly upgraded fridge, discreetly camouflaged in a cabinet, with shelves above for the glasses – sparkling and therefore also new, with none of the water stains office glasses usually get from being rinsed in the Ladies' – and cracked open the lid of the Gordon's. Evidently I was his first patient. One by one he held the glasses up to the light and dribbled in the gin as if a rationing Plimsoll Line had been etched on there. Then, relieved the hard part was over, he splashed in the tonic almost to the rims. Handed me mine, took a noisy sip from his, and gestured at me with his glass by way of reassurance. Safe to drink. He'd tried it first. Surely we can be grown up about this.

'Margaret, please. Don't you see we're really on the same side? I'm no happier about this than you are, but we have to play their game. They own the shop. In the final analysis we have no option but to go along with them in principle and retrieve what we can so that we can move for–'

'You sound like General Jaruzelski justifying martial law as the only means of keeping the Soviets at bay.'

Nelson cleared his throat. 'Yes. Well, I'm sure the poor fellow was under pressure too.'

'You are Our Great Leader,' I snapped back. 'It's your job to protect your people against the vicious onslaughts of the invader.' But remembered that Jaruzelski's collusion had, in effect, kept the invader out. Nelson, luckily, like General Eddington, is not too hot on Central Europe.

'I'm trying to. At this moment in time I am working hard to take us forward and ensure the continued employment of a majority proportion of the staff roll.'

'You mean they want to sack us.'

'We may have to let some people go.'

'Who? How many?'

'Who, they've left up to me. How many depends on how we do.'

'How we do what?'

'Well . . .' He made a point of permitting himself a small smile. 'If you had stayed on last Friday you would have known.'

'Well, since I didn't, and you did, and here we are, why don't you tell me?'

'Yes, why don't I! The *Intelligence Review*, the *Defence Review* and all the others which are currently monthly are to come out weekly. The articles are to be shorter and snappier to appeal to a wider industry. They want a faster turnaround, more advertising space and a less discursive style. They don't feel there's room for . . . what shall we say, Margaret? . . . academic types.'

'You mean, they want a glossy surface but no awkward analytical content, no attention to detail.'

'Well, you do fuss over the details of language too much, surely you'll agree with that.'

'It's not possible to be too fussy about language, Nelson. Content, interpretation, nuance – everything depends entirely on how it's expressed. Alter the structure of a sentence, move a comma – and you're changing the meaning. People need to be aware of that, and if they're not they have no business putting important things on paper. But you seem to be in favour of any old slapdash –'

'Now, now, Margaret.' It was at this point that Nelson must have remembered about arm-patting. For all I know the horse-whispering workshop may have gone into 'Body Language and Tactile Inputs to Human Resource Management', and here was his first real-life opportunity to test theory, so often a wonderful thing, against the nitty-gritty. Carefully he put down his glass and began to lift a consoling palm, but I saw it coming and stepped so smartly to one side that some of my untasted and now hand-warmed drink watered the mushroom field. Feeling himself rebuffed, Nelson's features took offence and his voice hardened. 'Don't forget that being in opposition is a luxury,' he said, turning away both from me and the theory that had just failed him. 'Anyone can snipe from the sidelines.'

'And don't you forget that being in government is a privilege. They can withdraw your directorship just as easily as they gave it to you, so don't imagine mouthing the party line will guarantee your position. If it's simply money they're after, Nelson, the minute you don't deliver you'll get your cards. Meanwhile, luxury or no, I reserve the right to insist that accuracy and reliability on matters of international security is what I was appointed to provide. I grant it was before your time, but these issues aren't simple so I'm not about to simplify them.'

'I hear what you say, Margaret.'

'But?'

'Well. You know. Perhaps. I was just thinking. Maybe you could get the pieces out faster.'

'Maybe I could. If some of the people you feel we should commission to write them would respond more promptly to the queries I send them.'

'Perhaps if you didn't send so many queries –'

'Nelson. If they'd only bloody do their own research properly instead of dashing off any old thing on the understanding that we do it for them to save their bacon, I wouldn't have to.'

'Other journals aren't as . . . fastidious as you are, Margaret.'

'Other journals don't have the responsibilities we do.'

'Gardnor McKinley think we can afford to let up a little.'

'And what? Have the world's Ministries of Defence take decisions on the basis of inaccurate information?'

'Don't you think they do their own research?'

'Judging by the number of calls and emails I get from the minions who work for them, no, I don't.'

'Oh, Margaret!'

Isn't it wonderful how much can be conveyed in the tone of three short syllables, or rather in the tone of three syllables since it is in the nature of all syllables to be short? The falling arc of that 'Oh', the further dip on the 'Marg', and the return to base of the 'ret'. So much clenched-fisted pent-up patience, like an impeccable parent who has ransacked all the recommended manuals for advice on how to deal with serial obduracy, but to no avail. Nelson's toothless twins cannot have tested his equanimity as I did. And yet I maintain, as he knows full well – hence of course the sighing cadence of his voice – that it is my job to test equanimity, that it is indeed the job of every analyst and editor. In this world, in my world, we are testers of equanimity, not the gurus of inner harmony and peace. But it was nearly six o'clock. Perhaps Nelson had had a gruelling day trying to fill advertising space. He should be going home.

'Look,' I said, sounding I thought conciliatory, 'I can see you're in an invidious position. Why don't you get off home to the family and let me get back to my files and we can sort this out another day.'

I'd misjudged him. There wasn't another day.

Peter's leaving 'do's are always the same: the table in the conference room cleared for waxy paper plates; the two little secretaries – one black, one white – inseparable Milly and Sharon, ripping open the bags of crisps; under the table the cardboard boxes of wine, but only two bottles opened at a time in the hope that not all of it will be drunk and the odd one can be held over for next time; colleagues from my home department and anyone passing down the corridor taking advantage of the earlier than usual end to the working day – and the free booze, tanking up as if they were about to be sent on a fact-finding mission to Tehran or somewhere in Saudi; Nelson Barkworth, editor-in-chief (as he likes others to call him), waiting until the cheery faces round him are that little bit cheerier, and pinker (we're not yet ethnically representative in our staffing policy, Milly notwithstanding), flushed enough for him to say his piece.

He had to trawl through my personal file, whistled up from Human Resources, because he only joined Peter's eleven months ago, brought in to shake the place up, or down, and to take us forward into the twenty-first century. Or so he threatened at the time (he'll be lucky if he's still here when it arrives). He and I had had, as he put it, pausing delicately, our little disagreements. Everyone laughed, which of course was the purpose of the delicate pause, and looked at me.

I began by quoting the old chestnut about truth being the first casualty of war blah blah, but how, when Gardnor McKinley took over, I had decided it had instead become the first casualty of the bottom line. I knew my colleagues expected me to say something of the sort, in order to get up Nelson's nose. Without exception, they hoped I would do that, whether or not they believed it themselves. (I have become, over the years, the nearest approximation to Court Jester at Peter's – but without, clearly, the licence granted to jesters by the kingly authority. In private I liked to characterise myself as a prize fighter, urged on to more heroic efforts by fans clustered in safety on the other side of the ropes, absorbing the punches that might in fairness have been distributed among them all. Also in private I had to acknowledge that no one had forced me into that rôle.)

Peter's Information Group, I pronounced, had once been worth working for: it had had clout in the world it served because it had integrity. Our research, our analysis was quoted even in the less specialist media and relied on by governments, NGOs, the UN – even when our findings did not accord with our readers' expectations, or assumptions, or presumptions. In a word, we were, and were seen to be, independent and therefore trustworthy. If we said that such and such a state's military hardware was equivalent to such and such another's, it was understood to be so. If we said that a given regime did not in fact possess the weaponry, or the nuclear preparedness credited to it by its adversaries, it was a tough call for those adversaries to demonstrate otherwise – all their many efforts to do so notwithstanding.

But now, I said, fixing what I wished could be a basilisk stare on Nelson's grim and immovable grin, we, or rather all of you, will find your efforts compromised because in 'the real world' what now counts is speed of delivery over reliability of content. I've told Nelson what I think this will do to Peter's reputation but he doesn't have a problem with it. (At this point my audience turned as one to inspect Nelson. He stood erect, fascinated by the door jamb, with his glass of white plonk poised below his jaw like a dentist's spittoon.) Now, I said, warming to my theme, I'm sure that for anyone who is on message the pay and conditions will improve, quite dramatically, won't they, Nelson, after some codded-up review of value for money. But the question you will have to ask yourselves is, is it worth it?

I regretted that last remark the minute I made it. I was the oldest of all my colleagues, on the brink of natural retirement – if those two words are not oxymoronic – and consequently inseparable from the occupational pension I'd been paying into for nearly thirty years. My youngest colleagues, if they chose to leave in the principled huff I'd implied they should consider, might find other jobs to suit them. But most of my colleagues were not youngest. What were they supposed to do in a real world that considered a man of fifty and a woman of forty over the hill? So my call to arms was hardly an act of valour, since I could sound off with impunity, and anyone still listening knew it.

I told them that it was information – the getting of and the suppressing of it – that had been behind everything I'd ever done, and that it had shaped everything I was. And then, for some reason best known to the lord of sauvignon blanc, I began to say that there was a reason for this and that it all lay in the fact that I'd been brought up in the Faith.

Gratifying mystification on the attentive faces. A closet Catholic? Surely not! I allowed a brief dramatic pause, and explained. 'By which I mean I am a Bolshevik, born and bred.'

It was one of those moments when I wished *I* had been the photographer in the family. It wasn't hard to imagine what they were thinking: wouldn't Peter's have had her vetted when she joined, given what we deal with, given who our clients are? Not so much now, of course, but way back then – in 1968! Student revolution and reds under the bed? There was the sort of silence you might expect if you revealed you'd been abused by your father in childhood, which is all the rage these days – the revelation rather than the abuse – and then they all went 'Oh!' in almost orchestrated unison. Highly satisfactory.

But what I saw on the face of our administrator, and my pal, Joyce, was a mixture of puzzlement and hurt. Hurt because I hadn't told her before, and puzzlement because, impenitent reader of colour supplements that she is, she is well up on the career and lifestyle of my brother, Roy. She knows he lives in a Holland Park mansion (God, how she has angled for an invitation to get in and see that), and is courted by celebrity. Of course her beloved supplements have done the 'deprived childhood on the council estate' to death. Roy did, after all, establish his reputation with his Somers Town portraits as well as all that *Vogue* and *Harper's Bazaar* malarkey. But it amuses me how narrow, how shallow, nay, are the minds of some of these profile writers. Where do they get their information? Why, from the mouth of the subject horse himself! So apparently they've seen no reason to look further than the streets around our flat in Levita House, than the playground of Argyle School, RAF Wilmslow, where he did his military service, and the John French Studio.

Some of the more enterprising hacks tracked down a few old military service conscript colleagues from the year of '56 to see if the young Roy Hoskins had made an impression on anyone then, and found that apart from a spat with another call-up victim that got him locked up for a spell and then punished with a spot of extra 'ablutions', no one could remember much. They were aware of him taking the odd squaddie snapshot but not much more. The incurious gossip-mongers didn't think to inquire any deeper. Yes, they knew we were effectively orphans raised by an aunt, they knew I existed and had me down as some sort of defence academic, they knew of course about my dreadful sister-in-law and her even more dreadful society wedding business. But the Comrades? They never thought to ask. Well, you wouldn't, would you, people might say. But if you don't poke about, what on earth do you expect to learn of any interest?

Back to poor Joyce. She's always been intrigued by the difference between us, Roy and me, especially as we are physically so similar: short and thin, grey-eyed, pepper-and-salt hair – brindled in my case, like a terrier's. Which is how my colleagues characterise me: small, and wiry, and teeth. I thought, seeing Joyce's expression, I shall have to make up to her for this, one of these fine days. She deserves better from me, kindly soul that she is. Now I think about it, I don't know why I came out with the Party background thing at all. I have no qualms about it, naturally, but it was irrelevant to the matter in hand. What would have been relevant would have been to entertain them further with Granddad's story of how he came back from the First World War reeling with disgust because they'd made him execute a comrade after a ten-minute Field General Court Martial had decided the man was a deserter. Outrage at injustice was what he said prompted him to join the nascent Party.

Shall I tell them, I wondered, how he had then tried to find out more about that Court Martial, but had been blocked by official secrecy, and how he thought it had all had to do with class: that the men who were executed were working class, but those who decided on the executions – and then buried the records – were . . . not? My colleagues, I thought, would titter queasily at this because class, we are assured, no longer exists. Race we can talk about – and should – and gender and sexuality, but not class. So then, shall I tell them instead about how his story had become our family myth – not in the contemporary usage that implies a fiction, but in the original, religious sense of imparting meaning to life; a myth passed from him to my father, who died young, and to my aunt who brought us up, and that it was in Granddad's honour, and for a small child's remembered love of him, that I, as the first member of my family to go to university, had decided to study history, military history specifically, and within that the First World War, most particularly all that was allowed to be known about those executions? But that when I was a graduate student there was so much that was still not allowed to be known, although it has all been published now. Shall I tell them?

And then I thought, actually no. What's the point? Not any more. Let's all just drink up and go home. I've said what I meant to, and some. The ball's in their court now – poor sods.

* * *

An hour later everyone else had gone, leaving Joyce and me standing on the topmost of the five wide white steps that lead up to Peter's. I was clutching my Barkworth-presented bouquet – which I had somehow already managed to bedraggle – under one arm, and my huge 'Sorry you're leaving' card under the other. Surrounded by my expectant colleagues, I had had no option but to open it, and then pull the face they clearly hoped for. Easily done. The card had a winsome tabby kitten on it, all round eyes and cutesy sentimentality. Someone must have had fun choosing it: look, she'll really *hate* this! I hadn't read the messages. Those things are best done in private, and anyway I've attended my quotient of leaving parties and signed enough retirement cards to know the sort of thing to expect: some jocular, some spectacularly uninspired (wishing you well in your retirement), the inevitable clerihew from Mike Basildon of Nuclear Proliferation.

As the last one out, Joyce was setting the alarm, and what have you. She said, 'You know, you're going to have to give yourself a project of some sort or you'll go crazy.' (Dear Joyce. She is so good at forward planning the well-being of others.)

'Such as what?'

'I don't know. Something that will keep you researching. You can't go cold turkey. Not just like that. Anyway. Let's get you a cab home. My treat.'

As Joyce knows full well, I rarely take cabs. Added to this the circumstances and the wine provoked a sudden little stab of paranoia. Was she offering her treat because she hoped to be invited up? No one from Peter's, not even Joyce, has ever been inside my front door. I am no cook, no hostess, hospitality is not my forte. But almost as she spoke I sensed my face must have given me away.

Joyce is the kindest, most unthinkingly decent human being I have ever met. She gripped my flower-hugging forearm. 'Not to worry, Margaret. I'll only see you to the door. I know you.' She was treading carefully down the five steps, slightly drunk, as I was, on too much sauvignon, dispiritingly tepid, with only Twiglets and Cheerios and Doritos to blot it all up.

Evidently I was making a hash of clutching the bouquet, and, convinced that half the flowers would die and the rest fall out of the arrangement if she didn't rescue them, Joyce plucked the whole caboodle from my arms and suggested I 'hail a cab' while she finished locking up. 'What a wonderfully old-fashioned phrase,' I said. 'Hail a cab. Lovely!' I handed over the bouquet, wobbled down the steps to the pavement, with my hand up in case a taxi should be passing. To my astonishment, not only did one pass but it stopped where I stood. I scrambled in, Joyce on my tail, gave the driver my address and we swung away.

The bouquet made the confines of the cab smell like a florist's, and the driver said, 'Your birthday is it, love?' to Joyce, as she was holding the flowers. 'Not exactly,' I said, and thereafter we proceeded, stop–start through the rush hour, in silence. We were of course both dopy from the wine, always lethal in the afternoon. But as we turned into Somers Town Joyce stiffened, withdrew her spine from the backrest to sit tensed and upright. As departmental administrator she's had the addresses of all the staff but that doesn't mean she knows what these addresses imply. She was taken aback but didn't wish, and was too polite, to say so.

I decided to help her out and indicated the building opposite the gate to my block. I said, 'It'll be very convenient for the British Library, living here, when it opens. Mind you, I could have done with it earlier, when I was growing up. Except that I wouldn't have been given a reader's ticket, and now, of course . . .'

The usual two groups of lads were circling, one lot on foot (Bangladeshi) and the others on bikes (English), wary, preparing to snarl under their breath, as if young Richard Everett had been stabbed there only yesterday and not four years ago. The cyclists in their hoodies were bumping off the pavement onto the road and doing wheelies to get up onto it again. The Bangladeshis on their feet clustered and glowered. Bored to tears, every one of them. And seething.

Joyce flinched. She indicated the cyclists and said, 'They look a bit like my son and his friends, except that, I don't know, this lot look more like the real thing, if you see what I mean. Aren't you scared?'

'What of?' I said. 'They couldn't be less interested in me if they tried.'

I was leaning forward and telling the driver to stop anywhere

here, so he pulled up just past the lads on the bikes. I got out and reached into the cab for my flowers, but felt suddenly both awkward and churlish. In truth, I couldn't simply wave an airy farewell to Joyce, after all these years, and saunter into the estate, leaving her alone in the cab, on alien territory. What to do?

I shrugged and said, 'I can offer you a cup of instant, if you fancy it. Haven't got any real.' As invitations go I daresay it could have been more gracious but I plead inexperience. I turned into the gates.

'Hey, Margaret!' she shouted. 'Hang on a sec. Wait for me.'

The bike lads all yelled, 'Yeah, Margaret. Wait for her.' I gave them two fingers behind my back, but paused to allow Joyce to pay the cabby off, and noticed she got a receipt. So then, perhaps not her treat after all. The poor woman blushed. Clearly getting me home by taxi was part of Nelson Barkworth's instructions: a small generous act whose cost would come out of his pocket, or a corporate expense to ensure I was seen safely off the premises and all the way home to the other side of my front door.

We crossed to the stairs of my block together, Joyce cleaving to my side and throwing apprehensive glances at the surroundings. The courtyard I have traversed every day for most of my life was, I saw, partly bricked, with a single tree in the middle, a curved bench hugging its trunk. A small playground to one side was fenced in green mesh, huge spikes curving inward at the top. To my eyes these were to keep balls in; to Joyce's, no doubt, to keep people out. The ground floor windows were sensibly meshed to protect the glass – except, it is true, there were signs forbidding ball games on every wall. One door we passed was shielded in cast iron, and had been for so long that it had become invisible to me. The old note from the magistrates' court declaring the property closed had long blown away.

Joyce suddenly couldn't help herself. 'It looks like you all live under siege,' she blurted.

'Oh, don't be ridiculous!' I said. My block is rendered and could do with repainting to retrieve its original off-white. I pointed up to the fourth floor saying, 'That's me', aware, as I had not been before, of the satellite dishes clinging everywhere like fungus. The staircase is concrete.

Joyce said, 'You wouldn't want to fall on these steps, would you? They're so sharp.' It had never occurred to me that one might fall. As we climbed I heard Joyce's breath struggling somewhat. 'No wonder you're fit,' she said, 'although you don't carry the weight I do.' She slapped her child-bearing haunches.

There are four front doors on my landing, all of them black: two side by side look out over the courtyard, the two at each end face each other. Mine looks out over the courtyard. As I wielded my key I regretted inviting her. It seemed to me that what could not, or should not, be scrutinised was about to be judged. Every domestic detail would be squirrelled away to be laid out for my colleagues – erstwhile – on Monday morning: the short narrow hallway, the cramped square kitchen at its end with the white formica-topped table and the four chairs pushed tightly up against it. You needed only to look once to understand that these days nobody ever sits here.

I dumped my flowers in the sink and filled the kettle. 'You take it weakish, don't you?' I said, spooning the coffee into a couple of mugs. 'Shit! I'm not sure I've got milk.' I opened the fridge and there was some, but a precautionary sniff all but made me retch. I stuck my tongue out and poured the milk down the sink, unfortunately over the flower stalks. 'Do you mind it black?' Joyce said she did not. 'I have some biscuits,' I said. 'Hobnobs.' I keep them in a tin because I like my Hobnobs crisp. But when I put the tin on the table, Joyce burst into tinkling laughter.

'Margaret!' she said, and looked pointedly at the picture on its lid – an old scratched lid on which the very faded picture was of a tabby kitten.

'Good grief!' I tried to cover my embarrassment. 'We've . . . I've had this so long I don't see it any more. It's just a tin, you know. For biscuits. You don't look at things you live with, do you.' And you don't, until an interloper arrives, all agog with interpretation. I picked up a mug of coffee in each hand to go into the sitting room, said, 'You'll bring our furry friend, Joyce, won't you', and led her next door.

If anything, my sitting room is even more dispiriting than the kitchen. It's no longer possible to guess what colour the sofa used to be – brownish now, but flowered, perhaps, once. And the armchair, with the sentinel standard lamp behind it where I usually read, is a flattened, threadbare affair. Probably I ought to go out and buy vibrant, disguising throws. Clearly, bringing Joyce home had been a mistake. All it had done was point out to me previously invisible deficiencies. I ushered her to the sofa and retreated to my armchair.

Joyce sipped at her black coffee and nibbled the edges of her Hobnob. 'Have you lived here long?' she asked, in desperation, forgetting, I think, that I had already told her I had grown up here.

'All my life,' I said. 'First with my parents and my brother. And then with my aunt and my brother.'

'Oh dear, Margaret.' she said, mourning for me. 'I'm so sorry. Did your parents pass away young, then?'

'My father died, and my mother lost her marbles over it. I'm told. I don't remember it.'

'Not at all?'

'Absolutely nothing. I must have been too small.'

She didn't ask how small, for that would have been prying, and Joyce is too delicate to do that. Visibly longing to ask about my brother, she made a polite enquiry about my aunt instead.

'My aunt's lost her marbles too.' I said. 'She used to live here but now she can't. She's in a home.'

'Your wanderer's here again.' That's what he'd said on the phone, the youth (name of Matt) who always rang from HSBC, not his fault, but invariably at the least convenient moments. Although, as I hear myself say this, I detect something that sounds callous or, as the contemporary parlance would have it, 'uncaring'. But you have to picture it. On that particular occasion, as on so many others, I was in an editorial meeting when the call came, and Milly clipped in on her stilettos with the message. She's a sensible girl, is Milly, and doesn't disturb meetings for no reason. I took the call back at my desk.

Aunty Pam had pitched up at HSBC half an hour or so before, on the same quest as usual. Matt told me he'd managed to inveigle her into the small office upstairs at the back where she usually ended up, in order not to upset the customers. (Aunty Pam was happy enough to be in that room because she thought it was where she was meant to be anyway. In fact, when the phone had rung, she had snatched it up before Matt could stop her and announced, 'Temple Bar 2151', leaving the unfortunate Matt with some explaining to do.) 'I'll be with you in fifteen minutes,' I said, then rang Roy, who was of course not there, and left a message on his machine.

What is it about the language of finance that requires composite adjectives? Low-risk, high-yield, well-managed, widely spread. Thank God Aunty Pam hadn't a notion where she was. The headquarters of the Communist Party becoming a branch of one of the world's largest globalising banks would not have seemed an irony to her, because Aunty Pam doesn't do irony.

What I've never been able to understand, and no neurologist has ever been able to explain to me is this: having managed to make her way to 16 King Street through a quarter that had changed beyond recognition since the Party shut up shop there, how was it that when she arrived she couldn't see there was something wrong with the building, something not quite familiar? Was it that her addled brain fished out a vision of how it ought to look, obliterating what was there? Or did she literally not see it? The large mottled tiles on the floor; the bleeping ATMs and paying-in machines; the wall-mounted screen with the FTSE 100 share prices in green, red and blue, flickering and changing like a demented airport arrivals board; the stripe of red carpet leading to the seating areas and the desks; the Thomas Cook exchange rate directly opposite the entrance; the outlandish giant terracotta pot of variegated ferns. Did she really not take in any of this?

One sight of her and Matt's heart must have sunk. Here comes batty Miss Hoskins again, with her querulous demand to pick up Mr Pollitt's letters, with her obdurate refusal (no, lad, I know what needs doing round here, I've been coming here more years than you've had hot dinners) to be persuaded that, 'really, Miss Hoskins, there is no Mr Pollitt here at all and never has been.' (Ouch!) 'This is a bank, Miss Hoskins. It's been our bank since 1992, and before that it was the Midland Bank.' And young Matt hadn't what it takes to imagine a time when it wasn't a bank, because that was before he was born. So from his point of view there indeed never had been any Mr Pollitt here.

By the time I got there, Aunty Pam was drinking the sweet

tea they'd made her and eating a rich tea biscuit, and telling the miserable young man how glad she was to see him neat in a suit and white shirt. She only wished more of the young ones would realise that the capitalist state wasn't going to crumble before a gang of careless scruffs. That was in the days when John Bates was still our MD, and he'd had an elderly relative or two to look after in his time. 'Don't worry, Margaret,' he'd said as I was galloping out of the door. 'See what you can arrange for your aunt, and stay home with her in the meantime. It sounds as if she really shouldn't be on her own any more.' Decent man, John Bates. He didn't know the half of it. Aunty Pam shouldn't have been on her own for a long time, but I had to work, and she didn't want to leave where she'd lived for fifty-odd years. Now she was going to have to.

It's Roy who pays, of course. Conscience money, I call it.

Poor Joyce had sat patiently, all tact and tiny sips, while my mind was elsewhere. When she saw that I was back with her she leaned towards my armchair and said, 'What are you doing this evening? I mean, you could come over to ours for supper if you'd like and I could run you back afterwards. I'm doing a Spag Bol, and it's your favourite, isn't it?'

I shook my head, said it was a sweet offer but my nephew was coming over and we were going to my brother's house. 'He's got a new exhibition,' I said, 'Or, rather, an old one. They're doing it on the box. Eleven o'clock BBC2.' To allow her the option to watch – which of course I knew she would. I could see the mention of Roy's house had set her imagination working, that she could barely restrain herself from asking me to wangle that invitation.

'I'll be on my way, then,' she said. And then she asked, God alone knows why, 'How was it, growing up with your brother and your aunt. Did you all get on?'

'Get on?' How could she be so obtuse? 'It wasn't a question of getting on. It was damn near the best time of my life.'

Roy

How the fuck did those pashas do it? I've enough trouble with only two women, but at least they're not under the one roof. Jesus Christ! Well, they will be tonight and I'm the stupid bugger who'll have to carry the can for that one. Poor old Gina. I feel for her, to be perfectly honest, because I know Mig gets up her nose – and the other way about, but my wife can't expect me to junk my sister. Nor vice versa.

What Gina said, when I warned her, was, 'Why couldn't Margaret come to the private view like everyone else? She never comes, does she? You'd think she was boycotting your shows on purpose, or something.' Or something, more like. It isn't the shows Mig's boycotting. Then I got the old one: 'Why does she always have to have special treatment?' I say, 'Because she's my sister and she has been all my life. Don't you get special treatment too?' And she says, 'It's different.' That's true. It is different. But tonight, I said, what with Mig getting her cards and out on her ear, we'll be doing whatever suits her.

I told Gina, if Mig drops her pistachio shells on the carpets, I'll hoover them up myself before the cleaner comes. Fact is, I'm the one shoving the hoover round as often as not 'cos I quite like doing it, especially on those carpets. Got them in Persia on a contract for *Vogue*, thirty years back, it must be, and I love them as much now as I did when I set eyes on them. They've got a depth of colour you don't see anywhere else. *Vogue*'d already picked the place – all stone columns and ancient ruins and not my scene, but the money was good and it was a way of getting out there, Peacock Throne and the rest of it. *Vogue* picked the backdrop. I picked the carpets but then had a helluva runaround getting them out the country and back home. All perfectly kosher. It was the weight was the problem.

It's not that Gina gets twitchy about carpets, it's that she can't hack it when Mig doesn't notice, or doesn't seem to care, if a bit of sodding shell lands on the floor. And, I said, if Mig wants to smoke in the house, she's fucking going to. None of this taking her fags out to the terrace. She's just lost her job, I said, and she put her whole life into that. You don't need to tell me, she said. But what's she going to do with her whole life now? Be hanging round here all the time? Don't be silly, Gina, I said. That's the last thing she'd want to do. Don't be so sure, she said. But she went to get the nuts and put them out anyway.

Don't get me wrong. We've got a good thing going, Gina and me. You don't laugh at thirty-five years, not these days you don't. Married in June 1963, and met over a wedding too – this is early history when I was still making a living, part-time, out of weddings and christenings and cheesy family portraits. We used to polychrome them by hand back then. Made everyone look rosy. Terrible. When I wasn't doing that, I was playing second fiddle to the second fiddle in John French's studio, then got promoted up a fiddle. Lucky for me I'd kept up my call-up muscle, all the clobber he had me carrying around for him whenever he decided to do a street shoot. Luckier for me, not too often. Mostly it was studios, and I learned more from him about lighting – stuff I decided to unlearn later – than I could've from anybody else.

When I first went for the job he asked me if I knew how to use filters and incandescent light, and what speed film would I use for a moving street shoot on a bad day? And I said, "Course. Sure. Depends.' I'd've been a fool not to. But I didn't know what the fuck he was talking about. I'd fancied myself as a photographer before I started with him and found out in about ten minutes I didn't know the first thing. He only took me on because *he* fancied *me*. Came onto me just the once and then didn't bother. I reckon he was right to give it a try, though. Everything's worth a try.

But this wedding, the one where I met Gina, was in Godalming, a joke of a place if you ask me. Chocolate-box church and mock Tudor reception. After it, when I was going through the negatives I thought, hello, what's this? There were more pictures of the gorgeous bridesmaid with the black hair than there were of the sodding bride! Oh yeah? I said to myself. Old camera done a bit of its own selecting, has it? Well, it wasn't hard to find out who she was and bingo, next thing she knew I'd got me some legover in the grass on a nice spring day. I reckon it was a turn-on for her too, dating a jobbing photographer who'd come off a council estate. I was her bit of rough. And fair dos, she was the glossiest thing I'd set eyes on. Still is. Fantastic.

Was I thinking wedding bells? Not a chance, and no more was she, but eleventh shag and Dougie's on the way. Not that I was counting. The way she sees it is he was in the wings waiting to be born. Asking to be born. And I go with that. I'm not going to say I wasn't knocked back when she told me she was knocked up, and I'm not going say what was the first thing that came into my head because it's what would have come into any bloke's head, but to be perfectly honest I'd played the field a fair bit by then, starting when I was on National Service, like a lot of us did because we hadn't been away from home before. And anyway, as sixties totty goes, Gina was pretty hard to beat. And then I thought, but Jesus Christ, I'm going to be a father! A fucking father!

I was twenty-six, which wasn't that young to be starting a family. Not in those days. And it hit me then. If I was going to be anything like my dad, I might be snuffing it in five years' time. I hadn't given that one a thought before either. Funny that, isn't it? (And now I'm pushing twice the age the poor sod was he when he went.) So yeah, let's have this kid, I decided. Since I'm the last one left in the Hoskins line, let's keep it going. But, if I'm really honest, it wasn't my dad I had in mind but my granddad. I wish he'd lived long enough to see Dougie. He'd have really loved the kid. Doted on him. Now there was a man with a lot of love in him.

But it wasn't just Dougie waiting to be born, it was a couple of careers as well. I'd been a snapper on more duff weddings than any halfway decent ones – the set-up, the flowers, the order of ceremony, the décor at the receptions, the colours, they were all the same. Always the fucking same. Meant to be the best day of someone's life but you couldn't have told one from another, and you'd think, if this is how it starts, if this is the most exciting it gets, what's the rest of their lives going to be like?

After I'd banged on about this for a few weeks Gina said, all right then, I bet I can do it better. And of course the first wedding she organised was ours. Talk about things coming together. Because of her family there were pictures in all the right glossies, not done by me of course, with captions like, 'Society girl in a field of flowers' and 'Glamorous Gina McLaren weds up-and-coming photographer Roy Hoskins, at a reception to remember'. (If I wasn't up-and-coming before, I sure was afterwards.) Gina did that wedding like a flower child before there were flower children, and set the trend. Trestle tables in a meadow – classy ones, mind you, a daisy-chain round her neck, and a floating muslin peasant-style dress with Dougie tucked away snug as you like underneath and nobody the wiser, except Mig, of course, and Gina's parents.

They weren't exactly over the moon about me but what could they do? P (that's my aunt) wasn't over the moon either. I can still see her in her coat and her lace-ups standing up to her ankles in grass looking down in the mouth with a glass of champagne in her hand, wishing it was a cup of tea. She wasn't a happy bunny in those days anyway. Of course Mig went ballistic. You're throwing your life away, she said. You don't have to get married just because some girl's gone and got herself pregnant – doesn't say much for sisterhood, that one, does it? But I suppose that was a tad before sisterhood got invented. And, as I say, Mig and Gina have never hit it off.

The in-laws bought us this maisonette in Camden Town, basement and ground floor, when Gina said she didn't want to live in Surrey any more, and we were away. With Dougie boxed up in his carry cot my lovely wife branched out. She did receptions on boats, in London buses, in black and white like forties films, themed every which way you can think. And they keep coming. She's made a mint, probably more than I have if we counted it. It's just that they don't make TV programmes about her, though *Vogue* and *Cosmo* and *Good Housekeeping* and *Harper's Bazaar* have all done profiles. Even *Vanity Fair*. Come out more like ads, though, if you think.

But they did something for me too, those weddings. Back then it was all set-piece shots, groups on the stairs of the Register Office or in the church doorway, then bride's family, groom's family, couple and in-laws, and on and on. It was what they wanted for the album so they had to have it, all smiling like they were trying to reach their ears, stiff as squaddies on parade. Tripod stuff. Sharp focus all round, full face. Nothing interesting. You could fall asleep doing it. But I'd shelled out on a little Leica, and once they were all knocking back the bubbly I'd prowl round snapping away. Nobody notices the photographer 'cos he's not on the guest list, and you're invisible – just so long as you don't say anything.

Some of the women must've bought what they were wearing straight out of Yves Saint-Laurent or Pierre Balmain. One or two of them even knew how to wear it. So I tagged after them and got them from every angle – on the move with the hemline in a curve going one way and their hair the other. Snatches of other faces, a forearm and a hand raising a glass, someone scowling in the background just out of focus. Not one of them looking directly into the lens. Bits of other people's arms and legs leaving the frame, coming into the frame, but all directing your eye onto the million-dollar girl in the expensive get-up.

I'd leave the tripod shots with the studio to process, but I took the Leica and everything in it home. Gina hadn't been as sold on the basement as I was, but basement means dark room and I reckon I spent more time playing at chemistry down there than I did above ground. Forgot what ordinary air smells like and didn't care either. I took my favourite prints to John – when I was still calling him Mr French. I owe that guy everything, 'cos whatever else he was he wasn't mean. If he thought you had something in you, he'd push for you. So he pushed for me, and I was offered jobs by a couple of editors. But I didn't want to be locked into anyone's house style, so I said, if it's all right by you I'd rather be paid contract by contract and tout myself around.

That wasn't all it was, of course. I can say it now, looking back, but I couldn't've said it then. That world, the glossies, the people who belonged in it – I might just as well have been a foreigner. I couldn't work out what went on in their heads – took me a good few years to figure out too: answer is, not much. And, let's be fair, they couldn't make me out either. I didn't want to try and be like them but I was afraid that if I got my feet under their table, properly, I might start turning into them, without noticing it. So I thought, better stay the outsider, Roy, then at least you'll know what you're doing and why. And I was quids in doing it. I'd be lying if I said I wasn't. When you're not like the rest of them, everybody remembers you, and in a crowded field that helps. Anyway, I never regretted it, keeping on the outside. Freelance may have given the bank manager a frown or two between the eyebrows, but I was my own man, so eventually I could lay down my own rules. No Mayfair. No parks. No regency indoors. No porches. No more sodding stone columns and ancient ruins.

I had a subways series, with my girls sharp as crystal in this gorgeous point of stillness while the rest of the world was whooshing off somewhere on a train. New York and Paris suited better than London for those. I put the models on roofs, what looked like near the edge, and snapped them from below so if you had vertigo you'd better not look. I had them swinging through factories, between the trash cans in alleyways – anywhere, only not studios. If some tosser of an editor wanted his pictures nice and tidy he had plenty of other people who could give him that. Leave me out, I said. Glamour's great. I'm all for it. And I've got nothing against making a lot of dough. But there's still a real world out there, and it's mine, where I come from. So Beauty can strut her stuff in my Beast.

And then, you know what? Some new shoot is commissioned but all out of nowhere you think, no. No more of this. I've had it up to here. Time to do something new. We'd already moved, upmarket, Gina and Dougie and me, to Holland Park and the Pile – more Gina's earnings than mine, I don't mind saying. I won't knock it. The area's very smart, good nosh up the road in Notting Hill, leafy and all the rest of it. But you don't know who your neighbours are. All you ever see of them is next door's Filipina maid brushing down the front steps while her husband's polishing the boss's Roller. So I decided to take me a professional trip down memory lane and went back to Somers Town. Not that I hadn't been going anyway, every week when I was in England, lugging Dougie, not lugging Dougie, to see Mig and have the odd get together with P. But once we'd left Camden Town it wasn't as easy. Needed explaining. Needed a bit of subterfuge from time to time.

I had my first solo exhibition in . . . Jesus, what's my memory like! . . . 1970, I think it was. 'The Somers Town Portraits': all the old geezers from the estate, all the old bags, the teenage mums and their kids, the two women who ran the launderette like something out of *Eastenders*, the guy from the roadies' café on Chalton Street who always had a fag stuck to his lip, bottom right-hand corner. The characters who showed up every Friday for the market. Every one of them people you'd pass on the street and not give a second look, but every one of them with a name.

They were good pictures, some of them set up, some caught on the hop. My favourite was this hod carrier slinging bricks in an arc to a brickie who had his hand out like a baseball player without his mitten. I'd shot that one in two versions. One fast with a flash, so the brick was sharp, and suspended in the air midway between the two guys; they've both got their right hand out, the one who's just let go and the one who's just hoping to make the catch, and you can see they've only got eyes for that brick. But I did another version, slow enough to freeze the two guys while what I wanted was a blurred curve of movement between them, and in this one it looks like they're dancing, linked by the tips of their fingers by this misty grey rainbow. I can't remember how many bricks the poor kid had to keep slinging till I got the exposure right – enough to build the Great Wall of China probably. In the end I couldn't make up my mind which version I liked best so I kept 'em both. Proud of them, I was. Proud of them all, in different ways. All GSP black and white, of course. Could've done colour, but colour doesn't suit Somers Town. And I'm talking film here, not Bangladeshis. They weren't around then, anyway.

For some reason that show hit the spot, pushed the buttons of the time. The press came, the punters came, and I was more or less a gallery cert from then on in. Thames and Hudson. Arena. You name it. Funny thing is, P wouldn't let me take her. Not once. Foot down. No, lad, you're not coming near me with that contraption. Of course I could have cheated and got her when she wasn't looking, but then what would I have done with the photo? I don't take pictures to keep them hidden. I didn't do Mig either, although she's Somers Town through and through. You don't put Mig on display. If any of them had come to the gallery the other 'portraits' would've asked. They'd've said, where's Margaret? But of course none of them had ever been to a gallery, not then and probably not now either.

The private view yesterday evening wasn't bad. Same old same old. Canapés and critics. Telly types in earlier for the show because it was a retrospective – made me feel a bit like I was already in the grave (what's the difference between a retrospective and a posthumous? Only that in one of them you're definitely a stiff), and of course a lot of ballyhoo about the early pics. I'd had a run-in with the gallery over those anyway. I'd warned them I was going to put up some stuff from a long time ago but I hadn't told them what they were going to find when they unpacked. All I'd said was if they had any objections I'd pull the whole lot.

Poor Gina, though. People had kept coming up to her to ask her to explain, and of course she couldn't. I knew it had upset her; humiliated her, is what she'd said. 'What's it all mean?' she'd hissed at me.

But Mig didn't need telling. I got her sat on a sofa, nuts and ashtray and a tumbler of Château Lafitte – which is how she likes it (Gina reckons she can't tell the difference between that and Bulgarian plonk, but so what) – and poured one for myself in a proper glass. She took a glug and picked up the catalogue. 'So what's all the fuss about?' she said, flicking through all the old stuff she knew – though she did linger over the odd one that took her fancy again. 'Oh, yes,' she'd go, and tap it with her unlit fag, 'Yes. That one *is* good, isn't it. I always did like that one. But where are they, the ones Douglas was going on about? Where are your great mystery . . . Oh! What the f— ? Oh, you idiot!'

She had this huge grin on her face but a dollop of extra shine in the eyes.

Dougie and Gina were on the other sofa, sat side by side holding their glasses by the stems, legs crossed, stiff and silent as a pair of strangers in the doctor's waiting room. You could feel them sort of crouching and watching, 'cos they hadn't understood and I hadn't said anything yet. I was going to. I'd told 'em both: all will be revealed. In due course. But sorry, guys, Mig has to get first whack at these. Unfair, I suppose, since they'd already seen them, but couldn't make head or tail. But a photographic retrospective means looking back, thinking back, not just the gallery or the punters, but the photographer. It's remembering. It's fishing out what you thought you'd forgotten. And if it's genuine, if it's really going to be about the past, then it'd better be all of it. Or as much as you can dredge up at the last chance saloon.

And OK, it was a bit up the old arse, I'll give you that, hanging these sodding great blanks, framed in black like I always do, with just titles and nothing else to go on. But when you're in my game and you get to my age, I reckon you should be able to do what you want.

'D'you remember, Mig?' I said, though I saw she'd got them straight off. 'D'you remember?'

She said, 'How could I not? Every one – nearly. *Origins*. It was raining, wasn't it? Drizzling? And *Cucumber Ascending* – you pretentious prick! You were so mean, the pair of you. But then, we did . . . Oh, look, *The Argument*. It makes me blush now, Poor Aunty Pam, although she did . . . and *The Revolutionary*. Ah, yes I remember it well, eh, Roy? But what's –?'

Gina smashed her glass down and it broke. 'Can't the two of you shut up!' she yelled. 'What's any of it with those bloody silly names? *Cucumber Ascending*, for God's sake, Roy. And *Origins*. What's *Origins*, for crying out loud?'

Part 4

Pictures in an Exhibition

1948
Origins

Roy, Margaret and Pam

'Paul Cooke brought us presents when he come last week.'

'I like Paul Cooke.'

'You always say that, Mig.'

'Well, I always like him! He plays nice games and things. When he come last week –'

'Came, Margaret. Not "come".'

'When he came last week he said we could play hide and seek all afternoon but not here 'cos there's nowhere to hide in, so he said we should go out into the Fields where there's lots of places and –'

'He said it was presents for Christmas, though Christmas was weeks ago. He had Christmas with us last year, didn't he, but he couldn't this year . . .'

'His mother's getting on, love, I told you, so he had to go back home to be with his own folk, as a young man should. Still, he's a good lad, and he made it up to you. And as a matter of fact he did take you out into Coram's Fields, a bit of a step, I thought from here for Margaret's short legs, but –'

'He gave me a piggy back!'

'Well, aren't you the lucky one!'

'Yes and he –'

'Oh, shush, Mig. I want to say. He give me . . . gave me this camera. It's a Brownie, and you look in here, the viewfinder it's called, and when you can see what you want the photo to be, you click this bit. And then you get a picture.'

'But Roy can't get no pictures 'cos Paul Cooke didn't give him no film to put in.'

'"*Any* pictures", "*any* film", love. Not "no film". And no, he didn't, because film's expensive and so's the developing of it, and I can't afford that and no more can Paul Cooke.'

'Yes but –'

'It doesn't matter, though. Paul Cooke said the best pictures are the ones you see and then you take them in your head.'

'And keep them in your head, he said.'

'Yes.'

'Your head'll be all full up of pictures and you won't have room for anything else.'

'Oh yes he will, my girl. Our Roy's got a big enough head for all sorts of things, don't you think?'

'Yes and –'

'I took some pictures yesterday, really good ones, when we went to Coram's Fields. Paul Cooke said to look for stuff to take, but it had to be interesting, he said. Not just any old thing. He said having a camera makes you see things you don't see when you're not looking.'

'Well then, Roy. Say what you found, love. Everyone's waiting.'

'I saw some feet. Not real feet. I mean, I saw footprints. Black ones. But they was all wrong because it was just one foot. And I showed them to Paul Cooke, and he said, so tell me what's happening here, Sherlock. What do these footprints say to you? So I looked at them and it was all the person's right foot, very big, so the person must've been big, and it was a man's shoe, so it was a big man in his shoes, hopping, it looked like. There was a footprint and then miles away there was another one just the same and then another one, all just the right foot, and it would've been these giant hops. So I took pictures of the footprints. And Paul Cooke said we was going the wrong way and instead of following the footprints we should go back to where they started. To their origins, he said. And Mig said, "What's origins?", didn't you, Mig? And he said it's where things begin from.'

'Yes and –'

'It's my story, Mig. You can tell yours after. So we went back and traced where the footprints all come . . . came from. And we had to go out of the Fields and along the pavement and round to Guilford Street, on the other side from the fence, and we found this giant splash of black against the wall of a house. It was a white wall and Paul Cooke said somebody must've dropped a can of black paint and then trod in the spill with just one foot. And then wherever he stepped he left a print, but only with that foot.'

'No but –'

'What, Mig?'

'It could have been a different man stepped in the paint. Not the man what dropped it.'

'It don't matter, Mig. It's the prints what . . . who mattered. It don't matter whose they were. They looked funny, that's all.'

'It does matter. It does.'

'Why?'

'It just does.'

'Oh Mig! You're so –'

'That's enough of that. People don't want to listen to the pair of you argy-bargying. And it's soon time for your tea, so get off and get yourselves washed, and keep your nonsense to yourselves.'

Pam

Paul Cooke's been so good to Roy and Margaret ever since our Bill died. It started one evening when we were leaving King Street, not long after Annie had gone home to her parents' and I'd moved myself in here. He'd popped by for something from the *Worker* – that's not in King Street, by the way, but in Farringdon Road – and he said to me, 'How are those children getting along?' And I said something like, 'So-so, you know.' He said he could remember what it was like to be Roy's age because all in all it wasn't that long ago for him, which was true. And then he said, 'I could take them out to the park, if you like, of a weekend.' I said, 'What park's that, then?' Folk'll be laughing at me, I know, as Coram's Fields isn't half a mile from here it turns out, but I didn't know it because it's not on my route. You have to go east to Coram's Fields, but my way's west to King Street, there and back, there and back. When would I have the time to go round the local streets just to be looking at them! But I was glad he offered, and touched all the same. He had no need to offer, and I thought it might be a good thing if he did get them out of the house, especially for our Roy, because a boy needs a man round him.

It was a time when Roy was always scrapping in the school playground, little fists going everywhere, bloody noses all round. He was only small but even though he's a good-natured lad at heart sometimes he can lose his temper and you won't know why. And I thought, my goodness, that lad could do with a father to sort his head out for him, and then up pops young Paul Cooke and offers himself, right on cue. Of course he couldn't be a father-figure, he'd be more like an older brother, but it would help. All they have is women teachers at school, and then there's just me at home and little Margaret. Paul said he was offering for his sake, not theirs, because Coram's Fields won't let a grown man in without kiddies to accompany him. It's a good place to remember being a child, he said, and it's not been there more than ten years or so, as a park for playing in.

I don't recall that we had parks specially laid on for playing in. It was mainly streets then, as it is now. And it's made me try to remember what our Bill was like as a lad but all I can think of is that he was soft. In a good way, mind, but always soft. And Roy's not like that. He's in trouble for his scrapping more days than not, and I get tired of going round to the school when the headmistress calls. They make a joke of it in King Street. If the phone goes and someone asks for me, there can only be one reason. Mr Pollitt says Roy is practising for the struggle, and he laughs, but that's only to make me feel better about it. I know that Mr Pollitt doesn't think people should go about settling their quarrels with their fists. On the other hand, Roy is short for his age. I see it in the playground and on the street, and he has to stand up for himself or the other lads would walk all over him. And I daresay he's taken to lashing out to show them he can, and make them keep their distance.

He has his eye open for Margaret as well, so all she has to do is run to her brother if there's any trouble and he sorts it out for her. They're together all the time, those two, when they're let, more than usual brothers and sisters are. They make me think of those Start-Rite twins on the poster for the kiddies' shoes, the little boy and girl holding hands and walking off into the hills and underneath it says, 'Children's Feet Have Far To Go'. That's what they're like. Hand in hand all the way. They were having a bit of a set-to just now, but that's just children. We were like it too, I daresay, and most of the time Margaret couldn't want a better brother than the one she's got. But not so long ago it started getting worse. I'm talking about the trouble at their school. The last time the headmistress called, it was to complain that *Margaret* had been fighting.

I got the pair of them and sat them down and told them to explain themselves. Roy announced, like it was his great achievement, that he'd been teaching his sister to box, holding a pillow round his arm and telling her to hit it harder and harder, and so on. 'But what on earth for?' I asked him. 'What's all the fighting and scrapping for? Can't you be two minutes in the playground without taking your fist to some poor lad's nose?' 'It's family honour,' he said, and stuck his chin in the air. What a phrase to come out with! I had no idea where he'd picked up something like that, 'family honour' indeed. I had to try not to smile.

'Why, Roy?' I said. 'Have they been saying something about you and Margaret?' 'Not us,' he said. 'It's Daddy. They keep saying he was a coward.' It turned out there'd been some afternoon when the lads at break time had been swapping stories about what their fathers did in the war, and Roy had said his drove the ambulances. And then some other little fellow had come up with how he'd heard different, he'd heard that Bill had only stayed back because he was a conchie, which meant he had to be a coward.

Roy was right: it was family honour, but how do you explain politics to children? Roy and Margaret were too young for me to explain to them, and they were certainly too young to explain to their classmates, who were too young – too ignorant's the word, too ignorant to understand, even if they wanted to, even if they waited to. It wouldn't have done any good pointing out that Bill had died of a heart attack, and it was his heart that kept him out of the army. People knew he'd declared as a conscientious objector before that. People had talked about it then and, so it sounds, are still talking about it now. Well, they would, wouldn't they? And what's a lad to do? If someone accuses your father of being a coward, they'll think *you're* a coward if you don't fight. I didn't know what to say. In one way I was proud of our Roy, but I was worried about the trouble he'd be in with the headmistress, who's a patient woman, and the other parents, who only know that their Alfie or Sally's come home with a black eye. All I said was, 'Well, try and keep yourselves to yourselves as much as you can.' That was why, when Paul Cooke offered to take Roy and Margaret out sometimes, I accepted.

That first time he told the children how important their father had been (which wasn't true), and how our Bill had welcomed Paul when he first came to London (and that *was* true). And he talked all about the *Worker*, and what being a photographer there meant – finding out about things and finding ways of telling people things that the capitalist press likes to keep hidden – but in pictures. Then he started taking them with him to watch the paper being printed, and he showed them how they laid the text round his photographs. Other people there took to the children as well, and said good things to them about our Bill, and some of them said how they remembered Annie as a lovely young lady. I wasn't too sure about all that, all that talking about their mother and father to a couple of children who'd as good as lost both. It's my belief these things are best left undisturbed, so the children can forget. *I* don't mention their parents except when it can't be helped, and I think that's best. I only had to mention my worry to Paul Cooke once, and he dropped it after that. Like I say – he's a good lad, that one.

Anyway, after a while, he seemed to be visiting here as often as he wasn't. Maybe he was lonely too, I don't know. But it's been a great thing to see him with the children, and all the running about with them he's prepared to do. When he came by last week he'd brought a book of fairy tales for Margaret and that Brownie box camera for Roy. First he sat Margaret on his knee so she could stroke his beard, which she likes to do, although to my mind at nine she's too old to be sitting on people's laps, but he doesn't mind, seemingly.

Then he showed our Roy how to work the camera. The children were over the moon, but I'm ashamed to say I didn't have quite the right reaction. I thought those fairy tales were too advanced for Margaret, for all she's turned out to be a quick reader. Long stories and so many words on the page. Better for someone else to read aloud than for a child to do all by herself – and I don't have the time. And I didn't quite like all the business of princes and princesses either. But Paul Cooke laughed at me and said, 'Ease up, Pam. It's not only princes and princesses. It's about justice too. Evil always gets punished in the end.' 'Not much like life, then, is it,' I said, but I let it go. 'But the camera,' I said. 'I can't afford film and all the developing. And no more can you.' 'He doesn't need film,' said Paul Cooke, sure of himself. 'It's only a toy to help him learn how to look.' 'He doesn't need to learn how to look,' I said. 'He does too much looking as it is, for my liking.'

Roy was pleased as punch, and spent the whole evening holding the camera and looking down into it, pretending to take pictures. And since then he's hasn't been anywhere without it – school apart. Just as well he hasn't got any film or there'd be more pictures stuck all over the walls than we've got walls to stick them.

1951
Cucumber Ascending

Roy

Paul Cooke said last week we should all go to the Festival of Britain, it's been on long enough. He said, if we don't go soon it'll be gone and we'll have missed it. He invited us, and paid for it an' all. And it was five bob each! He had to talk Aunty Pam round. She said he shouldn't waste his money, just as she wouldn't waste hers on something that was all show and only show and wouldn't last. 'Whose life is it going to change?' she said. 'Not yours. Not mine. And not all those others who'll be following each other like sheep to get in, making the rich richer than they already are. Can't they spend the people's money on the houses and hospitals the people need?' Paul Cooke said, 'Ah, but Pam, it's a bit of fun. And if it doesn't do people any good at least it won't do them any harm. It'll be a laugh and it's time we all had a laugh.' She said, 'I'll cut you some sandwiches, then.' So we knew we was going.

But we didn't know it was going to be so bloomin' big. It's everywhere, not just in the one place. The Pleasure Gardens at Battersea's the best and we spent hours there, looking and not doing anything much 'cos we didn't know what to choose. Then Paul Cooke said what about the Tree Walk, and we done that. I done a Tarzan at Mig, pretending to swing through the jungle in the air. Felt like a little kid again. Then we went on the centrifugal Rotor, though in a way I wish we'd done the Big Dipper. We'd have been able to see right across London from the big dipper, whole panorama, but when Mig saw the Rotor her eyes popped, and anyway it was good.

Margaret

It's funny. You stand against the wall and it goes round, spinning faster and faster, and squashes you flat against the wall and it's going so fast you can't leave the wall but it pushes you up it. And then the floor disappears. We all screamed. But it squashes you to the wall so hard you can wriggle round and you stick to the wall all the time. I wriggled round till I was upside-down, like a starfish, and Roy made himself into a starfish too and he put his hands up and I had mine down and we held onto each other. I was a bit scared, though. What if it stopped? We'd all just sort of plop off, wouldn't we? Onto our heads.

Roy

The top of Mig's head was nearly touching the top of mine, so that when I tried to look up I couldn't see her, really. All I could see was her toes sticking out. And her skirt was spread against the wall instead of falling over her head. I thought all the girls' skirts would've fallen over their heads but they didn't. The trouble was some kid opposite was sick and we wanted to get out then, quick. I thought it was going to spin round and splatter us all over.

Then we went to see the Guinness Clock. We didn't have to wait long 'cos it gets going every quarter-hour. There's a kind of whirligig thing on the top and whatnot. Mig went for the toucan, this model toucan hopping like he was dancing round a tree, with 'Guinness Time' written on it, the letters hanging off like fruits. Paul Cooke said he likes Guinness, but he never tells the others because a lot of people at the *Worker* and in King Street don't drink, and don't like it when other people do. He said one day, when I'm older, quite soon, in a year maybe, he'll buy me a pint. He says it's sweet and bitter all at the same time, and the best bit's the froth. Anyway, I knew not to split on him about Guinness to Aunty Pam, so when we came home we didn't even mention the clock. But I took a picture of it.

Then we took the boat to the exhibition place. It was threepence for the tickets and it went under the bridges, of course. Paul Cooke said that at night the bridges is all lit up, every one of them, decorated with lights from end to end, hanging on them, so I thought, right, we'll have to go back in the dark and see that. But I didn't say so then 'cos I didn't know, did I, if Paul Cooke was more our friend or more a grown-up who'd have to tell Aunty Pam.

At the main festival place there was the Dome of Discovery, they called it, landed like a flying saucer just down from Mars. It was flippin' enormous! But in front of it was the Skylon, going right up into the sky and you thought it was going to take off any minute, right up into space. Take the messages back to Mars! It had these legs, like a grasshopper's, knees like a grasshopper's, thin and bent and spindly, but actually they was anchoring it to the ground and stopping it falling over. It's made of aluminium, woven. Like a net. I took a picture of it, very quick, because I really did think it might shoot away if I didn't. I know that's rubbish, but that's how it made me feel. Paul Cooke said he thought it was futuristic, and supposed to be a rocket, but he said what it really reminded him of was a giant cigar. Mig said she thought it was a cucumber and that made Paul Cooke and me laugh, a lot. Can you imagine? People going to all the trouble to fix this huge cucumber on cables for thousands of visitors to pay to see. Mig was angry that we laughed, and she said, why was a cucumber sillier than a cigar? And Paul Cooke said of course she was right. He said, whatever it's meant to be it's lit up at night. But because it gets dark so late at the moment we couldn't see it lit up. We will, though.

But everything was all different colours, and painted bright and new-looking. They had these coloured balls on sticks, poking out from the walls everywhere, and painted panels, and bits of ceiling hanging down from the real ceiling, like scenery in a theatre or something, where you could be moving bits about and changing them all the time. And I thought, everything's always been the same before but now everything's going to be different, and we can change it all and make it really new and modern.

I got this strange feeling when I thought about our flat, which has always been there and always been the same. But if I had them panels and stuff, I'd be able to move everything about and it would all be different. I wish it could be different instead of all brown. The carpet is, the settee is, the wardrobes – everything. It *smells* brown, brown like it's going to be brown for ever. But at the festival it wasn't like that. There was lots of yellow. Really bright yellow, sharp as lemons. The chairs in the cafeteria was yellow, and the walls had yellow, though Mig said she saw lots of stuff in pink, but that's because she's a girl. Girls always see everything as pink, I reckon.

They had flowers planted out in giant pots everywhere, concrete pots like cones what never existed before. And they'd made these bins, for rubbish, that might've come from space, with the Dome. I thought they were fantastic. Aunty Pam wasn't impressed when I told her, though. She laughed at me for thinking rubbish bins was beautiful, but that was because she'd wanted us to go into the Dome and learn about science and stuff. Well, we did go in, but it was boring. Like school. They wanted you to follow everyone and go round in the one direction to learn things in that order, but Paul Cooke said we didn't have to so we ducked out. And it was a laugh 'cos there was this enormous queue that we was in for something, and we was waiting and waiting, and Paul Cooke said to stay put, to keep our places while he went to see how long it was going to take, and then he come back and he was grinning and shaking his head. He said Aunty Pam had been right and we *was* all a lot of sheep because when he got to the front of the queue there was nothing there. He said, look at what we've become! All so obedient and queuing for nothing!

I said we would, and we did. Last night. We went to bed, normal time, first Mig at 8.30, then me at 9.30, and, though Mig swore she wouldn't fall asleep, of course she did. She always falls asleep the minute she's in bed – like a puppy, Aunty Pam says. Aunty Pam says it's enviable, so I suppose she doesn't get to sleep easy. Anyway, I had to wake Mig by shaking her and whispering and shaking her again, with my hand over her mouth 'cos she could've woke up scared and made a noise. Aunty Pam was in the living room with her mending and listening to the Third Programme, which is what she does every night – listens to the Third Programme and does mending, or ironing or something. Our flat is so small that if we made a noise Aunty Pam would have to hear it. But Mig woke up quiet and remembered she was meant to stay awake. She'd kept her clothes on, like I'd said to. We went out creeping, very slow, carrying our shoes. The thing is, Aunty Pam expects us to be asleep so she don't come and check on us or nothing like that. She used to when we was young, but not now.

We didn't put our shoes on till we got right down the bottom neither, 'cos they make a noise on the steps and one of the neighbours might've heard. We had to creep out the courtyard too, going round the edge, in case someone was looking out. But it was raining. It's been raining all this summer, so we had to take our coats, but at least that meant there wouldn't be people sitting out, what could've peached on us to Aunty Pam. And I was right. There wasn't nobody in the yard. They was probably at the Festival, that's what I thought. I had enough money for the tram, the one that goes under the river all the way. I could've walked it, but I thought it was a bit far for Mig – it's about two miles, I think, from ours to the other side of the river. Mig said she could manage but I thought it would take us too long. I had my camera, of course.

The thing was that even from the tram, before it dipped down under the river, you could see lights on the other side of the water. You could see the sky was a different colour. Like one side of the river was all lit up and our side, on the north, was all dark. It was like going into another country. When we got there, there was hundreds of people, thousands, all wandering round, which was much more interesting than seeing the same thing in the daytime. And the Skylon was . . . I don't know how to say it, but it was shining from the inside like it was alive. You couldn't see its legs and cables at all, they'd disappeared in the dark, and you couldn't see its edges. It was just shining and flying. We stood there for ages staring at it. It was so beautiful I thought I was going to start blubbing – and who does that? I've never felt like that before. Not just from looking at something. I didn't, of course. But I ducked under the cables and rolled right under the Skylon and took a load of pictures from underneath. You look up from underneath and you think you're going to be sucked up by it, disappear up the point and out into space. There was this geezer standing near us and he comes up sudden and says, 'I don't think your pictures will come out, sonny. Not with a little box Brownie like what you've got.' And Mig says, very sharp like she does, 'Of course they'll come out. They always do. He takes the best pictures in the world, you know, and we've kept them all.' He scarpered.

It wasn't really raining no more, just drizzling, and there was little humped lights set into the ground, with people walking on them, and Geraldo's Embassy Orchestra playing music. We stood there watching, me and Mig, and after a bit two people started dancing, with their coats on, over these lights in the ground, to the music. Very slow, like they didn't really want other people to notice. But then some more people joined in, and I said to Mig, let's do it too. Let's dance together. Dance with me. So she did.

I took her hand like the other men was doing with their partners, and held her round the waist, like them. She had her hand on my shoulder and I saw her eyes shining. She had her head against mine and we danced, closer and closer, and I couldn't tell if it was my heart I felt beating or hers. I just wanted to go on holding her and being there. I suppose it was like being at one of them balls long ago, except that it was out of doors in the wet and we all had our coats on. And all you could hear was the music and the feet moving.

Margaret

I was like Cinderella. We weren't touching the ground. We were floating, and I was so warm. It had stopped raining and the air was fresh. Everything smelled different. Roy was close and I felt butterflies inside me. But I was always afraid it was going to be midnight and it would all stop. Then we'd have to go home and be ordinary again.

1956
The Argument

Roy

I heard them all the way down the stairwell bawling each other out. You could even hear them from the courtyard. The neighbours was all hanging out their doors getting an earful, 'cos it's not like them two. Aunty P and Mig screaming! I thought, so I get the call-up, pack my bags, hop on the train and this pair start fucking killing each other while my back's turned. Is that how it's been all this time? I'm hardly home two weeks, hardly unpacked for Chrissake, just time to get myself a bit of a job.

I shot up the stairs, two at a time, with my equipment . . . well, if I'm perfectly honest it's not mine as mine goes. It belongs to the studio, but they let me cart it round, since most days I go directly from job to job, without clocking into HQ. Dreary stuff: weddings, christenings, family portraits. You know the sort of thing: Mummy and the kiddiwinks for Daddy to have on his desk in the office. Not what I thought being a photographer was going to be, but at least they let me use their darkroom to develop the pictures I took while I was in Wilmslow – that's fucking RAF fucking Wilmslow. Not charity, though. They dock some off my wages for it, but beggars and the rest of it. At least Aunty P's good about it. Don't ask me too much for the rent, and that's decent of her, 'cos she thinks photography – or the sort I'm stuck with – isn't a real job, so I call that special. She perked up when I showed her the prints from a weekend shoot I done last week at the East India Docks. 'That's more like it,' she said. Knew she would. Didn't tell her I was only messing about, trying out.

So there's me, chugging up the stairs with cameras and lenses thwacking me all the way, lugging the flowers they'd had at the studio what was left over, the neighbours on every floor staring up like they was looking at an eclipse, and me worrying that P and Mig was going to finish each other off before I got in there and stopped them. Then suddenly it all goes quiet, and I'm thinking, shit! They *have* finished each other off. But by the time I made it in they were just stood there, run out of puff the pair of them, nose to nose over our table, leaning across it, panting and glaring. Like a couple of street fighters taking a breather. Aunty P had her right fist bunched up like a tennis ball on the end of her thin little arm and Mig had the teapot drawn back by her ear like a shot-putter, and you couldn't've said which one was going to let fly the first.

They was both breathing so hard you'd have thought *they'd* been hoofing it up the stairs, not me. All I could think of was they looked like they'd frozen in a frame, ready and waiting. So I pulled up a camera and panned across the opposite wall. I got that blue and white enamel jar Aunty P keeps the tea in, her biscuit tin with the kitten on the lid, the bottle of Zal Pine Fluid half empty with the light coming through it, greened up, then P's packet of Spangles, her favourites, and the little green checked curtain under the sink bulging like a belly round the bucket with the floor cloth. Nothing changed since I went off to my call-up. Then right behind Aunty P the kettle on the stove starts whistling, and Aunty P and Mig both jump. So I get them in focus and say, 'Watch the birdie! Click!' (No film loaded. That's for tomorrow.)

They turned on me together, snarling, and I thought, bloody hell! What did *I* do to deserve that?

Margaret

I'd been reading the paper like I always do, mostly because of Paul Cooke. The *Worker* sent him to Hungary at the end of October, along with Peter Fryer – because of the uprising. He was so excited. He came to tell us the day before he left, 'cos he hadn't known he was going, and we said how much we'd miss him. Aunty Pam gave him a hug and said, 'You show it like it is, lad. We've had enough of the sniping and distortions they're putting out in the capitalist press.' 'Count on me,' he said. 'Someone's got to get it right, and that'll be Peter and me.' Then he added, just for me, 'You can keep a watch on our progress by his dispatches, Mig. We'll be going all round the country so you'll know where we are from them.' Roy wasn't there then, of course, since he'd been called up, though it wasn't long before he came back. But anyway he doesn't read the papers. He's not interested like I am, and never has been, which used to drive Aunty Pam wild. She kept trying to get him interested but he just wasn't. Not in any of it.

She used to try to get him to come out with me to the Young Communist League stuff but he wouldn't. Not the summer camps or the rallies. Nothing. He wouldn't even look at *Challenge*, although she'd got us the subscription. He'd smile at her and make her a cup of tea, but he wouldn't join the YCL and he wouldn't read the paper. She tried pushing him. 'You have to know what's going on out in the world, Roy,' she said. And he said, 'I do know. I live in it.' So she said, 'There's more to the world than the bit you live in.' And he said, 'The bit I'm in's enough for me.' Then she got shirty and said, 'You shouldn't forget where you come from and why. You owe it to your grandfather not to forget. If everybody was like you and only cared about themselves and what they want, nothing would ever get done for people.' And Roy said, 'You don't need to talk to me about Granddad, Aunty P. You know you don't, so it's not fair trying to use him to make me do things I'm not gonna do. No hard feelings, but I'm not.'

She went all white and quiet and I thought, Jesus, Roy's done it now. But Aunty Pam just said, 'You don't know anything, Roy. You young people aren't as clever as you think you are.' But all that was two years ago, before his papers came. Actually, that was a weird time, when they came. Because some people in King Street were saying the call-up was a good thing as it would train more soldiers for the coming struggle, but there were these articles every month in *Challenge* against it. I didn't want Roy to go, but he didn't seem to mind. He said, 'It'll get me out of here for a bit, Mig. I'm all cooped up in here. Don't you feel cooped up?'

Then he went. And after a bit we got a parcel in the post with all his ordinary clothes wrapped in brown paper. It was horrible. It was as if he was dead or something, and they'd sent on his 'effects'. But what it really was, 'cos he wrote to me, was that once they'd all been issued with uniforms, which didn't fit anybody, they had to give up their civilian clothes and have them sent away so they couldn't escape. So in fact, he was a prisoner of the State. They all were.

This time, though, it was me she was livid with.

It was all to do with Paul Cooke and me being scared that something could happen to him, since there'd been so much shooting in Hungary. The counter-revolutionaries had got arms from somewhere – from the Americans, people were saying – and they were prepared to target anyone, but especially a journalist or a photographer who'd come to find out the truth and report on it. Paul Cooke had said to me not to worry, he could look after himself, and Peter Fryer had been to Hungary before and knew lots of people, so he'd be fine.

But although I looked every day I couldn't find any dispatches from Peter. I mean, you know, not one. I did mention it to Aunty Pam Monday morning last week, just as we were going out. I said, 'Do you think he's all right, Paul Cooke? Do you think something's happened to him because there isn't one report from them, not a single one, and he said Peter would be filing every day he could.' 'I'm sure he's fine,' she said, 'but if you're that concerned I can ask them at the *Worker*.'

That same day I went to the library after school and I looked in *The Times* and the *Daily Telegraph*, and they were full of reports from Hungary, saying things like all the people had risen up against the Soviet-backed government that had oppressed them so long, that Soviet tanks had been firing on unarmed crowds, that little children were being killed on the streets and people were starving and all the sort of rubbish you'd expect from those papers, that Peter Fryer and Paul had gone out to correct. So it wasn't that nothing was going on. I mean, we knew it was from listening to the wireless, but since there were so many journalists from other newspapers writing it seemed odd that only Peter Fryer wasn't. It scared me all the more and I was sure something must have happened to them.

When Aunty Pam got home I asked her if she'd been in touch with the *Worker* about Paul Cooke and she put on a sort of guilty face and said she'd been so busy she'd forgotten. But there was something funny about her manner, and I thought – and I've never thought this before – I thought, I don't believe you. That was weird. I caught myself thinking it, and it was as if I was somebody else and I was watching myself and discussing with myself what my reactions were, all in slow motion. The thing about Aunty Pam is she's absolutely straight. She doesn't mess people about. If she says she thinks something then that's what she thinks, she doesn't pretend, or play jokes.

Of course I know she's been upset recently, with Mr Pollitt not being General Secretary any more because he's not well enough to do the job – overwork, according to Aunty Pam, and Mr Gollan's just not the same – and she's got so irritable and down-in-the-mouth I've had to try and keep out of her way, which is hard in this place, obviously. Especially at this time of year. So I've been staying longer at school, well, I've got exams coming up, and then going to the library. But I had this feeling when she put on the guilty look suddenly that she *was* pretending, and I thought if she's making it up then she's hiding something and the only way to find out is to go to the *Worker* and ask them myself. So next day I did.

They all said, 'Hello there', and how's school and so on and so on, the way some grown-ups do because they don't know what else to ask you. And Johnny Campbell came down the corridor and nodded at me and I thought, well, since he's the editor he's bound to know, isn't he? So I asked him. And he stopped dead and stared at me. Then he said, in a really harsh voice as if I'd done something awful like . . . I don't know . . . steal something, 'Those men don't work here any more. You'll have to make your enquiries somewhere else.' And he marched off with big shoulders, very stiff.

I didn't know what to think. I just stood there wondering whether to go home and bring it up with Aunty Pam, but I knew she'd have a fit if she thought I hadn't trusted her and gone behind her back. But I had to find out. The thing is, it was always Paul Cooke visiting us, ever since we were little. We never went to where he lived, and I couldn't think if we even had his address, otherwise I'd have gone round and found him – if he was there. If he was really safe. Then, while I was still standing there in the corridor Sandy Jacobs came out of her office. She's the television critic, which I think sounds like a lot of fun – we don't even have a television – and said, in a whispery voice, beckoning me, 'Come in here, Margaret.' Then she put her arm round my shoulders and sort of scooped me into her office and closed the door behind us.

It was like all their offices, with dusty papers everywhere so that you could hardly see the desk or the typewriter, and there was a huge pile of old copies of the *Radio Times*. She said to sit on that since there was only the one chair. So I sat on the *Radio Times* and she sat in her chair – one of those swivel ones on a tripod with casters but one of the casters was missing so it wobbled terribly. Anyway, she sat with her feet wide apart on the floor to keep her balance, and leant forwards over her elbows with her hands in a steeple and her chin on the top of the spire, and looked at me over her spectacles.

'You're old enough now, I expect,' she said, not really to me, more to herself. What for? I thought. 'Oh dear. This place is in a bit of turmoil, Margaret. Perhaps your aunt has been telling you.' But she hadn't. Aunty Pam hadn't told us a thing. So I just shook my head. 'Hasn't she? Well, I suppose it's understandable. It's . . . there are . . . let's say that just at the moment people aren't all seeing eye to eye. Not just here, but in King Street as well. Not in the way we did. And your young friend Paul has had a falling out with Johnny.'

'But is he all right?' I asked. 'That's what I came to find out. I've been trying to find their stuff in the paper and it's not there,

so I thought if Peter hadn't been writing it might be because . . .'
And she said, no, he had been writing. 'We haven't been printing
it, that's all.'

'But why?' I said. 'People have always said he's a good writer,
and Paul's the best photographer. Why wouldn't you . . .' And she
looked really disappointed then, as if someone had promised
her something and not given it or not done it but she had relied
on them. She said, 'It's because of *what* Peter wrote, Margaret.
He might just as well have been reporting for the *Manchester
Guardian*. He was sending us dispatches saying there was
no White Terror, that this was a revolution of the Hungarian
workers against Soviet oppression, and that their own army was
with them and that's where their weapons came from, not from
the Americans. It wasn't imperialism trying to regain ground, it
wasn't a counter-revolution trying to restore capitalism, it wasn't
the return of fascism, and so on and so on. So obviously we
couldn't print it.'

There was a half-empty bottle of Tizer on the window sill, and
above the window she had a big brown clock like a school clock
on the wall, ticking very noisily. I watched its second hand for
a bit while I was trying to think what to say. Sandy Jacobs has
always been friendly. She's terribly fat but in a cuddly way, like
somebody's giant teddy bear. It's weird because at that moment
I remembered how I used to think it might be cosy to sit on her
lap, but now I was nearly an adult. 'Was it true?' I asked. 'Was
it true, what he was writing?' 'Probably,' she said. Just like that.
Probably. 'Then why wouldn't you print it?' I asked, and she
said, very loud, 'What, and betray the USSR?'

I didn't get it. If it was true what he was writing, and Paul
Cooke had told us he and Peter were going out to get the truth
and tell everyone what they saw, which is what they were sent
out do . . . So I said, 'But what's the point? What's the point of
having a newspaper at all if you can't print something when it's
true?'

Sandy Jacobs just sat there very quietly and then she said,
'Well, you're not the first person to ask that question, and as a
matter of fact fourteen people have left.' Left the *Worker*? 'And the
Party,' she said. Left the Party? I'd never heard of anyone doing
that. I thought about what she'd said, and the way she'd said it.

And the fact that she was telling me at all, so I asked her, 'Are you going to leave too?' 'I'm thinking about it,' she said. 'Leaving the *Worker* is one thing. Easy enough, though God knows where any of us will get another job in that hostile world out there. But leaving the Party? I don't know. After so many years, and it's not as if what's happened in Hungary means that all the things that were wrong with this country have suddenly become better simply because the Soviet Union has made the odd mistake. Even if we were wrong to think the Russians had all the answers it doesn't mean that the fault is with communism. It just means they messed it up. The idea is as good as ever it was. But I don't know. People are all at each other's throats and it's so sad. We used to be such a close, happy crew, and now we've lost all that. And do you know, we didn't actually see the dispatches Peter sent, any of us, because Johnny decided we had to be protected from them. As if he didn't trust us to make our own judgement, or rather he didn't trust us to make the right judgement. Us, the *Worker* staff, would you believe it! Our editor doesn't think his own journalists should have access to what one of us writes. What's going on?'

Then she stood up. 'I haven't been very helpful to you, have I?' she said. 'Would you like a glass of Tizer?' Actually, I don't like Tizer. I don't like any fizzy drinks much at all because they make my nose feel funny, but she wanted to give it to me, as if it was in exchange for Paul Cooke. So I said all right, and she poured some from the bottle on the window sill into a cup she took out of her desk drawer and blew on to get the dust off. In fact, the Tizer was flat. 'Oh dear,' she said. 'I'm sorry. It's been there a long time. You can tell your aunt that I told you, if you want, but do it carefully. It'll upset her. And here. Give me a kiss.' So then, when I was seventeen and not seven, I got that squidgy cuddle, and it *was* warm and nice, except that since she'd never done it before I knew she was really using it to say goodbye.

When I got out onto Farringdon Road again I suddenly thought it hadn't crossed my mind to ask Sandy Jacobs how she knew what was in the forbidden dispatches if Johnny Campbell wouldn't let anyone see them. I wished Roy was there so that we could talk about it. We've always done everything together, and decided everything together. I didn't feel like confronting Aunty

Pam on my own, and Roy might think of a way of doing it that wouldn't get her going too much. He's usually much better at things like that than me. But he was on a job – a family portrait, the sort of job he hates most. He always says those things make him as certain as he can be he'll never marry or have kids if the result has to be these cheesy pictures. Perhaps I'd wait for him to come home and then talk to Aunty Pam. But I didn't get the chance. She was in before me and looking mighty suspicious.

'Where've you been, my girl?' she said, snappy before I'd even started. So of course I lied. I said I'd stayed back in school because I had some stuff to do. 'Oh no you didn't,' she said, like it was some sort of triumph. 'Your friend Jill came by with your maths book she'd borrowed, wanting to know where you'd rushed off to. So where was it?' And then of course I made it worse because she was talking to me as if I was still ten or something. 'I'm seventeen, Aunty Pam,' I said. 'And I haven't been anywhere bad.' 'Bad enough that you can't tell me,' she said. Well then, I thought, if she's going to be accusing me of stuff, there's two of us can do that. So I said, 'And why didn't you tell *me*?' 'Tell you what?' 'This morning. About Paul Cooke.'

You should have seen her face. 'Oh, I see! You've been down at the *Worker*, haven't you? And did you find out what you wanted, Miss Nosy Parker, always nosing around?' Which got me going, really got me going, since she knew I'd been worried for him. I'd said so that same morning, hadn't I, I'd told her. And she'd been pretending she didn't know anything. He could have been dead for all I knew. Then she said, 'He *is* dead as far as I'm concerned.' She sounded just like the editor, Johnny Campbell.

Sandy Jacobs had warned me Aunty Pam would be upset. But I didn't think she'd sound so . . . so . . . vicious. 'He's not setting foot in this house any more, Margaret, so you'd better get used to that. Not in my lifetime, he isn't. Not through that door, or sitting at that table, or drinking from those cups. Never, ever again.'

'Aunty Pam!'

'Don't "Aunty Pam" me with that shocked face, lass. There's such a thing as loyalty and it seems your young Paul Cooke, along with his friend Peter Fryer, doesn't know a thing about it. First little setback and he's running to the opposition with it. Did you know that? Did they tell you that? Peter took some of

110

his stories and gave them to the *Manchester Guardian*. The *Worker* wouldn't print his tittle-tattle so he resigns and scuttles to the other side. And your Paul supported him. What's to admire in that, eh?'

The *Manchester Guardian*! That's where Sandy Jacobs must have read it all. 'But the *Worker* should have printed his stories, shouldn't it,' I said, 'if they were true. That's what a good newspaper is for, that's what you always say. Find out the truth and tell it.'

'Who knows what's true and what's not, sometimes,' she said. 'But it's not the *Manchester Guardian* and that's for certain. And there are some things more important than the truth, whatever it turns out to be. And that's loyalty and friendship to the people you've grown up with and fought with. What he's done is betrayal. He's a traitor, is your Paul Cooke. As good as spat in our faces. And –'

'Traitor? Loyalty?' OK, I was shrieking. I don't shriek usually but she made me. 'Loyalty to what? Do people have to be loyal to your precious Party no matter what it does? What if it was a person? What if it was a person you knew, your friend or somebody you loved, or somebody in the family, and they did something like . . . like . . . I don't know, if they did something like murder someone or torture someone, and you found out. Would you say, Oh that's all right. Don't mind that. Got to stay loyal. Would you? If they'd tortured someone? And maybe they were going to do it again? Would you still be loyal, Aunty Pam? Would you? Is that what you expect people to do?'

'Don't be so stupid!' she shouted back. 'It's not for me to decide or you to decide, but you're too ignorant to understand what's involved. It's like Mr Pollitt has always said, it's a collective thing. You can't just decide off your own bat whether what's been done is right or not because it's always more complicated than people think. We're ordinary folk. We're not in the know. We've not been at all the meetings in the Central Committee in Moscow, have we? We don't know what's been going on in the meetings in Hungary or anywhere else. But there are people who know more than we do, so we have to take their lead. We have to or you'd have everyone going their own way and that's anarchy. And you can't run anything with anarchy, even if there's some youngsters who might think they'd like to. There's such a thing as holding together, hanging in together against the enemy, and when you can't be sure – and none of us, not even you, my girl, can be sure – when you can't be sure you have to listen to what the leadership says because they're likely to get closer to the truth than we are. Not just wave your fists about and strike off on your own, pouring dirt on people as you go, which is what your Paul Cooke has been and done. Spat in the face of his people, and that's why he's not setting foot here again.'

I said I'd invite him in, even she wouldn't. So she said it wasn't my house to invite anybody and I wasn't to forget it, and on and on. Then I said I'd find out where he lived and go and visit him there. 'And how will you find out where he lives, Miss Clever Clogs Know-it-all?' I said I'd ask the *Manchester Guardian*! I'd get a copy of it and get their address and ask them. So there! I know I shouldn't have. I knew it would make her furious, but I was furious too. I mean, all the years Roy and I have had to listen to her going on about Granddad and his fight for the truth over the First World War executions, and now she's not interested in the truth if it doesn't suit her. So I said so.

'Don't try telling me about my own father, Margaret. And that's not what your granddad said. He said the most important thing to remember was that it was always to do with class, and if he was right then, he's right now. But some people, *some people*, seem to have forgotten it.' She was leaning across the table at me and I was leaning across the table at her, and we were hating each other. Honestly we were. Hating each other.

And then suddenly Roy was standing in the doorway laughing at us and saying, 'Watch the birdie!'

Pam

I lost my temper when Margaret said that if I didn't let Paul Cooke back into our house she'd invite him in herself, and I'm not one to lose my temper that easy. But I can't believe what I said! I said that it wasn't her house to be inviting anybody in. The minute I'd said it I felt so bad, and so sorry for her. Maybe it wasn't her house, but then it's not mine either. It's where her parents should have been by rights, and *they* should have been having this argument with her, not me. I only live here because I moved in to take care of them when they were too small to look after themselves, but that won't be the case soon enough. We weren't to know it was going to be for good when Annie went back to her own folk. We weren't to know we'd never hear from her again. Not a letter, not a postcard on their birthdays, nothing.

To tell the truth, I never was sure what upset Roy and Margaret most – their father dying so suddenly, their mother disappearing the way she did, or when they understood their granddad had died. They did love him so, and it had all happened at once – is how it seemed. My heart went out to Margaret for all I was livid. But she didn't say – as she could have, and in her place I think I would have – well, it may not be my house but it's more mine than yours! She didn't say anything like that, but just went on about Paul Cooke. Maybe she'd got herself into such a state she wasn't listening to what I was saying, word for word. It was all arms waving and her face bright red.

When I remember how all those years back I thought it would be a good thing having Paul Cooke coming to visit because it would take the kiddies' minds off losing their parents, how I thought they needed a man in their lives – for all that Paul wasn't much more than a lad himself at the time! Well, you think one thing at one time and another at another. You can get too close to people sometimes, for good reasons and bad, and Paul Cooke . . . now I'm not saying he took advantage, not deliberately, but he grew to be so big in their lives. A Saturday wasn't a Saturday if he didn't stop by and the pair of them would sit watching the window and moping until they saw him cross the courtyard. I used to wonder what he saw in it for himself – his day off given over to a couple of children – but he never seemed to be doing it out of duty. There are people like that, aren't there, who like children just because they are children.

The trouble is he got to be so big in their lives before they had learned to discriminate. Margaret especially. She hasn't the experience to know there are times you have to let people go, when they don't do as they should. Friendship, comradeship – nothing in the world is as precious, but when you discover that someone you thought was a good and loyal person in fact isn't, you have to have the courage and the discrimination to cut them loose. No matter how much it tugs your heart. She doesn't know that yet, though this is teaching her, poor lass. Well. I can say that now – poor lass – but it's not how I felt at the time. Thank God for Roy!

My nephew will go a long way, that's my prediction. He's got ways to him that will open doors and soften hard hearts, just like his father in that way: natural charmers, the pair of them. Not that charm is a good thing in itself. There are too many sweet talkers around these days, and most of them are up to no good. But they have their moments, and this was one of Roy's. I was about to box our Margaret's ears, I swear, she was riling me that much with her chin in the air and her uppity manner as if she knew so much more about the world than those of us who've lived in it three times as long as she has.

So I was ready to box her ears for her and she looked as if she had it in mind to throw the teapot at me, and would have done, if Roy hadn't happened up the stairs with that camera of his. He shouts 'Watch the birdie!' and we turn on him, together, so he's drawn our fire. Yes, he'll go far. Then before I could say a word he pulled out this bouquet of flowers that he had behind his back and presented them to me like a young man cheering up his sweetheart. Don't mistake me. I knew perfectly well he hadn't gone out to buy them. He can't afford that sort of thing yet, if he ever will be able to, taking people's pictures, so I knew they must've come from one of those photographic studios, and they were surplus at the end of the day. Surplus to requirements. But it was the *way* he did it that beguiled me, that always does.

He wins you over, does our Roy, even when there's reason to be angry with him, without a fuss, so easygoing when he wants to be, but it's real, you think, it's genuine, you think. And maybe it is, too. Just like his father. Gets away with murder.

So I had my flowers. Margaret and I hadn't laid a finger on one another and Roy was all smiles. Then the pair of them went down the West End to listen to records in the booths at HMV. Margaret's got a thing for Pat Boone. Too syrupy for my taste, but she'll get over it. Roy says he's trying to convert her to jazz. Humphrey Lyttelton's the man, he says. I wouldn't know.

Part 5

1998

Roy

I zapped the box off. What I like about the *Arts Review* is you
know exactly what you're going to get: a forty-something woman
presenter so well briefed she should be in court, and three top-
notch wankers all trying to hog the camera. Roy Hoskins blah
blah, *the* chronicler of depersonalised 1950s conscripts with *Jankers
and Bull* blah blah, *the* most interesting fashion photographer of
his generation, *the* controversialist with his series *Before and After*
yawn yawn, and now *the* scourge of modern celebrity – with his
sculpted contrivances (actually, that's not bad) so undermining of
anyone who sits for him, too dangerous to accept, too dangerous
to refuse . . . Gimme a break! This is a retrospective. People who
watch this show know this stuff already. Get the fuck on with it!
I wanted to know what they were going say about my blanks.

And it was sweet! They fell over each other with their
theories. *Origins* was the Big Bang or a sperm going into an
egg, depending on who you listened to. *The Revolutionary* was
a self-portrait for Chrissake. But the best one was that *Cucumber
Ascending* was a Freudian euphemism. I thought Mig'd choke!
I had my arm round her while she was glugging away at her
tumbler of Château Lafitte and tapping the catalogue with her
cigarette. 'God,' she said, her voice all throat from laughing and
her fags, 'you really are an old mischief monkey, aren't you! This
has been a treat, Roy, really! I'm only sorry I didn't make it to the
opening. I'd have loved to see them all standing there with their
canapés and perceptions.'

Dougie was on the other sofa next to Gina. They hadn't said
a word, the pair of them. Stayed shtum all the time we were
flipping from one picture to the next, all through the show too.

'Dad,' said Dougie. 'Do you mind telling us now what all that
was about, Mum and me? We're feeling a bit left out here while
you and Aunty have your fun.'

'Sorry, son,' I said. 'It's just memory lane stuff. Not worth
going into right at the minute.'

'But it was worth making a whole section of an exhibition out of? Why? So you and Aunty could have a laugh at other people's expense? Just 'cos you know something the rest of us don't?'

'You're right, Dougie, you're right. But I haven't had so much fun in a long time.' Shit. Said the wrong thing. Out the corner of my eye I saw Gina get up with the magazine she'd been reading and sneak out the room. All hell to pay later.

'Nice one, Dad,' said Dougie. 'Now you've put Mum's back up. What's she done to deserve that?'

'Oh, she'll get over it.'

'She won't.'

'She will, Dougie. I know her. I've been married to her long enough to know. She will.'

'Well, I don't see why she should have to. Sorry, Aunty,' he said to Mig, and pushed off the sofa. Terrible, these sofas we've got. Once you're in, you're in. 'I've got stuff to do tomorrow,' he said. 'I should be going. You want a lift or are you staying on for more memory lane?'

Mig looked at Dougie, then at me. 'I'll stay on, Douglas. But thanks for bringing me over. I apologise if we've . . . it's just there are some things you can't –'

'Sure there are,' he said. 'Sure.' And he went. Gonna have to repair fences tomorrow, I thought. Other stuff now.

I sat there after they'd gone, sorry but not sorry – the way it can go – waiting for Mig to ask. She had that look on her face, turned in, turning things over, like someone who wants to ask a question but isn't sure they're ready for the answer. She doesn't miss a thing, and she wouldn't have missed this one. So I gave her knee a nudge with my elbow. 'Go on, then,' I said. 'Let's have it.' 'All right,' she said. 'What was *Broken Promise*?'

Spot on, darling.

Things you do as a kid. Things you think. They stay with you, even though they don't need to. You're all grown up and you're a rational man, and you know that when you swore you'd always do something – or never do it – all those years ago, decades, it was the kid thinking, but things have changed. But it goes on sitting there like a monkey on your shoulder and if you try and shake it off, tell it you don't need it any more, you get this cold hollow feeling you get when you've let somebody down. I said, trying it out. 'The picture's a broken promise and it's what I did.' Because she was sitting so close she had to lean away to look at me, like she was getting ready to drift away. I nearly grabbed her to pull her back but instead I pulled myself off the sofa and went over to the window. Lights on inside, dark outside, so nothing to see but my own face distorted in the glass. A face chewing on the next words.

'D'you remember,' I said, 'when Paul Cooke gave me that box Brownie and I started going round with it, I swore, cross my heart and hope to die, that I'd never take any pictures with it when you weren't there?' I couldn't see her face from where I was but I could hear her smiling when she said, yes, I remember. 'Well,' I said. 'I kept the promise with the camera, but I broke it with this picture.' 'I don't get you,' she said, which was fair enough. 'This picture,' I said, 'I took this one before we ever met Paul Cooke, before we ever heard of him. Before I had a camera. It took itself and it's been sat in my head, fully developed a good fifty years. More than. And it's the only one with me in it.' She said, 'What are you doing in it?'

I turned to face her and put my hand up to shoulder height, closed my eyes for a blink, and felt it there, warm, and hard, gripping mine. 'I was out with Granddad. You weren't there. I can't remember why you weren't. Maybe Nana'd kept you back 'cause you were too small for the walk. It must've been a Sunday if he wasn't at work. We were up on some hill, don't ask me which one, looking down over the houses, and he was talking about something and holding my hand. I don't remember what he was saying, not the words. But I can hear his voice, how it went, deep, it sounded to me, deeper than our dad's was, telling me something. Maybe a story, maybe he was pointing something out. I don't know. All I remember is that feeling of his hand holding mine, and that he was talking to me, not to anyone else. It was cold up there with the wind blowing round us like we were in the middle of all the winds picking on us, having a dance round us, but we were together and I was safe. I thought, so long as I held onto Granddad, so long as he kept holding onto me, I'd always be safe. So that's all it is, *Broken Promise*. This scrawny little kid on a hill with his granddad. But you never –'

Margaret

And then his face crumpled like a handkerchief released from a fist, eyes squeezed shut, lips clamped together. He'd flopped down onto the other sofa, his hands on the edge of the glass coffee table in front of him, gripping it till his knuckles were lumpy and skeletal, while his whole body shook and tears ran down his nose.

'Roy!' I had never seen him crying since we were children but I knew why he was. I struggled out of my seat to put my arms round him but his position didn't change. He went on clutching the table as if he dared not let go, as if holding onto that table was keeping his entire self in one piece. He was swallowing and gulping air through his nose, trying to regain control. I understood, and backed off.

We sat in silence, the two us, alone in this gracious sitting-room with its enormous windows giving over the landscaped, night-time garden where my brother and his wife sit on a balmy evening appreciating the handiwork of the two full-time gardeners on their books. Douglas had gone home. Gina, in her huff, had also gone – to bed, I assumed. There was silence but for the wailing of a distant Friday night siren. Behind my eyes I examined *Broken Promise*: there he stands, my brother, his baggy shorts whipped by the hill-top wind, hand in hand with our grandfather, dwarfed by Granddad, whose head bends slightly towards the little boy. He has one hand extended, still pointing towards something among the chimneys below that he must have been talking about a moment before. Roy's face, in profile, is not following that indicating finger but is gazing up at Granddad with that slight smile that always lifts the left side of his mouth more than the right. His eyes are fixed on Granddad's, with the unblinking wide look you see in a nursing baby when it's eye to eye with its mother. His small hand has disappeared in Granddad's large one. As I watched I began to feel, actually, distinctly feel both their hands wrapped around mine.

If it hadn't been for the war, we wouldn't have found ourselves in Openshaw for those four years, billeted on our grandparents. We would never have come to know and respect Nana's upright kindness. We would never have been in love, as we both were, with Granddad and his lumbering walk, his gentleness, and his constant and unfeigned interest in everything we said. I knew, without being told, that deep down for some reason he favoured Roy – perhaps because he was older, or the boy, or because he was drawn to him for some particular quality that was beyond explaining. I knew, but I was never envious. It was a preference I couldn't have faulted.

But now I needed to be on my own, to walk alone, as I like to do, with Roy's box Brownie pictures in my head.

Roy

'Where did I leave my jacket?' she said. 'Course she'd slung it over the back of a chair when she came in with Dougie, like she always does, and Gina had whisked it off and hung it properly away, like *she* always does. 'You off, then?' I said. 'I'd better be,' she said. 'Look at the time.' It was pushing one. 'I'll call you a cab,' I said, setting the old routine off – no, I'd rather walk, but you won't be safe, when have I ever not been, etc. etc. When we'd done that bit I got her her jacket, same snaggy old blue thing she won't get rid of because she likes the pockets – just right for her fags and lighter. 'I don't think I'll put it on just yet,' she said, folding it over her arm. 'It's like the blooming tropics out there, isn't it? Unseasonably so.'

That's Mig to a tee. Change the subject so she can piss off out of here for a bit of a think on her own. But I'm glad I showed her, and glad I told her. She could've misunderstood. After all, *Broken Promise* – what might she have thought when she knew these were all pictures from what Dougie used to call the olden days. I wouldn't've wanted her to think I was two-timing her way back when.

'Giss'a kiss, sis,' I whispered after we'd snuck down the stairs so as not to disturb Gina, and we had a hug in the open doorway fit to sail us back in time. We're like the pieces of a jigsaw puzzle, I think sometimes, Mig and me. Locked together like some fretsaw made us. But that's just between the two of us, and wouldn't go down well with Gina if I was to say so, which isn't exactly a surprise.

The thing is, all in all we've done all right, Gina and me. We've hung in there, with the odd rocky patch, same as everyone. You start with lust, and then it wears off. Not completely, not if your wife looks like mine, but time goes by and you get edgy. You see how green the grass is over there and you want a nibble. So I made a pact – with myself – that if I was going to go out and play, it would only ever be with foreign pussy, when I was on a shoot abroad, and only so long as both sides were clear what the game was: what happens on location stays on location. 'Calais rules,' as we say in the trade. No involvement, no emotions, no tears – and condoms all the way. It worked a treat until Gina found out. So what I said to her then was, 'I believe in equality. If you're the one who's away somewhere and you get the itch, then you go ahead and do what you have to, but I don't want to know about it. Let's just agree that we won't piss in our own pond.' Of course, it wasn't quite as easy as it sounds, but give or take . . . Anyway, we got through that and here we still are. No problems on that front now. The problems are all to do with Mig.

There's a hell of a lot I can give Gina – her special treatment – but I can't give her my past, I can't give her my childhood. It's like old soldiers – they can only really talk to each other. P isn't Gina's aunt, and she wouldn't want her anyway. She wouldn't want to have grown up the way me and Mig did, she only pretends she does to other people. The fact is, half the time she makes out Mig is envious of *her* because of our house and our lifestyle. And it doesn't matter what I say, she can't believe Mig couldn't give a monkey's arse that the flat she still lives in is so run-down it's only two steps from being a slum. She doesn't care what things look like and never has. You'd think, if your wife was going to worry about another woman, it would be because of a real affair or something of the sort, not your bleeding sister!

But Gina's not wrong. There is going to be a problem. For sodding sure there is. I go all the way with Gina on this one.

Margaret

I love my city at night, when I'm on my own. People think I ought to be afraid of walking alone through streets of strangers, or empty streets. But I believe that I'm as near invisible as dammit, so that even if there is evil intent in the passers-by they'll vent it on someone more substantial than me. And as a matter of fact that's been my experience all these years. Of course it does help to know where you're going, being familiar with your route, with the alleys and byways. And I dare say I'd be much more nervous in someone else's city, or an unfamiliar quarter of this one, where I wouldn't be able to interpret the loungers on the corner, the clusters of youth, the jostling and the shoving in the crowded places. But I've always lived here and have always loved to walk alone and I will insist to my dying day that what you do not fear need not be frightening.

I sensed as I set off that Roy was still standing in the porch outside his magnificent house, like a guard monitoring my departure for as long as I was in sight, so I strode out like a trooper to indicate my confidence, and thought I could as good as hear him give his small, throaty chuckle.

It was such a warm night – all the nights this early summer seem to be warm – and the closer I got to Notting Hill and then beyond, along the Bayswater Road towards Hyde Park Corner, the more crowded the pavements were. Everybody seemed to be pissed, some of them just a little, some of them, in the usual English way, lurching and spitting, and barging blindly into all comers. All that bellowing they do. But as I expected nobody noticed me and all I had to do was dodge.

It surprises even me how fast I can walk in spite of my paltry height. Aunty Pam used to say of the Hoskinses in general, 'The trouble with us, love, is that our tail's too near the daisies. Short stalks, that's us.' Short maybe, but my stalks are pretty serviceable. And when you walk with things on your mind, things to turn over, things to remember – things to imagine even – the miles roll by, and you can find yourself on a particular street with no memory of how you got there. I have to say I was a little optimistic to suppose that it would only take me something over an hour to make it home because when I got in I saw from my wall clock that it was half past two. I also saw the light on my answerphone flashing. I assumed it must be Roy checking up on me to be sure I'd got home in one piece. I don't have a mobile phone – I've never felt the need, although Douglas keeps threatening to get me one. But it wasn't Roy. It was Aunty Pam's care home letting me know she'd had a stroke.

I saw that the message had been left at eleven o'clock – more or less exactly when the programme about Roy's exhibition had begun. Well timed, Aunty Pam, I said aloud, but immediately took the sentiment back. If Aunty Pam wanted to be part of this family retrospective, what else could she do? And then, of course, I took that back as well. Who chooses when to have their stroke, or to have one at all? I rang the care home, counting the rings – thirty-three (well, it was unsocial hours) – and spoke to a person on night duty, whose sleepy voice grew more lively with every word. She told me the doctor had been in and had advised that, things being as they were with Aunty Pam, it was possibly not worth sending her to hospital for any tests. But the decision must be mine. I said, without hesitation, that I agreed with the doctor. She then said that Aunty Pam was, as she put it, as they always put these things, comfortable.

Comfortable in what sense, I asked, no doubt sounding tart. But this nurse was evidently used to badly behaved relatives, and emollience poured down the phone. 'Your aunt is asleep,' she said, 'but to be telling you the truth, at this stage there's not much to choose between her sort of sleep and a coma.' She sounded Irish, which I found reassuring, don't ask me why. 'Should I come in now?' I asked. 'Well, you could,' she said. 'But then again, there might not be that much difference in the morning, do you see?' 'But might she die overnight?' I asked. 'Well, she might. Indeed, she might. There's no telling,' she said.

If Aunty Pam was in a coma she wouldn't register if I was there or not. Yes, I know that people sit by a bedside singing or reading aloud or earnestly recounting their day's doings in the hope of penetrating a shut-down brain, and, who knows, perhaps these things work. But they do all that because they want that person restored to them as they were before the stroke. Aunty Pam before her stroke was not worth restoring. All right, all right. What I meant was that *she*, the original she, would not have thought herself worth restoring – to the lost mind and the absent person. So long as she really was 'comfortable', and might stop altogether in the midst of her comfort, wouldn't that be best? Without a doubt. But what if she wasn't in a coma, and only asleep, or in a coma but at the approach of death had some inapposite inkling of what was around her and in front of her – then it might matter if I was there, or not.

And what about Roy? Should I tell him now? At this hour? If she were to come round, even for a second, I knew whose face would be the one she'd most want to see, to carry away with her into wherever it is we all go. I tried to imagine him in his bed, lying rolled under his duvet next to Gina, his hand fumbling over the phone. But, odd as it may seem, I've never been into their bedroom. I don't know what it looks like, and don't wish to. I don't know how it's laid out – do they have a bedside table on either side of their king-size, with dinky trilling telephones and little marbled bedside lights, or perhaps stooping, Giacometti-like structures with halogen bulbs? It's extraordinary how Roy, who really does care how things look, has ceded the interior decoration to his wife. Not my business. Anyway, I thought, care homes have phones and, if need be, I'd call him from there. I checked my purse for 10p pieces in case they were required, noted I was doing that and approved the forethought. Noted the approval – and winced.

I did take a cab for this trip, north across town to Mill Hill, and because of the hour the cabbie must have known that all was not well as he didn't speak until we arrived. 'Hope it's all all right in there, darling,' he said, snapped up his fare, and sped away, leaving me standing in the suburban darkness on the gravelled driveway. I took a single crunching step towards the front door and a security light flashed the garden into view. The last time I was here, longer ago than I'm inclined to acknowledge, the shrubs were not yet in leaf. Now they stood about, bulging and sappy. A light snapped on in the front hall, so the security light had alerted them to my arrival, or a potential intruder's – although this neighbourhood is as unlike Somers Town as it could be, verdant and private and, for the most part, semi-detached. A burglar here would have profitable pickings once he navigated the bolted windows and the alarms. The front door, built to look panelled, swung open so they must have inspected me through a peephole and deemed me acceptable.

'Yes?' Hissed.

'I've come about my aunt.' I was whispering too. 'Pamela Hoskins. You called to say she's had a stroke.'

The nurse nodded. She had rounded cheeks and soft hair, and said, 'Oh yes. We spoke, didn't we? Her room's Daisy, but of course you'll know that.'

Her name tag told me she was Siobhan O'Halloran. I set off along the parquet corridor, Nurse O'Halloran padding softly behind, past closed doors behind which people lay sleeping, maybe released in their sleep from whatever troubled them in the daylight. Tomorrow – or rather today – was nudging in, possibly their last, with its ordinary awful routines.

When we reached Daisy Room I thought at first that Aunty Pam had done a bunk. She was so small and slight that the bedclothes didn't seem to be covering a body at all, but looked merely rumpled. I was glad the doctor, and then I, had decided to leave her be in her bed. Why torture a body whose mind has gone AWOL and whose span is shortly up anyway? She was breathing deeply but heavily, gasping on the inhalations as if she'd been holding down her breath and was inhaling now only because her body demanded it. I could just see her hair spread thinly on the pillow and the point of her nose thrust into the air. Her arms lay pinning the sheet and cotton blanket down, as if they'd tried one escape and she was taking no chances. There was a leatherette armchair next to the bed with its high back against the wall. I pulled it out so that I could face her, and sat down.

'She's not changed the tiniest bit since we rang you,' murmured Nurse O'Halloran. 'We've been checking her all the time, of course.' Of course. 'But you'll be wanting a little privacy, will you not? I'm only round the corner if you need me. You only have to say.' And she was gone.

For the first time I felt the distance I'd walked in my legs, so I stretched them out and rotated my ankles. The soles of my feet were sizzling, as if to reassure me that my own physical state in its momentary discomfort was, at least, very much alive. Now that I was here, I began to wonder why I'd come. Aunty Pam breathed on, in and out, in and out, slowly, stertorously, but without faltering. She could go on like this for ever. If I'd stayed at home, she would have been breathing like this in here with or without my company. If I were to go home now, the metronomic sound wouldn't be interrupted. Unless it simply stopped.

I leaned my head against the chair back and closed my eyes. There was something soporific about that regular breathing, like the sound of the sea on a shingle beach, tumbling the pebbles at the edge of the shore. Except, even as the metaphor came to my mind, I thought it an odd one to alight on because Aunty Pam had never been to the seaside with us. And in fact, those few visits to the sea that I've paid in my lifetime have been to the Mediterranean, where the coasts are rocks or sand and the sea holds its tongue. But, as must by now be clear, I have a pedantic turn of mind and a tendency to examine language even as I use it. So I assumed that the image of the stony beach was a literary one, born of reading rather than experience. The poem's shingle scrambling after the suck-ing surf is part of our heritage, and so we believe we know how it must sound. And then I thought, what an odd thing it was to be sitting at the bedside of my dying aunt, and to be thinking about suitable images to describe in my head and only for myself what the sound of her breathing reminded me of.

I opened my eyes again and in the stripes of light sliding through the Venetian blinds saw how thin the hand nearest to me was, how papery, and how ropy and raised the veins were on its back. It occurred to me that in these situations a person in my position would reach out, should reach out and take that hand in mine – to give comfort, and announce my presence. I should cradle it in one palm and with the other gently stroke it, as people do in films. But I couldn't bring myself to do that because – and I know this does me no credit – there was something about her hand that was like a premonition. In time, and perhaps not that much time either, my own hand would not look so different. Besides, Aunty Pam and I have never held each other's hands. It was not her style and it's not mine either. But perhaps at this moment she might want a touch or a caress; perhaps all the restraint that she'd grown up with and that by example she'd instilled into me should be put aside, because it was her last chance – and mine. Still I couldn't do it, even though I knew that, were he here, Roy would have been holding her hand.

The sun woke me, shafting directly onto my eyes and making me sweat. There was the usual early morning befuddlement and the reek of my own unwashed mouth, and only then the recognition of why I was here. Aunty Pam hadn't moved. Unless she had – entirely – to another world whose unwarranted existence would astonish her. Her eyes were open and glassy. She may have woken, then died just as I was dozing off. I bent over her to look down into her face, my back stiff from the chair, and apologised aloud but under my breath, because who knew how the thin the partition walls were. I imagined her disappointment that I hadn't managed to stay awake long enough to see her off, and what came to mind was Jesus reprimanding the relevant apostles in the Garden of Gethsemane.

What can I do for you now, Aunty Pam? I asked her staring eyes. I put out my hand to close them, but the feel of her under my fingertips, cool but not cold, disconcerted me. I got to my feet feeling aged and orphaned, bowed to her, rather formally, and raised a clenched fist. And thought, I'd better tell them out there.

Nurse O'Halloran, round her corner in a room the size of a cubby-hole, sensed my approach. A young woman with experience. 'Is she gone, then?' she whispered? 'Ah, dear me. It can't have been more than five minutes ago. She hadn't changed from the time before. Well, the poor soul will be better off this way, do you not think. Is there anybody you need to ring? It says here she had a nephew. Your brother, would it be?'

Another nurse, one I had not seen before, butted in with officious information. 'There's a payphone by the front door in the corridor,' she said, 'for the use of patients and relatives.'

'Did you ever hear the like!' said Siobhan O'Halloran. 'The woman's aunt is lying dead in her bed and we're sending her into the corridor to do her phoning. You stay right here, my dear, and use the one on this desk, just as long as you need. Alison and I will be going along to see to your aunt. And once we're back we'll get you a cup of tea. You could do with that, couldn't you? Of course you could!' And she swept off, round and dewy, all but dragging the infuriated Alison by her wrist.

Roy

Poor old P. Eager beaver, even after they put her out to grass. Tough as old boots, on her feet, certain how we had to be and behave – and how the rest of the world had to be and behave as well. Amazing woman. Amazing. But what a way to go after all this time, fizzles out and switches off. Not how she'd've planned it. I do feel sorry for her for the last years of her life. No. All of them. When did she ever have a good time, except she did her duty and duty was her number one thing?

Actually – and here's the joke – Gina can get a bee in her bonnet about duty too. She's been a real nag about me going to visit, which I never did because after P completely lost it I couldn't see the point. She wouldn't've known me from Adam, or Adam from Adam come to that, and so long as they were doing what I paid them to do, feed her properly, keep her warm and clean, and didn't push her about, I really couldn't see how she'd've been happier if I'd pitched up there and sat in front of her while she was flopped in her armchair like some kid's rag doll. If she didn't recognise Mig she wasn't going to recognise me. But, to be perfectly honest, I think Gina's bag was that it didn't *look* right that only Mig was going. Who to, I said? The staff? That Ms Vera Massie who runs the show? The other inmates who are all about as on the ball as P was? I said, 'If you think someone from this house ought to be going, if you think it matters that much, then *you* go. Permission granted.' 'But she's not my aunt,' she said. 'No,' I said. 'She isn't. So stop fussing. She's fine where she is, as fine as she can be, and seeing me or not seeing me isn't going to make the blindest bit of difference to her.' I had to get out the old A–Z, though, which is a bit of a giveaway, if ever there was one.

'Shall I come with you?' Gina said. But I said no, Mig was there. I'd be OK. She shrugged and pressed her lips together like she'd just freshened up her lipstick.

It was going to be an easy run. Saturday morning, last night's boozers all still tucked up. Kiss FM was playing 'Killing Me Softly', and had me humming along with it but bothering myself over my wife and my sister. What is it with the pair of them, I thought? They can't see what the other one's there for. Literally they can't. Mig thinks Gina's an upper-class airhead with nothing between the ears, and Gina thinks Mig's a dried-up old spinster, probably a dyke, who hasn't got any friends because she's frightened them all off, and hasn't got anything better to do except work. That's what they thought thirty-odd years ago, and evidently that's what they still think now. Only then it was worse 'cause as Gina saw it Mig was deliberately trying to make her life difficult by filling Dougie's head with nonsense. And yeah, maybe. I never thought I'd see it but Mig was head over heels with Dougie from the word go.

She had him over as often as she could get away with, right from when he was little, and took him all over the place. You name it. The zoo, the flicks, the theatre, museums. And all the time, talk talk talk. And she taught him. Oh yes, she taught him: Mig's creed. Always ask questions, never accept the answer. Great! So he comes home and Gina tells him, get in the bath, and it's why? Because you have to be clean. Why? Because you'll get ill if you don't. Which germs precisely? (What normal kid ever said 'precisely'?) Or, you'll smell if you don't. I don't mind smelling. What really put Gina's teeth on edge was that if ever *I* said, 'Your Aunty won't want to take you out any more if you smell', he'd hop straight in the bath like there was no tomorrow.

If she'd had her way Gina would've put a stop to Mig and Dougie's outings, but I wouldn't have it because our family's small enough as it is. I wasn't having him cut off from any bit of it. I reckoned he spent enough time with her parents, eating scones and swinging all over the climbing frame in their garden back in Godalming. The Hoskins side had to get a look-in as well. And anyway Dougie would've screamed the place down if Mig had been barred – and he had a good pair of lungs on him, the scallywag. But I could see where Gina was coming from. How are you supposed to bring your kid up when his mischievous aunty stymies you all the way?

But now it was *our* aunty who was gone.

When Mig called, the first thing I thought was, now's the time to get that pic. Now or never. Not being callous, but respectful. For the record. There's not even a snap of P anywhere that I've seen, not as a kid, not from King Street, not anywhere. If I didn't take a photo now, she'd only ever have existed on paper, and in our minds, Mig's and mine, and maybe in the memories of one or two of the old comrades – if any of them's still alive and compos.

I could've taken the Hasselblad but fished out the old Leica instead. Call it being sentimental but I reckoned it would round the story off, complete the Somers Town Portraits – all but one! You wouldn't think the Leica would still be going strong, but they had good engineers in those days. A sight better than some of the tinny stuff you get now. I've been experimenting with these new digital jobs. Cost a bomb but that'll come down soon enough and then everybody who isn't actually registered blind will think they're a photographer. But the way they work, it seems like we've come full circle. From polychrome to PhotoShop. I dunno. The way it looks to me is you'll end up spending more time fiddling around with a picture *after* you've taken it instead of preparing and thinking and really looking at what's in front of you. It's all going to be post-production now, if I'm not mistaken. Toys for kids, that's my feeling. But ageing codgers always say that about anything new. Like Dougie says, parents are analogue and kids are digital, and it's true. I'd have jumped on the digitals if they'd been there for the taking twenty years ago. Or if I was twenty.

P was pushing ninety. Got a bit smaller and a bit thinner every year till she disappeared into that dot in the middle of the screen, seemingly, like the old pictures on the telly did in the early days. Sucked into it and off into oblivion which, if you ask me, is a sight better place to be than where she's just been, poor old bat.

Mig was perched in this big black chair by P's bed, drinking tea and eating biscuits and looking like she'd been through a hedge backwards, up all night. 'You should've called me,' I said. She said she'd thought to but since P wasn't conscious she couldn't see the point.

They call it a care home, but there's not much home to it. You wouldn't live here if you didn't have to, you wouldn't move in by choice. First step in the door and you know what it is by the stink – old age and leaking bodies and bleach.

There was this nurse who kept popping in and out of the room, like a traffic warden on the prowl. 'Alison Taylor' it said on her badge, with a face like a Jack Russell. One look from her'd freeze the balls off you. Evidently taking snapshots of your dead aunt was a no-no. I tried to explain it wasn't going to be any old photo for the album, more what you'd call an icon. But it was no go. She put her hands on her hips, and screwed her eyes up at me with the corners of her mouth turned down. Ugly as hell. Poor cow was in a fix. She was supposed to be keeping all the other old biddies alive in their beds but what she was really wanting was to shove me out of there.

Then a doctor showed up – like some kid all dressed up in his daddy's gear, little smart-arse who took one look at what was going on, and got it wrong. I was a ghoul, so Mig, who'd fetched me over, must be ghoul's pimp. P was our victim and we were gloating over her corpse. He pushed past me, poking his elbow into my camera, and shone a torch into P's eyes. Stuck a finger on her pulse, at her wrist and in her neck, and said she was dead, which was supposed to be news. He had to do the death certificate so he picked up the notes from the bedside table to get the details. 'Hoskins,' he said. And then louder, 'Oh, I see. Hoskins! That Hoskins? You've got a show on, haven't you?' Must've been watching the box last night. Junior quack *and* arty type. I patted my camera. 'That's all right then,' he said. 'Just so long as you don't start taking pictures of me.' Pictures of him! He fancied himself, didn't he? But out of respect for P I kept quiet and cheered myself up with what she'd have said to him if she could.

P's bed was head to the window, pointing east, with the morning sun blasting straight in. If she'd've been alive she'd've been sweating under it. I crouched down at the foot of the bed to be lens-level with her face, and let the light flood in. Her bony old head would come out as a black silhouette, like a cast, with this giant halo radiating from it. Let's canonise her, why not? Then I went all round her, like she'd never let me when she was alive, looking, staring. Mig went out for a smoke but I hung on in there with P, suddenly not feeling so good about it because it felt like I was taking advantage. Corpses can't object. They don't jump up with their hands over their faces. They don't tell you to bugger off.

You'd think, wouldn't you, that in forty-odd years taking pictures I'd have had a corpse in one of them. But today was my first. To be perfectly honest, P's is the first I've ever laid eyes on. Except for my dad's, when I was a kid. But I was so scared then I didn't really look at him. I reckon I must've been looking everywhere else. Not now, though. I stared at P in a detached sort of way, a curious sort of way. What colour is she, I thought. People always say a corpse is white. P's bedsheets were white, but she wasn't. She was like not quite a person any more but not quite a waxwork either. Like the colour of putty, but putty was too dark. Raw pastry, then. No. This doesn't sound good but she looked dirtier than pastry. And the lines on her face, which I remembered as so deep you'd think someone had scratched them in, they'd been ironed out like she felt easier dead, relaxed, so to speak, and all the tension gone out of her. And it made me wonder whether the lines we all have on our faces are only there because of tension, and when we die they go. So whoever comes to visit us and stand around the bed will look down on us and notice how the lines have gone and think we must be at peace. Whatever that means. Poor old P. I don't think she did peace.

I closed the slats on the venetian blind and went round that bed with the light metre, thinking angles, thinking shapes, still not feeling so good but not holding back either, leaning into her face, pulling back out, and thought how still she was and how her eyes had sunk right down in her skull. P wasn't only my first corpse. She was the first of my models who hasn't been able to stare right back at me, if they wanted to. But what would they have seen? Not me, for sure, because I was behind my box of tricks, and my eyes were covered. They would have seen my knuckles and fingernails, my elbows and forearms, tufts of our Hoskins hair and bits of my eyebrows. But they wouldn't have seen *me*. It was all one way. Jesus Christ! How come I've never thought this before? P's stiff, camera-fodder without a voice, suddenly pipes up in my head: Left it a bit late to think of that, lad, didn't you?

People have a thing about photographs, and photographers. I'm not talking about the paparazzi boys from the press, but real photographers, where the picture – taking it and how you want it to turn out – is all that matters. OK, I'm rolling in it these days,

I'd be lying if I said I wasn't, but it doesn't change what I do. The money's one thing but the picture's another. Yes, I'm famous, and yes, some people get twitchy with what made me famous. They don't like the pictures, or they don't like the way I treat some of the celebs who've sat for me.

There was even a demo, back in the seventies, by some women's group outside the *Before and After* show when it opened 'cause it was almost all women I took in that series, not all, but almost – ordinary women, every sort, thin ones, fat ones, dressed up and then in the buff, showing off their cellulite and their dimpled arses. It was demeaning, according to the Wimmins Libbers, who hadn't got a brain cell between them, or an ounce of comparison. It wasn't demeaning. It was a celebration of ordinariness after I'd pigged out too long on the catwalk girls. They were gorgeous, don't get me wrong, but they were too gorgeous. Not their fault, and not too many brain cells there either, but it was like eating at Marco Pierre White's three times a day – when once a week will do.

P was still lying there – where was she going to go? And, apart from the first one into the sun, I still hadn't taken a single frame. Get on with it, man. Just do it! I focused closer into her, head on again, and remembered Paul Cooke. He was handing me the parcel with the box Brownie in it. It was so clear it was like I could feel I was unwrapping the paper all over again, like I had it in my hands. It was thick, and grainy, and inside was this cardboard box with Eastman Kodak Brownie No. 2, and the fat little cartoon boy in his school cap with stripes on it, and leggings, hugging his new camera and pulling faces at me.

The thing about the box Brownie was that you looked down into the viewfinder instead of holding the camera up to your eye. But now, with my thighs pressed up against the frame of P's deathbed, with my old Leica up to my eye, I realised I wasn't *looking* at P at all. I was *aiming* at her.

I don't know what happened but without thinking I'd backed off until I was pressed against the opposite wall, braced against it. It wasn't the old Leica in my hands any more but a service rifle, and it was Ali McDonald that we all just called Scottie who was in my sights. He was a big guy. Huge. Built like a Sherman and came from Deptford so the only Scottish thing about him was his name. He was a moaner. Complaining all the time that we were stuck in RAF Wilmslow and not on active duty where we could be putting bullets in people. There was plenty to complain about but for most of us that wasn't it. Scottie's beef was that the war in Korea was over and done with just as we all got our papers, while he'd been hoping to take a few pot shots at some commie slit-eye. But, since the emergency was still going in Malaya, plenty of commie slit-eye there, what were we all doing farting about in Cheshire, Compton Bassett Wiltshire next stop?

Every day, same fucking background noise: I'd show 'em, I'd let 'em know you don't fuck with the British, gimme one down the end of a barrel and watch the little yeller feller shit himself . . . until one day on exercises I'd had it up to here with him and thought, OK, sweetheart, let's see who shits himself now, and swung my rifle round until I had Scottie's heart fair and square under my finger. Live ammo that day, and everyone knew it. Shut your fucking face, I was saying over and over, out loud or to myself, I don't remember, shut your fucking ugly face. There was this silence. No twittery birds, no wind in the trees. Nothing. And at the end of my rifle stood Private Ali McDonald from Deptford, gone grey as the Nissan huts, and who was shitting himself now? We could all smell it.

Just for a moment, a split second, but long enough for me to enjoy, it was perfect. There was this big mouth, and he was terrified, total terror, and I had him there. It was like a rush I'd never had before, like a high you'd crave to get again. But then suddenly it wasn't Scottie, but some faceless guy with a blindfold on him in my sights, and I heard P banging on, like she'd done so many times, about Granddad, who'd never said a word about it to me because when we were in Openshaw I was too young for talk like that. And for the first time, I understood. Here I was, ready to squeeze that trigger, wanting to, really wanting to, but with Granddad they'd made him. No choice. And the man he and the others had fired on had simply been too frightened to go on fighting, although for all I knew he might have started out just the same as Scottie, all brag and bullshit.

The exhilaration went. It didn't drain away, it just went, flushed out, and I was empty and ashamed, though not because of Scottie. I dropped the rifle and they locked me up. And I was happy enough about that.

I felt sick then, sick of myself, and it filled my mouth so I had to drop the camera to my chest and spin away from P and her bed. I went over to one of the windows and if anyone was looking they'd think I was admiring the view. But I closed my eyes and leant my head on the glass, waiting for the sickness to pass.

Margaret

By the time I got back from the care home it was almost midday, and hot. But I was so tired I lay down on my bed in all my clothes, then and there, even in my shoes, and fell asleep with one leg dangling over the side. I do remember dreaming about being a student again, and something to do with a summer afternoon on a lake. Perhaps it was that dangling leg that prompted my unconscious to fish out a memory of a hand trailing from a rowing boat on the Serpentine, fingers dabbling through the slow water. I slept so long that someone with a more psychologically attuned mind than mine might say that I did it in order not to be awake. Poppycock. None the less, it was eight o'clock when I did wake up – eight o'clock the following morning – and all I could think of was a bath and breakfast. But I had none of the usual ingredients. The milk I'd had had gone down the drain when I made coffee for Joyce, and the flowers in the sink where I'd left them, my valedictory flowers, that I'd forgotten to put in a vase, had wilted beyond repair. There was no bread. There were no crackers. Not a box of cornflakes. Normally I eat breakfast at work, a good breakfast, and then work through. At weekends . . . I . . . What do I do at weekends? Anyway, normality was not the issue.

I got up off the bed and ran a shallow bath, thinking maybe I'll get a shower fitted. Of all the thoughts to come into my head as a result of Aunty Pam's death, I would never have imagined that the first would be the fitting of a shower. To begin with, as I sat in that bath, I tried to analyse why it was not only that I had thought about having a shower fitted at all, but also why I hadn't thought about that as soon as Aunty Pam had been, as it were, taken into care. Nobody had ever suggested she was going to come out of it. You could ask, of course, why we hadn't had a shower fitted while she was alive and well and living with me – or, rather, I with her. And the answer would be that Aunty Pam didn't like showers and I didn't care enough to go to war over it. But here I was, in our old enamel tub that has lost most of its surface, jade-green stains drooping beneath the taps, considering my options in the light of a new-found freedom. Aunty Pam wasn't here, and wouldn't be returning. But she had never been going to return.

Then I fell to those musings – is there anyone who hasn't had them? – about what may have been passing through her mind before she lay in her stroke-bound coma. Had her sense of herself remained, floating inaccessibly below the turmoil of her upper mind, resurfacing sporadically, sometimes even recognising itself before plunging back into the depths? And after the stroke had felled the turmoil, was Aunty Pam still there somewhere, reaching but unreachable? That was the one that made me shudder, as I suppose it makes us all shudder, partly out of compassion but mostly from solipsistic terror. I flinched with remorse. The more so because I wasn't mourning my aunt as I felt I should – hollowed by the loss of her and unable to imagine how my life could proceed without her. How I wish I could honestly say that was so. Instead, I was relieved that the awfulness of her last years was over, and that I was no longer responsible – and I can't swear which of those came first.

Without her Roy and I might have ended up in an orphanage, or separated. There would have been no one driving into me the importance of books and reading and schooling the way she did, who had never had the same chances. Without her curmudgeonly acceptance, Roy wouldn't have had the space to become the photographer he has. Without her we would have been so frighteningly alone. I salute her. I raise my glass to her. I thank her. She did what she had decided was her duty and so much more. But love? I didn't know if it was in her conceptual lexicon.

The water in my bath was cooling so I sank down and clamped my toes over the hot tap to add more, even though on this summer's day the atmosphere was steamy enough. That's one thing about these flats: even if it arrives in pipe-shaking belches, the water runs hot as a geyser. The empty flat – or rather the complete absence of Aunty Pam – and the now deep bath, long enough for my short self to lie full length in it, brought to mind again a memory I thought I'd managed to extinguish – until Roy rekindled it on Friday night. I was young at the time, although, all right, old enough to have had better judgement. It was summer then too. 1963. I was a junior lecturer and writing up my doctorate, at King's. Roy had just got married, ridiculously (on Midsummer's Eve, partying in a daisy field at Gina's behest – half the daisies were in her hair) and unnecessarily. Yes, she was pregnant. But the days of marriage automatically and precipitately following impregnation were behind us, I'd thought. And argued – to no avail.

Afterwards, Roy left us. Gina's parents had helped them buy a flat of their own, a Victorian conversion in St Augustine's Road near Camden Town. Easy walking distance for walkers, so we walked it. To be fair, Roy walked it most often, so often in fact that had someone ever dropped by to visit us they could have been forgiven for thinking he still lived here. We were on his way home. He was working part of the time out of a studio in Clerkenwell Road, Cowpers, as well as with John French. If anybody now recalls Cowpers it's only as the place where Roy Hoskins was employed when he began to make a reputation. At any rate, Roy to'd and fro'd while Gina stayed at home growing her baby.

She seemed at first to think this was a full-time occupation, sitting in the bay window and fluttering her fingers over her expanding belly. If I'd known that the result would be Douglas I'd have been as interested in the process as she was. I'd have been on my knees at her side whispering sweet subversion to the foetus under the dome. But I didn't know. How was I to know how I would feel from my very first viewing of my nephew? Even now I struggle with the sentiment to pin it down: compassion, of course, for anything quite so helpless, although that surprised me. But it was more a surge of recognition – we are of one flesh, thou and I. Later it became a journey of companionship with a sweet-natured child possessed of a sharp mind. I found it disconcertingly thrilling: to love so deeply and be loved in return, and nurture this growing little intellect with its independent spirit.

But I digress. My bath, fingers dimpling the water prompting recollections of youthful foolishness. *The Revolutionary*. Roy's photograph of *The Revolutionary*.

One evening after work my colleagues and I had decided to go for a quick pint at the Nell of Old Drury in Catherine Street.

It was one of those summer evenings when office workers and students and market traders from Covent Garden cluster on the pavements with their glasses brimming, and anyone who wants to pass by has to step off into the road. In those days Covent Garden was still the wholesale fruit and vegetable market and not the tourist honey-pot people know today, and this particular pub was a favourite with the traders, so the drinkers were a mixed bunch. I was on the outskirts of our particular crowd because to someone of my stature the middle brings claustrophobia, so it was easy enough for Jake to notice me as he negotiated the kerb.

'Comrade Margaret!' he exclaimed, and hoisted a clenched fist. He was unchanged – although I don't know why I say that since there is no particular reason why he should have changed. I had known him, as the word goes, when we were both undergraduates, and that hadn't been so very long before. His hair was still uncombed, his beard still goatee, but despite his beatnik accoutrements Jake Littlejohn always said he was a Trotskyist. Unfortunately he also had dark eyes that were both intense and twinkly, and therefore inescapable.

'Now don't you go anywhere,' he announced. 'I'll be back as soon as I've got myself one of those.' He nodded towards my glass and plunged through the crowd into the pub. How like Jake to suppose that without his instruction I might leave, despite the fact that my glass was full and I was with friends. But I was foolish enough to be flattered. Jake was one of those people who, arriving from the rear, gets served while others are still disputing the head of the queue. In a moment he was back, grinning over his beer which I knew was bound to be Watney's ale – his public drink of choice because it was what the workers drank. Not being a worker himself he had researched the matter. He dipped his beak into his drink and came up with froth all over his moustache, which he wiped off on his cuff. The years fell away. He drank like a man filmed stumbling out of the desert to capsize face down into the oasis. Eventually, when he had appeased his thirst he belched loudly – something he had learned to do at will because it irritated the bourgeoisie – and said, 'So where does the world find you, these days?'

'Still King's,' I said. 'Bit of teaching. Research.' Jake waited a moment, then shook his head, smiling through his beard. 'That all? You never did say more than you had to, did you?' (In those days, the days I'd known him, that was true, whatever may be the prevailing opinion now. In those days I'd been verbally more timid than I am today because I wasn't yet used to the company of well-heeled and confident people who talked all the time.) 'Well, in that case, let me tell you about me,' said Jake with enthusiasm. He sucked down the rest of his beer and dangled his glass by its handle from his little finger, tapping it against his thigh rhythmically so that the dregs ticked down his denim leg.

'I am glad, nay, delighted to be able to inform you that I too have been appointed to mislead the young. The people who appointed me probably don't see it quite that way, but, believe you me, that's what I'm going to do. The University of Reading doesn't know what's coming its way, but watch out for seismic shocks in the Home Counties. When the military-industrial complex is brought to its knees and history takes account, can you imagine the apoplectic faces behind their *Torygraphs* when they realise that it all began at the bottom of the lawn! All hail the revolution!' He swept his empty beer glass above his head, 'Long live the dawn of the Workers' State in our green and pleasant land! What are you doing at Kings?' 'Research, I told you,' I said. 'The First World War.' 'It's the third one you should be concentrating on,' he said. 'It'll come, you'll see. Probably on its way as we speak. Fancy another?' I shook my head and said I had to be off, which was quite untrue, and he said where, and I said home, and he said why, and I said because I had promised my aunt that I would cook tonight. At which Jake, perfectly reasonably, performed a theatrical splutter and asked me what I had against my aunt that I wished her dead so soon. 'I've got a much better idea,' he said. 'Why don't I come back with you, and *I'll* cook the dinner. That way, I get to meet your aunt, about whom I remember hearing so much, and she survives to tell the tale. I'll buy us a bottle of plonk, red preferably, and then we can all get smashed together.' I told him Aunty Pam didn't drink. 'Then you and I will have all the more. Who knows what else we can share. Come along, comrade,' he said putting his arm through mine, 'we've been here before. Say goodbye to your friends like a good girl. It's time your uncle Jake reawakened the revolution in your little heart.' The last said with a knowing leer in the voice.

God, how I love hindsight. The power of it. And I know, I know. But I was young and the pattern of my life had been disrupted by Gina. Hasn't everyone done something stupid for the wrong reasons, at least once? I walked him to the flat and on the way Jake bought not one, but two bottles of red wine that were not plonk, because he had grown up in a household that knew about fine wines and there is only so much that a man can reject. In the off-licence he made a point about arguing with the shopkeeper over the merits of the different vintages, about château this and château that, before buying what he'd decided he was going to get in the first place. I knew what he was doing. He was demonstrating to the unfortunate fellow that unsavoury types like himself could be knowledgeable in all sorts of unexpected ways, and that therefore this example of the petty bourgeoisie, this grocer, should beware of making judgements based on appearances. I should imagine that the grocer drew no such inference but put the cash in his till and turned to his next customer, raising his eyebrows behind Jake's departing back. You shrug, but you've made a sale.

Jake was delighted by the Ossulston estate. He stopped for a moment by the tree in the courtyard and took deep breaths, spreading his arms with a bottle of red wine grasped like a skittle in each hand, as if by this gesture he was embracing the surrounding blocks and all their inhabitants. He had come home, he seemed to say, the prodigal son returned, who was going to cook the fatted calf himself in a spirit of reconciliation. He sat down heavily on the bench under the tree and scanned his surroundings, window by window, with such attention that if any of our – in those days entirely peaceable – neighbours were in they could only assume this was a visitation from the law, in fancy dress. 'Yes!' he concluded, triumphant as a location scout. 'This is absolutely it. History begins tomorrow. To work, I say, to work!' And he revved himself to his feet with a strange noise in his throat, something between a Gallic rumble and a small growl, and strode off. But of course, since he didn't know which block, which stairway, which floor and what door was ours, he had to pause to let me take the lead, and in ceding the vanguard rôle lost some of his élan.

'Is she in yet?' he muttered, slightly breathless as we climbed the concrete steps. 'I shouldn't think so,' I said. Aunty Pam was always first into King Street and last out. I sensed relief in his silence and wondered why. When I opened the front door Jake crowded in behind me and surged into our kitchen to take a look. And he saw what Joyce saw, because essentially it hasn't changed. The kettle's new since then, of course and . . . actually, I can't remember what may have changed, but very little. As I remember, he displayed his disappointment, as if he'd been expecting something less domestically ordinary. Party symbols, perhaps, or Soviet posters dripping blood and Cyrillic.

I tried to look at the only kitchen I'd known through his eyes, but all I could see was that it was extremely small and clean, with a free-standing gas cooker and a sink with a scrubbed wooden drainer, a narrow cupboard painted a fading blue for plates and saucepans, a tiny square Formica table, and the four chairs. There were no smudges on the windows – Aunty Pam saw to that – and the floor was swept. Oh yes. Of course. The fridge isn't the same, but the one we had then must have been about the same size.

Jake put his two bottles on the table and rubbed his hands together. 'Now then. What were you going to cook?' 'I wasn't actually,' I said. 'We don't have dinner or supper or whatever in the evening. We have tea. I mean, really tea. Bread and butter, and maybe boiled eggs and some salad. You know, cress and beetroot.' 'No kidding?' he said, but opening the fridge as if he was checking up on me, bent, peered, and closed it again, dejected. 'I could whip us up an omelette and make a salad, perhaps, when she gets in. Let's see.' He opened the cupboard and pulled out our frying pan. Plonked it on the cooker. And then he began working his way along every shelf and drawer like a detective searching for the telling clue. Since I didn't know what he was looking for I couldn't help him and frankly I was astonished at his gall. Eventually, when there was nowhere further to look, all he had found to his liking was a couple of tumblers.

'Where's the corkscrew?' he demanded. 'We don't have one,' I said. 'I told you. Aunty Pam doesn't drink.' 'But you do,' he said, and I agreed this was so, but not at home. He plunged into his jacket pocket and pulled out a Swiss army knife, prised out its corkscrew, opened both bottles with a flourish of expertise, and stood them on the table – to breathe. Then he folded his arms over his chest and shook his head at me. 'Hopeless,' he said accusingly. 'How am I supposed to cook with nothing?' 'I didn't ask you to,' I said. 'What is it you're looking for, anyway?' 'Olive oil. Herbs. The basics, you know.'

'We've got the basics, young man,' said Aunty Pam, who was standing in the doorway glaring at this stranger going through her kitchen as if the cutlery was her underwear. 'And we're both quite well, thank you. So then, our Margaret. Aren't you going to introduce us?'

It had been a long time since Aunty Pam had called me 'our Margaret', but I understood what she was about. She'd taken one look at Jake, made her unfavourable judgement, and was putting him on the other side of her fence. 'This is Jake Littlejohn,' I said lamely. 'We were at university together. But he's a lecturer now.' 'Is he, indeed,' she said, as if he wasn't there, and taking off her jacket. 'And is he stopping?' Then she saw the two bottles and the tumblers on the table. 'I see. Well, don't mind me. You have your drinks, the pair of you, and if you'll excuse me I'll just see to the kettle.' She edged between Jake and the cupboard to get at the kettle to take it to the tap and then set it on the cooker, and it seemed that, wherever he was, he was in the way. We all stood in silence, listening to the kettle getting up steam. 'Has our Roy been by yet?' she asked, swilling hot water round the teapot. 'Well, if he comes, tell him I'm in the other room.' 'Don't you want anything to eat, Aunty Pam?' I asked. 'I'll see to myself, love. I've a meeting to get to anyway.' By this time she'd put the teapot and her cup and saucer and the milk jug on a tray. She'd taken our knitted tea cosy out of the drawer and slipped it over the pot; buttered a couple of slices of bread and spread them with jam, and was now standing in the doorway holding the tray as if she'd just salvaged everything on it from a fire. 'I wouldn't drink too much of that stuff without eating,' she said, pointing her nose towards the wine. 'It gives you the runs, never mind a bad head.' And she was gone.

For a moment Jake stood where he was, back pressed to the window, and I knew he felt let down. For a Trotskyist, of course, the Communist Party of Great Britain was anathema, Stalinist, and wedded to state capitalism. All the same, Aunty Pam was the real thing: working class, from somewhere up north, in the Party all her life, totally committed. But all she'd done was make a pot of tea and talk about food. I was sorry for him, and embarrassed too, because I thought she'd been gratuitously rude. So where half an hour before I'd been wondering how to get rid of him, now I was determined to make him like us, or at least me.

'A dour lot, are they, then, your CP people?' said Jake, dolloping his expensive wine into the tumblers. Dear me. Isn't it extraordinary how the allegiances can be buffeted by a few words! Now I found myself veering back towards Aunty Pam, never mind my immediate inclination to say that the CP were not my people – which would have made a Judas of me. 'Hear this,' proclaimed Jake, holding out a tumbler. 'There is nothing that a glass or three of really good wine can't put right. So smile.' And he put on such a wistful and winsome expression that I laughed, and drank his wine, and it was good.

There was some cheddar in the fridge which I cut into wedges and arranged on a plate, and we ate the wedges as we drank first one, then the other bottle of Saint-Emilion. Jake talked about his plans for the youth he intended to mislead, how he was going to warn them off all the books on the reading lists they'd been previously recommended by their teachers; indeed, how he was going to warn them off any book they had not discovered for themselves. I managed not to wonder aloud if he had forsaken Trotsky for the anarchists. Instead we began a discussion about whether one student's recommendation to another would therefore also be suspect or whether it was only the opinions handed down by the established staff that should be ignored. But then, if that were so, would not Jake himself, as a member of faculty, belong to the same category, which would mean that, if his students were really listening to what he advised, they ought by definition to reject his advice, and as a consequence have to read the books he'd proscribed to spite him.

We spent some time devising a list of recommended books that students should not read, and, by contrast, a list of books that students should be commanded not to read, in the expectation that they would. Drinking steadily, we argued over each title, and, amiable as it was, our dissension was charged and exhilarating. I was smoking roll-ups, Jake had his Gitanes, and although the kitchen window was wide open our smoke sat on the still air. We didn't notice Aunty Pam leave for her meeting and we didn't hear her return.

'You'll have missed your train, young man,' she said, looming in the doorway like Banquo's ghost. 'Wherever it is you were going. You'll have to make do with the settee. Our Roy used to sleep on it well enough, though he's shorter than you are, but one night won't kill you – unless you've already been and poisoned yourselves with the alcohol. Margaret'll see to you.' And like Banquo's ghost she melted away, leaving us staring groggily at the space she'd occupied. I was suddenly aware how dry my mouth was, my inner lips puckered by the red wine. All I wanted was to drink a lot of water and stretch out in my bed. 'I'll get you some sheets,' I mumbled, and blundered out to make up the sofa for our guest.

Now, our bathroom is next to the kitchen, on the end wall. The sitting room is the other side of the kitchen, then comes my room, and Aunty Pam's is – was – at the far end of our thin hall. Maybe I'd shown Jake round when we first came in because he seemed to understand the layout. He watched me spreading a sheet over the sofa cushions and said, suddenly, 'I fancy a bath. It won't wake "her up north", will it?' I was too tipsy to bridle at his mock Lancashire but simply waved a 'help yourself' hand towards the bathroom, thought, oh damn, I want to brush my teeth, thought what the hell, I'd rather get to sleep, and stumbled into my room and out of my clothes. But I hadn't drunk the water I wanted, and now really needed, so I wrapped my dressing gown round me and went back to the kitchen. I didn't look into the sitting room but I could hear the taps running and saw the bathroom door was ajar so I assumed Jake wasn't in there yet. Brushing my teeth had become an option again. I slipped in and grabbed my toothbrush.

The door closed behind me and there stood Jake in the altogether, a murky outline in the mirror wrapped in a fog of steam. 'Share an ablution with me, Comrade Margaret, and I promise I'll scrub your back. I scrub a mean back, I do.' He plucked at my dressing gown while I was trying to bat him off. 'Oh, come along, give us a kiss,' he whispered, and pulled me towards him. And I have to presume I let him because I found myself all tangled in his arms with his bearded face pressed on

150

mine, his tongue rooting in my mouth and the tip of his penis prodding my midriff. The old revulsion washed over me that was not entirely to do with his behaviour, a revulsion so violent that in one move I was able to shove him away, crashing back against the opposite wall.

Roy

I came in and I thought, where the fuck did she dig this one up? And *why*? What I can't remember is why I'd gone home – I mean to Ossulston Street – on a Saturday morning. This creep was tucked up against the kitchen table smoking a Gitane, and all he had on was his jeans. The rest was bare torso, bare feet, bed hair, and looking like he hadn't washed yet. If ever.

He had a mug of coffee, *my* old mug, in front of him, and he was sounding off about something at P, batting his forefinger in her face like a teacher with a dumb kid who hasn't got what it takes. I got there just when he was saying, '. . . and what you people don't seem to get is that revolution can't be a one-off because it only takes about ten minutes before the people who made it become the bosses who use the fact that they made it to keep it to themselves, and justify whatever they do next. That's what's happened in your precious Soviet Union. The Workers' State was betrayed. It was there, but it was lost when the Politburo decreed that the revolution was "The Revolution"' – he wiggled his forefingers in the air – 'the one and only, and you can bet your bottom dollar they didn't want any more because that'd mean them all losing the top jobs, the power and the gravy train. And so you . . .'

P suddenly bent across the table and grabbed him by one of his fingers. He was so surprised he shut up but his mouth was like a beak, still saying 'oo'. 'Did you strip the settee?' she said. 'What?' 'Did you take the sheets off the settee? You didn't, did you? You got up and lit up and came in here and sat yourself down, and waited for our Margaret to make you your coffee. And then you started on your speeches. Now where I come from, when you stop the night in someone's house you tidy up after yourself. And if you've got something to say you do your talking afterwards.'

Mig's boyfriend yanked his finger out of P's fist, laced his fingers behind his head and tipped back on his chair. He half closed his eyes like he thought it made him look like Marlon Brando and sneered up at her. 'Well, well, well,' he said, with a drawl straight out of Chelsea. 'The great CPGB staffers turn out to be a crowd of petit-bourgeois after all. Just as we thought. Half the world is trying to make revolution and you're making beds. What sad little lives you must all lead. Tight-arsed, small-minded, the lot of you. Now I get why you're so frigid, Comrade Margaret. And I'm sorry for you, I really am. But you know what? You should strike out on your own. Remember what we talked about last night? It's called not always doing what people expect. It's called being your own person. It's called non-compliance. And that's what you need, little girl. A bit of non-compliance. And let Aunty here look after herself. She's the past and you're the future.'

That was it. I couldn't stop myself, and didn't want to. I jumped into the kitchen, cupped my hands into a lens, focused close to his face and said, 'Gotcha!' Then I kicked the chair legs out from under him and he was flat on his back with his knees in the air. I went in for another close-up, and another, and from a different angle, click. After that all he could do was roll himself to all fours and scramble away. We stood there, the three of us, lined up, while he grabbed the rest of his clothes from off the sofa and shot down the stairs with his gear under his arm. Then we all went out the door onto the outside landing and looked down on him in the courtyard. He was sitting on the bench under the tree putting on his shoes. But when he pulled his shirt over his head he saw us there, all bunched up together, so he raised his fist like some kid pretending to be a revolutionary. Then he got up and went out the gates trying to look like he didn't care.

'Spoilt child, that one,' said P, for us all. 'Thinks it's a game. You're best off without, Margaret love.' 'I was never with,' she said.

I followed her into the sitting room where she was pulling the sheets off the sofa, wrinkling her nose, and muttering to herself.

'What are you saying?' I asked.

'I'm not saying,' she said. 'I'm declaiming. *Sotto voce*.

"Hurrah for revolution and more cannon-shot!

A beggar on horseback lashes a beggar on foot.

Hurrah for revolution and cannon come again!

The beggars have changed places, but the lash goes on."'

'You better not let P hear you,' I said. 'No,' she said. 'Hence the *sotto voce.*'

I took the other ends of the sheet from her and we started folding it, till she swore and dropped her corners. 'Let's not bother,' she said. 'I'll take it all to the launderette. Wash him out. Yuck!'

Well, I was with her on that. But there was one thing he'd said that stuck with me. 'Mig?' I said. 'What?' she said. 'Are you going to stay on here for ever?' She said, 'As opposed to?' I said, 'Moving out somewhere.' 'What, and leave Aunty Pam on her own?' 'But you can't stay with her for the rest of your life. Or hers,' I said. 'Watch me,' she said.

P's funeral. Cremation is what it was. We're not religious, Mig and me. Don't see how we could be, though I suppose we could've done what kids do and gone the opposite way, but we couldn't be arsed, neither one of us. But rituals make you feel better so long as you can get enough people to join in. When it's just the two of you, though, it doesn't do the business. What's the point of getting married when it's just you and the registrar and the witnesses? Or baby-naming with only the parents, whoever's doing the naming – and the baby, of course? We'd have laid on a bash for P if we'd thought some sort of crowd would turn out for her, but who was going to show? Her King Street mob had likely already snuffed it, except for a few ancient intellectual types holed up in Highgate and along Hampstead Heath. But it was just as Mig said it would be, not one of them made it to the crematorium. 'They're snobs, you know, the comrades,' she said. 'To a man and woman. Aunty Pam was only a secretary, after all. Why would they bother honouring her?'

Gina offered to come, since she's a good girl, and so did Dougie, but it wasn't enough of a crowd to have Mig and Gina in the one room again, and, if not Gina, then not Dougie either. I reckon he couldn't much remember P anyway. Mig used to bring him back to the flat on wet Saturdays to brainwash him when he was still a toddler and P kept tripping over his Duplo. Brainwashing is what Gina called it, and still calls it. But I've said to her that

154

if Dougie's done so well, spotted his opportunities before other people did and made himself a mint ahead of time, we ought to be thanking Mig for giving him an independent mind. 'Who'd've thought,' I said, 'that these dot-com companies were going to be so big ten years ago? *Five* years ago? Dougie did, didn't he? And we laughed. We said, we both said – you did too, Gina – nobody can make money selling something that doesn't exist except as a brand name. And now look!' At least she cheers up when I say the last thing Mig wanted to do was turn Dougie into a digital entrepreneur fleecing the pink pound. The two he's got that are really pulling in the dosh are his travel sites homotels.com and soqueerandsofar.com and biggaysout.com, which does what it says on the tin, I reckon. God knows what old P would've made of that. Lucky for her she'd lost the plot by then and never had to get her head round it. Lucky for us too. Can't imagine how I'd have started trying to explain.

Anyways. In the end it was just the three of us at Golders Green crematorium. P in her box, and Mig and me sitting dumb as a couple of bottles in the front pew, staring at it. We didn't even have anyone officiating, which put the administrators in a twitch. We said we didn't need anyone, that we'd sit together and think about her a bit, and keep silence. They probably thought we were Quakers. When we were ready, we said, we'd press the button ourselves. They got really uptight about that.

'Apparently button-pressing is a reserved occupation,' Mig said. She'd told the geezer in the office she knew where they kept the button and we could promise to do it within the twenty minutes of the single booking. 'I guarantee there'll be no overrun,' she said. 'And if it's crucial we won't do it too soon either in case you have any worries about the oven not being ready, or overbooked, leading to an unforeseen mingling of ashes.' Then she said, 'How does anyone know they've actually got their person's ashes anyway?' This really put their backs up and the hatch came down over the finger on the button. Health and Safety, they said.

We jammed ourselves together, the two of us, at the end of the empty pew. P's coffin was on its runners just a step away, with our red roses jumbled all over the lid. There was this pair of dinky double doors like Toytown prison gates, locked for the moment but ready and waiting to open up. And over them, high up, was a stone portico, like a gable, on a couple of green marble columns. But it was phony – stuck onto the brick wall, like a piece of scenery from an opera, like an entrance to a cathedral leading nowhere. Except you knew where it led. It wasn't a church or a synagogue, but I suppose the dark marble and the portico were meant to make you think of ancient temples and everyone's beliefs – but they weren't going to say which ones, since all sorts get themselves turned to cinders in here. Multicultural death. All the rage.

We sat there and breathed in the crematorium air. They all have a smell to them, functional places, don't they? In schools it's feet and farts, in proper churches it's dusty hassocks and old paper, though the exotic ones have candles and incense and old lady whispers. In hospitals it's bad food and shit and baby oil, village halls it's cup-a-soup, and crematoriums it's, I dunno . . . damp overcoats, maybe. No coats today, though. Not this summer. I was thinking of that more than I was thinking of P till Mig said, in a doctor's-waiting-room voice (funny, that, since there was nothing to stop her talking out loud), 'Do you remember when we were here last?' And I said, "Course I do. Harry Pollitt's in 1960, and such a crowd they couldn't get them all in. Now *there* was an occasion!'

It was just as hot then, though that was July. Me scampering about taking pictures, for all I was worth. A gathering like that was a gift. Of course, in those days I was still just jobbing – without an 'oeuvre' yet, but that subject matter would've been part of my retrospective – in the catalogue under 'documentary' – if it hadn't been for the flood from a burst pipe at the studios the winter after. Most of the prints and negatives I'd stored there were destroyed.

Paul Robeson was my main man rather than the Soviet ambassador or the Chinese delegation. Harry Pollitt's wife was in a dark funeral car but once she'd got out we didn't know which one she was, and P didn't tell us. Harry's old Wolseley'd been brought up for the ride by his chauffeur, who doubled as his bodyguard, they said. Some other Party bigwig inherited him, I suppose. I did get a good shot of Paul Robeson in the rose garden afterwards, like this big black tower, head and shoulders above the other mourners, looking like a horse in a herd of donkeys. But he was out of place everywhere, poor bloke. Too black and communist in America, just too black in Moscow, too famous in London. Did he sing? Can't have. We wouldn't have forgotten that.

'Time's up,' Mig was murmuring, tapping her watch. 'I'll go whistle up the jobsworth.' He must have been lurking at the door because they were straight back. He strutted down the aisle ahead of her, pressed his button, stopped there with his chest out for a second so's we'd notice he was being properly respectful, and cleared off. P slid away between the purple curtains and out through the prison gates, so we left her to it while we made a dignified exit, arm in arm with our noses in the air, past the little commissars' sentry box, and out into the sunshine.

We'd agreed that P ought to get a niche in Commies' Corner, where she belonged, cosied up with all the old warhorses. Mig had sorted it, though she'd had to put up a fight. First they said the Cloister Garden was full, then when Mig pointed to an empty space they tried to make out P didn't have the right credentials, like only top-notch Bolsheviks could make it past the selection committee. I reckon Mig may have had one or two things to tell them and if I try I might feel sorry for the geezer on the other side of the argument. She says she delivered a lecture on the nature of Marxist ideals in general and the CPGB in particular, loyal service, years of toil and all the rest of it. Whatever she said, they gave in and the niche was made over, probably just to shut her up. So we went round to check it out.

On the way we passed beds where they'd planted the roses in straight lines, each one with a white plastic tag telling you its name, and under the roses were these small square plaques on sticks, like lollipops. Bill Nash 1921–1983, fertiliser for Alpine Sunset, which you'd think should've been a blaze of red and orange but was only pink with a bit of yellow in it. Next to him was Sarah Fitzgibbon under Blessings. She was pink too, and Rex Macintyre, died aged only forty-two, but some wag had seen to it he was still hard at work. His rose was called Sexy Rexy – still pink, though. But then I saw I'd got it wrong because a sign in the lawn the other side of the path said that

that was where ashes were buried, so it must be manure, not people, under the roses.

They've got the Cloister Garden round a corner of the main building, right up against a red-brick wall by an arch covered all over in ivy. They're all there: William Rust, born 24 April 1903, died 3 February 1949, it said. Foundation Member Communist Party, Secretary Young Communist League 1923–1929, Executive Member Communist Party 1923–1949, Editor *Daily Worker* 1930–1949. George Alison, 20 May 1895–11 September 1951. Foundation Member CP, blah blah . . . Albert Inkpin, 1884–1944, Foundation Secretary of CP of Great Britain. Julia Inkpin, his wife and comrade. A. F. Papworth, 1899–1980, incorruptible fighter, blah blah . . . John Gollan, 1911–1977, CPGB General Secretary, 1956 –1975. And of course old Harry himself, 1890–1960, Foundation Member of the Communist Party 1920, General Secretary 1929–1956, Chairman 1956–1960. Not Raj Palme Dutt, though.

'I wonder, where did they put the great theorist?' said Mig. 'What shall we say on P's?' I asked. 'I dunno,' she said. 'How about Pamela Hoskins 1912–1998. Daughter of Foundation Member Communist Party, indefatigable stenographer and loyal secretary? It doesn't have the ring of the others, quite, does it?' 'Who cares?' I said. 'I mean, look at them all in the wall there! You'd never guess about all the quarrels and the in-fighting.' 'Like a flipping synod,' she said. 'Not Cloister Garden for nothing.'

We sat on a wooden bench in the sun, Mig and me, and looked out at the garden, at the rosebeds and the striped lawns that had just been mowed, and we listened to the faraway traffic rolling like waves, and the birds singing because none of it bothered them. The tarmac paths had been swept and were being swept all over again, and the whole place looked like some hospital matron had it under her thumb, it was so tidy. Not a weed in sight. Everything clean, all the beds properly made, corners trim like they should be, all in nice neat rows. I thought, this is how you know it's a place of death 'cause they're not leaving anything to chance.

Out of the blue Mig suddenly goes all shaky on me. 'Hey, sis, what's with you?' I put my arm round her. She pointed back at the jigsaw of plaques behind us like they were a job lot she'd put up for auction. 'It's getting too much,' she said. 'This interring of relatives.' 'It's only been three,' I said. 'By our age, that's normal, isn't it?' 'This one, maybe. Not the first. Not Bill. And actually, Granddad. He can't have been that old when he died, can he? Younger than we are, at any rate.' And I said that was true. We'd picked up that he'd died suddenly as well. There'd been whispering about it, not meant for us kids to hear. 'But I don't think *he* had a dicky heart,' I said. 'Somebody would've said, wouldn't they, later? What with Bill?'

We sat for a bit and she said, 'And now who's left?' 'We are,' I said, and gave her a bit of a squeeze. 'You and me. We're left.'

Mig's had a call from the care home asking her to collect P's 'effects'. She told them they could go ahead and bin the lot, but the manageress said if they did that they'd be contravening the terms of their contract with us, paragraph this, line that, only next of kin are authorised to dispose of the property of the deceased. And since I'd signed the contract way back when – because I'd be the one signing the cheques – I'd have to be the one to go round and pick the stuff up.

They'd packed it the way removers stash away crockery, in a cardboard carton sealed at the seams with tape. I'd had the idea to just look over whatever P had left behind and nod it through to the nearest charity shop, but Ms Vera Massie wasn't having that. The whole bleeding box, everything in it, all the tape round it, was going to have to leave the premises, and to be sure it did she hoiked it up herself, nearly falling over 'cause it was heavier than she'd expected. It sent her feet in their little black heels skittering about all over the parquet. 'My condolences, Mr Hoskins,' she squeaked, dancing along with the box all the way down the hall like something out of Tom and Jerry. She wasn't going to put it down for a second till we'd got the other side of the front door. But the minute we were on the drive where the Alfa was parked up, she shoved the box against my chest and said, like I'd accused her of something, 'We did everything we could for her, you know. We made sure she was comfortable right to the end of her stay with us.' I smiled and grinned at her like you do, but how the fuck they'd have known what P found comfortable beats me.

The boot wouldn't close over the box and I wished I'd borrowed Dougie's Range Rover. In the end, I crammed it on the back seat, shook Ms Massie's hand, and drove slow as a hearse full of new-laid eggs, like it was P and not her raggy old clothes jiggling there behind me.

Along the way south from the gardened semis of Mill Hill back to Somers Town, I wondered whether Mig would stay put in the flat now that P was never coming back. Then I thought about the picture I'd taken of P laid out in her bed, and started planning how best to develop it. Then I was trying to decide what was the closest to Mig's I could park, since it's asking for trouble leaving a car like this one anywhere near the Ossulston estate. In the end I pulled up on Brunswick Square, near Coram's Fields, where we used to go and play hide and seek through the colonnades. Then I got to thinking about Mig again. No work and now no P either. Crisis time. Can't talk that one through with Gina. I'll give Dougie a ring and sound him out, see what he thinks, although all he's got in his head is his new plans. For Mig's sake I know he'd drop everything and come right round.

I found a spot to park just round the corner from the Renoir cinema. Anyone who doesn't know it should give it a go: out-of-the-way little arthouse that shows a lot of foreign-language films, for people who like that sort of thing. I hauled the box out the back seat and set it on the roof so's I could slide it onto one shoulder. Size was the issue, not the weight. I couldn't balance it with one arm. So I put it on my head and held it up there with both hands, like an African woman trekking off for water. I swayed down Judd Street, trying to look like I was only doing what everybody does on a sunny afternoon in London, but there wasn't anyone about to laugh – or clap. Judd Street always seems so quiet you wonder what really goes on behind those mansion block walls. So fucking respectable looking.

Then I was thinking about P again, and about people dying, and turning points – that deserter's execution in the Great War that made Granddad join the Party, then his death that people wouldn't talk about, then our dad's death that drove our mum clean off her head but landed us with P, and her with us, more like, and now P's. What next? Where was this one going to take us? Mig didn't have to play the good little niece now. She was free. But freedom's scary. Still, she could do what she liked with the place, couldn't she? And then I thought, fuck, no! What if they don't let her stay on? I think the council only allowed P to take the tenancy over on compassionate grounds, because of us. But there are rules about inheriting tenancies, just like there are rules for everything. I expect some character from Housing will pop up with a book of regulations and Mig'll find herself bundled into a bedsit. She probably wouldn't mind for herself but Christ knows where she's going to put her reference books when they all come back from Peter's – next week, she said. Maybe she'll give them to Oxfam, though I can't think which poor sod'll want them. Or she could make a bonfire of them in the courtyard. That'd bring the types from the council roaring in. Cause for eviction. Then where'd we be? We've got space for her, of course, at the Pile, but I don't see Gina wearing it. Or Mig, come to that. I could afford to buy her a place somewhere, no problem. So could Dougie, and he would too, but she'd never accept it.

When I crossed the Euston Road and turned into Chalton Street I could see her sitting out at one of the pavement tables where the truckers have their greasy breakfasts under the young hornbeams the council put in a few years back. Mig's always had a taste for greasy breakfasts, with a packet of fags and tea so strong it's orange. I took a bet with myself this was what she'd be having, never mind it was mid-afternoon. She waved her fag at me over the plate she'd wiped clean, then toed it out as she stood up to help me get the box down. 'Blimey!' she said, and I sat down. A man came out the café strapped in a butcher's apron. He swiped up her plate and raised his eyebrows at me. I shook my head and he went back inside, whistling 'Delilah'. Where the fuck's he been all this time, I thought. Some woman I didn't know came by with a bursting red and white plastic laundry bag on wheels, for the launderette next door. She nodded at Mig, so I supposed she must live on our block, Mig nodded back, and they said how're you doing and OK to each other and I felt like a tourist.

Mig lit another fag. 'Procrastinating,' she excused herself. 'Sorry.' 'I'll be back in a tick,' I said. Knowing Mig, the fridge would be empty. I crossed the road to the Londis mini-market and bought milk and coffee, and some chocolate digestives for the biscuit tin. Then I remembered what she really likes is Hobnobs, so I changed them. Looked like it was going to be a long afternoon.

Margaret

I hadn't put a foot in Aunty Pam's room since she left – although, of course, she didn't 'leave': she was removed. I hadn't even opened the door. I think – odd as it sounds even to me, especially to me – that somewhere in my unconscious I was afraid I might be found out, that just as I was having a little private rummage Aunty Pam would sprout through the lino and confront me, not batty, but fully marbled, as it were, never having been a patient or resident or client or whatever is the word – customer, no doubt – of a care home for the elderly mentally infirm. That's part of it. The other side is something else, and has nothing to do with Aunty Pam.

At Peter's, operating on the assumption that much of the information we wanted someone else was trying to hide, all subjects were fair game. True trade figures as opposed to the published ones; which ministry of which nation was getting into bed with which supplier; what spoken but unwritten deals had been struck that would at some future date allow country X to run a pipeline through country Y, contrary to known and stated policy, possibly in return for armaments whose route of delivery would be circuitous and country of origin unclear. So if everyone wasn't lying all the time they were certainly not always telling the truth either, which was why scepticism was the first tool in our drawer, checking and rechecking because we always assumed someone was trying to hide something from us. Qualms were not so much a luxury as an irrelevance. But, for me, that only applied to these ministers, or CEOs, or Brigadier-Generals or 'special attachés' at whichever embassy, in their professional capacity.

How they lived when they got home from that capacity didn't interest me unless it turned out that their wives were also in some skulduggery up to their necks, or that their mistresses were, or their closeted gay lovers were the route to further deals. (I notice that my assumption was that it was always men I was dealing with. Well, it *was* always men, and largely still is.) What was it to me, went my reasoning, what their relationship was like with an unbending father who could never be pleased? Why should I wish to flay the personality, skin by skin, until the trembling core stood naked and diminished on general display? Hoodwinking the electorate, where there was one, was one thing. Keeping your soul to yourself quite another, and as it happens I stand by that still. So if Aunty Pam, who had no oil wells or defence contracts in her gift, wanted to keep things to herself, it wasn't for me to prevent her. I'm not one to go poking into other people's private lives.

Roy

There was about as much air as you get in a mausoleum. Like Lenin's fucking tomb. So the first thing I noticed was the smell. Not just that little old lady smell, it was somehow . . . metallic, like dirty coins. We dumped the box on P's bed and I backed into the doorway, seeing her with my nose, got this picture of her standing there, up on a chair, wiping the windows in her tweedy skirt and buttoned cardigan. Mig took one breath, shot across the room and opened one of the windows.

The room was tidy like you'd expect. Two tidy women on their tod in a small flat. But I didn't know if, at the end, it was maybe Mig who kept P and her bedroom clean like a thank-you for the way she used to scrub us. Or revenge. Or perhaps P had managed that well enough for herself. Of course this used to be our parents' room, the big old iron bed where P slept was the one they'd had, and where our dad copped it.

Time doesn't half pass when you turn your back. These days Dougie's fucking older than Dad was! That one hasn't hit me before.

I get this idea in my mind of a portrait I might put together, three generations in one frame, but two of them never met. Somewhere at the Pile I've got a snapshot of our mum and dad. There's no date on it so I can't say if it was taken when me and Mig were already on the scene. But they're in the living room, our living room, here in this flat, and Bill has his hands on Annie's shoulders, and they're staring into each other's eyes like there's no one else in the world, so I think they didn't even know anyone was taking the picture at all. She's got long hair swept up in one of those forties styles, and though the print is grainy you know she's wearing a good, strong, dark lipstick. And you know from the look on his face that he'd have her decked out in yards and yards of New Look if he could – except that he died before it came in. Poor Bill, never got the chance to show off what he could do for his gorgeous wife. Never got the chance to dress her up. I reckon if he'd only had the dosh he'd've been like me – spot a classy outfit on the rail a mile off and get a kick out of buying it.

I dug this snap out a few years ago, and showed it to Mig, who stared at it like she was trying to remember who it was of. Then she shook her head and gave it back. 'Is that our mother?' Stupid cow, making it out she didn't remember! 'Course she remembered. I just wanted to remind her what our mum had used to look like: all young love, and passion. Clear skin, white teeth, laughing eyes. A moment's joy. But of course once P'd gone and told us – when was it, Mig must've just left school – that she'd known for years Annie was so bonkers she'd been sectioned into a loony-bin somewhere near Nottingham, no picture of pretty Annie stood a chance. We had this picture of a mad witchy woman with wild hair and staring eyes.

At the time, me and Mig, we'd thought we might go up there and see if they'd let us visit. See our mother. See if she recognised us. See if we recognised her, more like. Pop round and look in on the other grandparents as well, while we were about it, Surprise them. Give 'em the heebie-bloody-jeebies, with any luck. Serve them fucking well right if they both had heart attacks and dropped dead on the spot – unless they *were* already dead. If I had grandchildren I'd want to see them. I'd want to know them, make them mine. Not that I'm going to, ta very much, Dougie. We didn't go in the end. Perhaps we should've. But Annie and Bill – they were never it. Not as far as Mig and me were concerned. Never.

Anyways. Here I am, playing with the idea of slipping in a self-portrait and airbrushing Annie out – like the comrades kept doing – and photoshopping an all-male threesome: grandfather, father, son. Of course, I'll come over as the grandfather, won't I, and Bill will look a complete prat, mooning down at nothing. Unless that's where I insert Dougie. But Dougie when? As he is now, typical Hoskins with wiry hair and bony face, or when he was a snub-nosed, nappy-toting toddler? Best would be if I had a snap of Granddad as well, get the four of us in, but we've never had one. I'd have enlarged it if we had.

They'd changed something in P's room. The bed, when we were kids, wasn't up against the wall, I'm sure of that. Me and Mig used to try and get in with Mum and Dad in the early mornings when they were still asleep. We'd creep up on them, thinking if we could only slip under the covers, one from each side, they'd let us stay put. But they always managed to wake up in time.

Things shrink when you grow. Space shrinks. So this room of P's was smaller than it used to be, and the big old bed was still a big old bed, but not the huge fucking thing it used to be. Wrought iron with brass pine-cones on the corners. Used to belong to some geezer in King Street who'd copped it and their son or daughter, dunno which, had given it to Bill as a retrospective wedding-and-moving-to-London present. Good way to start your married life – in a dead man's bed – but then all old beds are dead people's somewhere along the line. I put my hand round one of the pine-cones and it felt smooth as silk, like generations of hands had been stroking it to get it that way. The mirror though. And the blotches on it. That was the same. And I thought, just like I did when I was a kid, what's the point of a mirror you can't see yourself in? Wouldn't have worried P. She didn't look in mirrors. She used to watch me trying to slick down my hair and make it sit the way the other lads' did – sleek but with a quiff, and she'd laugh. 'You with a head like a bottle brush, what are you trying that for?'

P was always old to us. But of course she can't've been more than mid-thirties when she took us on, poor cow. Did that stop her having a life of her own? I looked over at Mig, who was standing by the window she'd just opened and not saying a word, and I guessed she was thinking the same as me. So I went across to her and took her hand, and rubbed her fingers. We were both blinking. Comic to look at probably.

'Let's go for it, shall we?' she said and opened the wardrobe at the foot of the bed. It was almost empty, as it would be. Most of P's clothes were in the box on the bed – all those brown skirts, and cardigans and brogues. Was there ever a time before we barged into her life when she put on her glad rags and went out on the town? Would she have gone alone? With girlfriends? With some lover? But I couldn't see her in anyone's arms. She was kept too busy by the comrades. Well, and us.

I said we ought to take a butcher's under the mattress. That set Mig laughing. She asked what I expected to find there. Family treasures? Wads of cash? But she lifted a corner all the same.

Then she was hunting through the sewing box on the dressing table for a pair of scissors, and snickety-snacked away at the packing tape until the top of the box popped up, and it was like more waves of P's smell bursting out.

Mig climbed up onto the bed and sat with her back against the headrest, the box between her knees. 'You ready?' she said. I said, 'I am.'

Margaret

Roy got onto the bed too, the opposite end, and settled his back against the frame. It's a solid affair, this bed our parents conceived us in, riding high off the ground with its brass finials and iron frame on rusted casters. Old-fashioned. You'd sail in her, I fancy. So there we sat, face to face, with Aunty Pam's giant box crouching between us, and held our breath. It's as if, I thought, we're expecting something or someone to spring out of it and shout Boo! I have to say I felt queasy about proceeding, but I told myself that what with Aunty Pam being now nothing more than cinders, and given that I don't believe in anyone's immortal soul, no harm could be done her by foraging through the fag ends of her biography at this stage. And yet, and yet.

'C'mon, Mig.' Like me Roy had taken off his shoes and socks – it was fearfully hot – and we had the soles of our feet pressed against each other, his left to my right, as though we were going to play the rowing game. He scratched one of my soles with his toe, remembering of course where I'm most ticklish. 'You shit!' I said, jerking my foot away to rub off the tickle. And my doing so flipped the flaps of the box open. We both leaned forward. Neatly buttoned cardigans, three, had been laid over neatly buttoned blouses, also three, folded with the professionalism you see the young things wielding in department stores. Under the blouses were the skirts. No underwear to be seen – they must have junked it, with good reason probably, and no nightdresses either. Her one coat, her shoes, worn at the outside heel implying bandy legs that I had never noticed.

At the bottom was a small pile of newsprint, all old editions of the *Worker*. Why on earth had she kept them and how had she managed to smuggle them out with her to the care home? There must be something significant in these particular editions that in a moment of lucidity, or perhaps not, she'd decided was worth the hoarding. 'Look at the dates,' I said, flinging them out. 'Maybe there's something relevant.'

1 January 1930. The very first edition to come off the presses,

when Aunty Pam would have been eighteen. Collectors' item by now. Next in the pile was 18 March 1953 – too many days after Stalin's death to have anything of interest, surely. 4 April 1959, 22 June 1938, 29 February 1949, 28 June 1960 – that one made sense, Harry Pollitt's obituary – but on and on they went, in no particular order until 23 April 1966. A framing edition, so to speak, the last to be printed under the *Daily Worker* rubric. Arise, *Morning Star*! My God, were we going to have to plough all the way through every one of them hunting for clues? Even after it went tabloid in the 1980s, the *Morning Star* wasn't the most entertaining or stimulating of breakfast reads, though the comrades will have been grateful it wasn't *Pravda*. We shared a glance, without hope; we sighed, we shrugged, picked up a newspaper, each of us, and began.

Roy had bought Hobnobs, bless him, and placed the biscuit tin (with its embarrassing tabby kitten on the lid) equidistant between us. The cookies decreased in number, crumbs gritted Aunty Pam's lilac candlewick bedspread, and we grew jittery on caffeine. But nothing that we read – not a headline, not an article, not a review, not a sports report, not an editorial – explained why Aunty Pam had filed these editions away. 'I'm jacking it in,' groaned Roy, lacing his fingers and stretching his arms over his head. 'I've had enough reading to last me a year. And I know Sundays are for sitting in bed reading the papers, but come on, Mig, not *these* fucking papers.' I was inclined to agree but disinclined to throw in the towel just yet.

'I wonder,' I said, reaching for another paper and the penultimate Hobnob, 'are we perhaps looking for the wrong thing?' Wisely, Roy didn't reply. 'I mean,' I continued, 'whatever it is in each case could be a single word, standing in for something else, dammit!' – and I gave the newspaper I'd just pulled out of the box a vicious shake.

A clip of closely written sheets floated out, surfed the still air for a moment, and came to rest face down between Roy's knees. He picked it up and turned the pages over. Read the first few words. 'Oh, Jesus,' he said. 'You'd best come here.' I pushed the box and its remaining *Workers* to the edge of the bed till it crashed onto the floor, and then crawled over the mattress to my brother. He put his arm round my shoulders and, snuggled close, we settled down to read Aunty Pam's familiar uncluttered handwriting.

July 14th 1960

My dear Harry,
    I never thought I'd be writing to you. There was never
going to be the need because I didn't once stop to ask
myself what would happen if you died. But of course,
since you were always 20 years older than me, it was
bound to happen one day, wasn't it? Would you believe
it, but I thought what I might do was tell you all about
your funeral – how it went, who was there, what their
faces were like, what they all said. I'd let you know about
the weather, and about the songs we sang, and about the
speeches, and where we all went afterwards. I had it in
my mind to do that because of course you weren't there
to know. What a silly fool I am! And how you'd laugh at
me! If you weren't there to know then, you're not here to
know now. But you see, for me, you are and you always
will be here.
    The strange thing is that for the first time in my life I
feel as if I've got you all to myself. I'll not pretend that
Marjorie isn't sad, or that your children aren't grieving.
And I know as well as anyone that all round the country,
in the factories and the shipyards, in the mines and the
docks, they've all been weeping for you, Harry, because
of the man you were to each one of them, not just as Harry
Pollitt, biggest and best man of the Party, but as Harry
Pollitt the outstretched hand, and the kind question,
and the concern for the children, and the memory for
the wives' names, and who had been ill and whether
they were better now. They'll mourn, and maybe they'll
remember, but their memories can't touch mine.
    Oh, Harry. I never told anybody, not even you, because
it wouldn't have been right, and because you might
have been so embarrassed you'd have said I should stop
working for you. It was better to keep quiet than to run
that risk. I knew you'd never do the wrong thing even if
you were tempted. And how was I to know if you *were*
tempted? I couldn't guess if you ever looked at me as
anything more than your reliable little secretary, the

child stenographer you gave the job to out of kindness, for all I know. I made sure I didn't put a foot wrong, never lost a letter, always checked my spelling and laid things out as they should be. I was always neatly turned out, and never was late for an appointment or a meeting. That way, I thought you'd keep me by you, and you did. I did wonder sometimes, from a look in your eye, from the little smile you shared with me when no one else was looking, I did wonder then that maybe there was more to it than just a friendship between a boss and his employee. But I never said anything to you about how I felt. I shouldn't have been able to bear it if I'd told you and then it had turned out that everything I thought there might be between us had never really been there, not on your side, at any rate.

But we had some good times together, didn't we? We had some of the best conversations, didn't we, in the back of that old black Wolseley they used to drive you about in, which once belonged to the Chief Constable of Bedfordshire! He'd never have sold it on if he'd known who was going to buy it, would he? We were always very correct, of course, because of your driver, except when we started off with the Music Hall, and your favourite, 'Daisy, Daisy, Give me your answer, do.' And it was just the two of us singing!

We had a good laugh too, so many times. Do you remember telling me about that day in Moscow when they took you for an official tour of the condom factory and showed off the French letters to you, blowing them up like balloons, and all the while across town Nikita Khrushchev was telling the people at the 20th Party Congress that Stalin had committed crimes and made mistakes. They were keeping you out of the way, of course, because people only wash their dirty linen in front of the family.

It made me angry, that, after we'd laughed about it. You were the leader of the Party in this country and they should have let you in on the secret. But you didn't bear a grudge. You just smiled and said you took it as a compliment that they'd show off condoms to a man of your age, and that you understood how painful it must have been to be talking about those things, so the Russians would naturally only want to be among other Russians to do it. After all, you didn't even agree with Khrushchev, did you? You thought he'd gone too far and that it was despicable to mock Stalin after he was dead, and cowardly. You thought that when the world as a whole was so hostile to what we were trying to do, and what they had been trying to do in the USSR, people were quite right to try and keep it to themselves.

It was loyalty that mattered to you most, wasn't it, Harry. Loyalty to your group, loyalty to your trade union, loyalty to the Party of course, but loyalty to your promises as well. That was why you stuck by Marjorie all those years, even though I knew you were never really happy with her, and actually she wasn't all that happy with you either. But you weren't going to be the one to duck out, no matter how awkward it got. I admired you so much for that.

But I can tell you now, Harry, that I came so close once or twice to letting it all out, to grabbing your hand, which I've wished so many times, so many, many times, would take mine and hold it. And I would imagine and make up in my mind how one day you would stop in the doorway as you were leaving, when it was just the two of us hanging back of an evening in King Street after the rest of them had gone home, and you'd come back to me, and you'd say, 'Pam, I've tried so hard not to tell you this but I can't keep it in any more. I love you just as much as your Bill used to love his Annie.' And then I'd picture how you'd put your arms round me, and I'd put mine round you, and we'd kiss right there in the doorway, no matter that someone might see. In a way I wanted them to see. I wanted them to know that you loved me as much as I'd always loved you, although it had had to be a secret for years and years and years.

There'll be people who'd say, if they knew, that I've thrown my life away, wasted it hanging around the stage door waiting for the leading man to come out. But I don't see it like that, even though I'm 48 now and never was anybody's idea of a looker. What does it matter that I'm too old to find somebody else? There isn't somebody else after you, Harry, and there couldn't be. I've done the work I believed in at the best time to do it, in the best place, with the best man at the helm. I've seen the two kiddies through as well as I could, even though I expect Bill and Annie might have done it another way. Annie would probably not mind as much as I do that our Roy runs about with his camera snapping away at the young mothers twinkling at their babies' christenings, but maybe it'll come to something one of these days. It's just that I really do think the lad has a talent and it's wasted on what he's doing. It's what he thinks too, I know he does because he tells me so, but he's always been the optimistic type. He says, don't worry, I'll make a name for myself one of these days and you'll be proud.

Well, Harry, do you know, I don't want him to make a name for himself if he doesn't get famous for the right reason. But he's a tricky one to deal with is our Roy. He listens, and he smiles, and he gives me a peck on the cheek – and then he goes away and does just what he wanted in the first place. Not like Margaret. Margaret's like me. She stands her ground and argues the case point by point. It's not just that she wants to win, she wants you to know that she has, and why. He's a charmer, she's a little fighting terrier. Most people would rather have the charmers. So I worry for Margaret. She's only 21 but I can smell the spinster on her. That's a terrible thing to say, isn't it, about any young woman, and especially coming from the likes of me. But I had the Party, I had the struggle, I had you in my secrets, and what's better than that to see a person through? Margaret's got a good brain on her, and she's always worked hard at her books just as I told her she should, but I don't know where it's going to take her. I never thought I'd hear myself say this but I'd like to see her settled with some nice young man. Can you believe it, Harry? The trouble is our Margaret doesn't seem so keen. She doesn't think much of the young men she meets at the University and she keeps herself so dowdy that I expect they don't even see her coming down the street like a little brown mouse.

Do you know, I was two years younger than Margaret is now, more or less, when I lost my heart to you right from the first day? There'll be those who say the twenty years means you were old enough to be my father, which is as may be, but you'd seen the world already and had put your thoughts together about it, which isn't what most of the lads I came up against had done. Perhaps that's what Margaret is waiting for, especially as she lost her father so young.

It doesn't seem to have taken Roy the same way, but maybe it's different for the lads. Let's see what sort of young woman takes his fancy when the time comes, though I haven't seen that he's got any special girl, even though he's 24, unless he's keeping her a secret, which isn't his way. Everything's out in the open with our Roy. If he could only afford it he'd like a car – one of those sports cars the well-heeled youngsters drive around in with the roof down. He'd like to move away from here too, just as soon as he can, and even though he hasn't the money for it he's already got it all planned.

You won't mind, will you, Harry, if I write to you from time to time? Sometimes, you know, writing things down clears the rubbish from a person's head. It used to be a help to me talking to you about the children. You gave me such good advice and I did my best to follow it. Be clear what you mean to do, you said. It doesn't really matter what it is just so long as they know, and just so long as you stick to it. It's ambiguity that's bad for kiddies, you said, just as it is for anybody, even for a nation. People need to know where they are and what's expected of them, and then they can get on with their business without having to worry too much. Thinking for oneself is the best thing there is, but not in a vacuum, you said. There has to be a context, there has to be a framework, a set of rules and a true morality. It's when

175

people give up on the ideas of what's right and what's wrong that the world falls apart, or when the only thing that guides a person is self-interest.

Ah, dear Harry. You worked so hard, so much too hard that it killed you. You knew it would but you couldn't prevent yourself, could you? I tried to believe you'd be strong enough to get over those bouts of illness because I hadn't the courage to face the truth – that you were wearing yourself out for the cause. It wasn't worth it, Harry. Can you imagine I'm saying this? And you wouldn't catch me saying it in King Street, not aloud in front of everybody, but as far as I'm concerned there isn't a cause in this world that's worth the loss of you. There you are, I've said it. Are you disappointed in me now? Do you think I've lost my mettle, or that all that kept me nose down for the Party was the hope that one day you'd see me as the woman who loved you more than anyone else possibly could? Well, in a way it's true, Harry. I was in the Party because I was brought up to believe in it, and I did and still do. But without knowing I'd be seeing you every day in King Street, would I have stayed the course? I won't answer that, but I can tell you this. Those months at the start of the war, when you fell out with Moscow and Mr Dutt, when they made you stand down from your post and sent you back north to write your book and sit out the crisis, I thought I'd die then, Harry. I didn't think I could bear it.

And what do I have to do now? Live without you another 20-odd years, till I'm 70 like you, and can go to my grave? I tell you, I've wished so fervently that I could believe in a God and a heaven and an afterlife. I wouldn't care which one or what it would be like, so long as you were there too and I could join you. The rest of my life wouldn't be so hard then. It would be like the title of your book, 'Serving My Time'. In the end I'd get out from behind these bars and we could be together again, and in another existence, a different sort of existence, you'd maybe take me as I always longed you would.

Try as I may, Harry, I can't make myself believe, so,

you see, my life sentence has begun, and without you to look forward to there won't be any remission. But never is too long to bear! Never see the warmth of your eyes again, never hear your voice again, your way of laughing, never feel your presence in the room with me. It's too hard, Harry, and I don't know how I shall be able to manage it. I shall have to be like God and create and re-create you every day as I walk across to King Street. The day I don't carry you in my head will be my last, Harry. But don't you fret. I'll do what's expected to keep the flag flying, and nobody will be any the wiser. Your Pam will be as staunch and stalwart and reliable as ever she was.

Roy

She hadn't signed her letter. Perhaps she hadn't finished it, or got interrupted. The handwriting was strong and neat like it'd always been – all those lists she used to make, the notes she used to leave us – and it ended at the bottom of a page, so there could've been another one that had slipped out the clip. But the ending did seem like an ending. Poor old P. She finished up living longer without her Harry than she'd had with him, thinking she'd pop off at seventy but going on till she was nearly ninety. That was a long time too long, by anybody's reckoning, when you've lost all you ever wanted. And he never knew. His wife never knew. Did P ever have a wish that Marjorie would come a cropper in some accident? Quick and clean and painless, but it would finish her off? And then did she feel terrible for wishing it? It would've cleared the way for her. But would she have told him then? While she was comforting him? I don't think she could've done that. Though if she'd waited, she might have got him later. Except that he went and died on her. He was old enough to be her dad. She'd said it herself. And dads die.

I picked up the letter, gave it a little shake, and let it go so that it floated down onto the bed. 'You'd never've known,' I said, 'would you? You wouldn't've thought she had it in her. Stupid geezer couldn't see what was under his own nose. Or he wasn't looking. Or he didn't fancy her, poor old bint. Don't you reckon, Mig? Mig?'

She hadn't said a word. Not made a sound, which isn't like her. I let my head flop sideways onto hers, and felt her stiffen ever so slightly. So I shovelled myself round to look at her and the bedspread scrunched up under me. Mig was sat there not moving, but staring down into her lap, and her face was pale and tight like someone had come at her from behind, laced his fingers over her nose and pulled the skin right back.

She lifted her head and looked me right in the eye. 'I know what she meant,' she said. 'I know exactly what she meant. I know about love too, and how it feels when you can only love one person. But I know something she didn't. Harry Pollitt didn't love Marjorie, but he didn't love Aunty Pam either. He was having affairs all over the place. Can you imagine how she'd have felt if loving him so much she'd had to bear him loving someone else and I – '

But quick as a cat I put my hand over her mouth to stop her saying any more. I got what she was about. Of course I did. I've always known this was going to happen one day. It had been on the cards as long as I can remember, if I'm honest, but I'd been dreading it. I said, and it wasn't easy, 'Listen, my old darling. Listen up carefully. I don't love anyone like I love you. Not Gina, not even Dougie. And I never will. You and me, we're like one person. We've grown up the same, we think the same – even if you use more words to say it than anyone needs. We understand one another like no one understands us. But remember P and her frigging loyalty? Well, that's one thing she got into my head more than she ever thought, and when Gina and I got hitched I knew that whatever else happened that's how things were going to have to stay. I know you think I only married Gina because she was up the duff. But I *wanted* to, sweetheart. And I'm glad I did. And for Chrissake you're my sister, Mig. My fucking *sister*! Don't you get it? I love you to bits but that's not the point. You're my sister. We can't change that, and there are some things I don't do, because I can't – I don't want to and I can't. I mean that. Can't and don't want to. Don't you get it?'

She was so quiet, and I was sticking knives in her. Crap timing but what could I do? I held onto her like you hold onto a little kid that's had a nightmare but can't wake up. But I knew I'd hollowed her out saying what I'd said, gouged her out, because once some things have been said there can't be any more dreams. P'd had the right idea. She'd kept her mouth shut.

Margaret

The phone woke me, ringing distantly, beyond the fringes of consciousness. It took me a moment to realise I was not on my own bed but sprawled across Aunty Pam's. I tried to clear my eyes and my head, struggling to remember why I was here, then saw the mess of newspapers on the floor and the upturned cardboard box that had held her last possessions. Roy had disappeared.

I could have left the phone to ring itself out but am incapable of doing so, and was glad of that when I reached it. It was Douglas. I felt thick-tongued as I answered, dry-tongued the way one gets from sleeping in the daytime. Clearly something in my voice sounded odd because he asked me if I was all right, or – in ironic tones – whether I'd been hitting the bottle. Then he asked me to come out to dinner 'When?' I said. He said, 'Now.' 'What?' I said. 'Now, like now this minute?' – looking at my watch and seeing it was nearly seven o'clock. 'Yes,' he said. 'That sort of now.' He was parked outside on Chalton Street, he said, but because of the local lads who were hanging around the gates in a group he didn't want to leave his car. I'd have to freshen up, I told him – which provoked a knowing chuckle, and he said not to worry, not to hurry, he had music in the car.

This time I really did regret the lack of a shower. A deluge of cold water would have been just the job, sharp as iced needles, a flagellation of iced needles. But as I sloshed water over my face and the back of my neck like a cowboy under a pump, as I rinsed my teeth, I felt my spirits tumble. And all the while downstairs Douglas was waiting patiently with his music. I must be as auntly as it was possible to be, in the usual way.

I did the rounds of the flat to close windows. Aunty Pam's room reproached my slovenliness. But it wasn't going anywhere and could wait. In my rush, though, I left my bag behind, although not, thank the Lord, my keys – as always in my pocket. I hurried down the four flights of stairs, gathering myself into proper dignity, squaring my shoulders. For you, Douglas, I promised, I am unaltered and unalterable.

Of all his various vehicles Douglas had chosen to show up in his latest toy, a black square contraption, taller than a taxi, built to traverse the Veldt in the rainy season. It dwarfed him. But, gallant as ever, he jumped down to open the passenger door for me.

'Douglas,' I said. 'I've forgotten my handbag.'

'You don't need your bag,' he said. 'It's my treat.'

'My fags. I haven't got my fags.'

'The place I'm taking you to is non-smoking anyway. So is my car.' Such is the power of money, I thought in some desperation. He who pays the bill dictates the non-smoking venue.

'All right,' I said, 'I'll invite you, and we can go round the corner to my local Greeks where the non-smoking area is by the toilets.'

And he said, 'You can't invite me because I invited you first, and your bag is upstairs.'

'My Greeks will give me tick.'

'I won't come with you, Aunty. I don't want to die young of passive smoking, or leave with a sore throat and stinking clothes. I have planned my future and it's long, fit, healthy and fragrant. Can you get in OK?' I was aware of the lads sniggering as I hauled myself up into his car's ridiculous height, no doubt looking as ungainly as I felt. The car, I now realised, was expertly parked in a space only slightly larger than its length but facing the wrong way.

'You're facing the wrong way, Douglas.'

'I know. I figured that would save you having to climb in from the road side. Don't worry. I'll manage a U-ey.' When I was installed and properly belted in place, Douglas slipped his key into the ignition and said, 'Anyway, what's with the "You're facing the wrong way"? You're the one who's always said rules were there to be broken.'

We keep having this argument as if it was our signature tune: a sort of perennial overture; our ritual private curtain-raiser.

'I said questioned, not necessarily broken. And it depends on the rules. Who made them, and why and who for.'

'Don't you mean "for whom"?'

'Impudence!'

'Yes. But you did bring me up to question all authority, didn't you.'

'There's a difference,' I said, 'between learning to regard authority with proper scepticism and deliberately flouting rules and laws that have been arrived at for the public good.'

'But wouldn't the authorities say that what they represent *is* the public good? I mean, aren't you just saying you want me to disobey the rules you don't admire and obey the ones you do. What happens to your principles if I do it the other way round? I might be incredibly impressed by important people in high places or even by government ministers, but want to park my car wherever it suits me and stuff everyone else. You don't believe anyone has the right to tell you what to think but you're trying to become a traffic cop. Try again, Aunty.'

'Oh, Douglas, really. I never said you should question authority just because you didn't fancy doing something. That's a travesty of my argument. I said people should question the motives behind what they were being exhorted to do because as often as not authorities have one aim only, which is to go on being authorities. I didn't mean a free-for-all, with everyone thinking that what suits them personally is the only criterion for judging what's right.'

'And that's how you think things are now, is it?'

'It sometimes seems remarkably like it.'

Douglas started his engine and hummed the car out of its illegal space. 'Well, to cheer you up I won't do the U-ey, I'll reverse.'

And he did, coaxing his pet with one hand on the steering wheel, at ease and at home in the way that people who ride all day are at ease in the saddle. I'm not doing badly, I thought, with a frisson of self-congratulation. Perhaps I am as expert in my own small way as my nephew is with his driving. And must remain so. I sighed to indicate contentment and leant back in my seat, noticing how comfortable in fact it truly was, how much more comfortable than any other armchair of my acquaintance. And now that I happened to look out of the window at the traffic, largely stationary in parallel lanes on either side of us, I saw how much higher I was than lesser passengers in lesser vehicles and was on the point of enjoying the sensation when I caught myself at it.

Suddenly Douglas looked ahead, looked behind, and said, 'Don't go away. I'll be back in a minute', leaped out of the car and sped through the waiting lane to his left and onto the pavement, where I lost sight of him. Now what? What if the traffic moved and I was driverless? What if a traffic policeman on a motorbike were to roar up and demand an explanation? 'Excuse me, madam. Would you mind informing me of the whereabouts of the driver of this vehicle?' Concealment would be called for to protect my nephew. Driver? I'm afraid he was taken ill. We had to call an ambulance. 'Ambulance made it through this traffic, did it, madam?' I was squirming in my seat, looking around for Douglas in approaching panic, but now here he was, returned, levering himself in, satisfied, smiling. Had he needed to pee and noticed, or knew of, a nicely placed urinal?

I said, 'Where on earth did you go? Where have you been, Douglas? I was afraid the police would arrive and ask awkward questions.'

'How could they?' he asked, reasonably. 'We're so stuck in traffic they wouldn't have been able to get through either.'

'On a motorbike, they might. Or a helicopter.'

'What's got into you, Aunty?' he said. 'You're not usually so antsy. Must be nicotine deprivation, you poor old junkie. So I got you these.' He fished in his pocket. 'Because I hate to see people suffer.' Twenty Marlboro Lites. My brand. And a green Bic lighter. My colour. As so often, I thought that it was only because my beloved nephew is gay that he notices these details. 'But you can use the car lighter . . . there. You just press it.'

'But this is a non-smoking car,' I said.

'As I say, I hate to see people suffer.'

'Douglas, I can't!' I said.

'I think you're going to have to, under the circumstances. If you feel that bad about it, puff out of the window.' And from a button by his side he opened mine to exact smoke-puffer's height.

In truth I had been wondering how I was going to get through the evening without a cigarette. So I lit up, trying to persuade myself it was acceptable to do that in his fragrant car only because he was insisting, and then stowed my booty into my cardigan pocket for safekeeping. Cardigans, especially those with sizeable pockets, may be considered inelegant by some, but they are practical. But what a sweet child he is. Really.

'Aunty, I'm worried about you,' he said.

'The cigarettes?'

'No. Your mood. You're not yourself.'

'Oh, Douglas. But that's the sorrow of it,' I said, although with care. 'I am completely and too much myself. I wish it were otherwise, and then at least you'd be having a nicer evening.'

'I always have a nice evening with you.'

'I can't imagine why.'

'Nor can I.' He leaned across to kiss my cheek but found himself held at a distance by his seat belt. His lips smacked the air two inches from my face. 'Look,' he said. 'This is where obeying the law gets you. It leaves deserving aunts un-kissed. Therefore . . .' He snapped the seat belt open. 'Down with the law.' His lips met their target. 'Now aren't you proud of my independent spirit?'

'Never prouder,' I said, and meant it.

Hooper's. Our destination of Douglas's choice: the walls are white, of course, the floors are ceramic, the ceiling soars as in a church and is inset with halogen spotlights. The tables and chairs are spare and unadorned. Actually, the decor is so stark that it could be a works canteen. The acoustic is like some factory at any rate, except you sense that the prices will make you wince. But Douglas wasn't wincing. A young waiter with a startling white apron like a length of tablecloth lashed snugly around his slim black-clad hips leapt to ease me into my chair. 'Good to see you, Mr Hoskins,' he said. Looked at me, and back at Douglas. 'And to meet your mother?' Douglas winked at me because this happens so often.

A basket of bread arrived along with a tiny glass jug of green olive oil with a curved red chilli pepper lurking in it, like the poor benighted tequila worm. They brought a bottle of sparkling mineral water and two tall glasses filled almost to the brim with chunky ice cubes. Two menus so crisp they seemed newly minted, untouched by previous diners. Fortunately for me, the text designer had had the foresight to keep the print large.

'I don't suppose,' said Douglas scanning his menu, 'that you'd risk breaking tradition by not having soup?'

'You don't suppose correctly. Carrot and coriander.'

'What is it with you and Dad? He always has soup. Always, even when it's as hot as it is today.'

'Habit. Aunty Pam used to create marvellous soups from apparently nothing. Has he been here too?' I wriggled slightly on my chair as if trying to gauge whether Roy might have sat here before me, opposite our boy.

'No. But what about a nice goat's cheese bruschetta?'

'Carrot and coriander, I'm afraid.'

'Or scallops on a bed of pureed flageolet beans? Or – '

'Carrot and coriander.'

'Oh, Aunty!'

'If my choice is boring, entertain yourself with yours.'

'I shall have to. That is to say I would.'

'But?'

'Their carrot and coriander soup is the best.'

'Dear child.'

'What will you have to drink?'

'What will you?'

'For the sake of you and your public weal, only this.' He tapped the bottle of mineral water. 'You wouldn't have me done for drunk driving, would you?'

'Then I'll join you.'

'No, have some wine. A glass at least. Have some Chablis.' My 'brand'. He ordered it. 'Now, what will you have to follow?' I watched my nephew consider his menu again and thought that at his age I had known little of restaurants and menus and how to behave with aplomb in moneyed places. In some ways the young seem so much older than their years, yet in others such unburdened children or, rather, not unburdened if that implies that there has been a burden but one that's been removed, but *less* burdened. I almost thought 'carefree', but in this age of AIDS (oh Douglas, be careful!), and global warming and global markets 'carefree' might be going too far. And of course in my day, it never crossed anyone's mind that they mightn't get a job. But Douglas had invented his out of thin air. Soaking in the bath under a duvet of bubbles in a miasma of essential oils – ylang-ylang had apparently been the inspirational fragrance.

'How's the wine?'

I gulped at my glass. I hadn't noticed it arrive. I could have sworn no waiter put it there. 'Delicious.' It was. 'I wish I could transmit to you how delicious, or better still see you drinking a glass of your own, but as you're so responsible I can only salute you.' I raised the glass. 'Of course, I suppose you could drink with me, leave your lorry here overnight, and pick it up in the morning when you're sober again.'

'In the morning by the time I got here it would have fallen foul of the parking restrictions and been clamped. Besides . . .' And he stopped.

'Besides?'

'In the morning, Aunty, I'm going away.'

'Away?'

'To America.'

'How contemporary. In my day people went on holiday overland to Afghanistan in pursuit of discomfort.'

'People, but not you?'

'No, not me.'

'Too frivolous for you?'

'They weren't being frivolous. They were finding themselves. Too brave for me.'

'I can't imagine you shrinking from tribal horsemen, Aunty. I can see you being intrepid and striding over the crags wearing a white safari hat and sending the natives running for cover. What scared you?'

'The prospect of finding myself. Of all quests, the one best avoided.'

'I think you had a lover you didn't want to leave behind.'

'Poppycock!'

'Aunty.' Douglas clasped his hands over mine with their piece of crusty bread and gazed at me mournfully.

'Don't be sentimental, Douglas. You're the wrong generation for that.'

'Don't be fooled, we're a very sentimental generation. You should've seen the hankies at the cinema when we all went to see *Bambi*.'

'You were about five, Douglas. I know. I took you.'

'So? I'm still a member of the same generation.'

'But possibly not the same person. In the thirty-odd years since then, all your cells will have been renewed, your earliest memories forgotten, your moral person formed and your experiences, with or without *Bambi*, will have so altered who you are, genetics notwithstanding, that someone clever might be able to make a case in court (if ever you came up in court now for a crime committed in your childhood, which of course couldn't happen because, as I know you, you could not have committed a crime in your childhood, you were much too nice and well brought up for that), such a person could argue that you cannot now be tried in retrospect because the child who committed the crime and you are not now one and the same.'

'I thought I couldn't be tried after twenty years because of the statute of limitations.'

'I was speaking philosophically, not legally. Have you never heard of Theseus's Ship? Where did your parents send you to school!' (Very expensively, to begin with, to some institution that swiftly expelled him for a thoroughly laudable transgression, which now slips my mind. Holland Park comprehensive gave him asylum, although I'm not convinced he was properly grateful.)

'I'm not going on holiday, Aunty.'

'Business? I thought the whole purpose of commerce these days was that it was "e", and you could do it anywhere. Yours in particular.'

'Yes, business,' he said. 'As a matter of fact, I'm starting a new website. Yessir.com. It's going to provide butlers for the gay American scene. "Male domestic staff trained in England, for that special occasion – or more permanently. Uniforms acceptable but no nudity or menial chores without prior agreement." What d'you reckon?'

'But you'll have to be in England to find your butlers, won't you?' I protested feebly. 'Vet them, see they're properly trained for . . . for whatever.'

'No, I won't.' he said. 'Or at least not all the time. I can delegate. But it's not the point. It's New York. *You* know, Aunty. I've told you before I'm more comfortable there. I want to "relocate". Permanently, if I can.'

He had indeed told me he felt more at ease in New York, many times. On every return, in fact. But I had supposed that regular doses, if that's not an unfortunate expression, of New York club life and whatever else, was enough to do the trick. 'But Douglas. They won't let you! Green Cards and all the rest of it.' Grasping at straws, I was well aware.

'Well, I think they will. I mean, it's kind of in hand.'

So he had been making arrangements all this while, and I hadn't known. No one had told me. Not even Roy – who would have understood that I might find the news . . . disconcerting. Must I lose my nephew too?

There was a smudge on my wine glass which I hadn't seen earlier and which didn't look as if it came from any of my fingers. But to be certain I placed one carefully over the smudge and then examined the place for similarities. Without my glasses I couldn't make out the details but the size was most definitely different. Not my print. Surely, I thought, a place like Hooper's has fine large dishwashers to bring their wine glasses out sparkling and pristine. They shouldn't be allowed to get away with smudges on the crockery. If I were to raise the matter now, it would embarrass Douglas. I was his guest and I believe guests should never embarrass their hosts. Unless it's ethically necessary and this wasn't an ethical matter, except for the size of the bill. It might not be so very large, though, because I wasn't as hungry as I'd thought I was. What I needed now was a cigarette rather than soup and what have you. But not in this place. This aggressively non-smoking place. To light up here would be worse than calling attention to the smudge on the wine glass, and not fair on Douglas, who was sitting opposite me in complete silence. Then he took pity, trying to be kind.

'Look,' he said, 'I'm not going for good now. It's more of a recce. I might be back within a fortnight and, who knows, perhaps I'll have changed my mind. Or the INS will have turned me down.'

'Perhaps.' God willing. If only I could believe in him just this once. But my orisons would be as useless as kneeling Claudius's.

'Ma said I should tell you. Break it to you, was what she said.' Had they discussed this then, behind my back? The restaurant, the menu, the 'breaking' of his news?

The lithe little waiter had slipped a huge shallow bowl of carrot and coriander soup in front of me while Douglas was talking. A spiral of cream speckled with chopped coriander floated on its orange surface like a piece of paisley. The steam was fragrant and my appetite nudged me. I took up my spoon, dipped it and fed myself. I saw Douglas, who must have been waiting for me to begin – oh, that upbringing – dipping his spoon, feeding himself; saw his face as I had known it when he was a toddler brought round by his father so that we could take him to the park, swinging his tight light body between us. Wheee! Roy, and Douglas and I.

As I swallowed my spoonful a knot of despair rose in my throat and collided with the soup. Just in time I buried my face in the giant napkin the waiter had spread over my lap, and before Douglas could push back his chair I was lurching between the tables and their startled diners making for the Ladies'. There, safer, and alone with the mottled marble and black tiles, I stared into the mirror at my soup-stained agony. I turned on the taps and swilled my face in running water.

Then I lit a cigarette. High in the ceiling where I hadn't thought to look, a cigarette-seeking alarm started yowling for help.

I don't know how Douglas extricated us from the ensuing pandemonium, but he was clearly torn between concern for me – and hilarity. As he drove me home through the now traffic-free streets he described how all the waiters and the manager had rushed for the women's loos as if, as he put it, they were moonlighting for the fire service; how some of the diners had leapt from their chairs as if they were expecting the entire restaurant to be imminently ablaze while others had sat on, apprehensive, but determined to demonstrate impressive *sang froid*. Douglas himself had chased after the restaurant staff fearing they might sluice me out with a fire extinguisher. I was, I thought to myself, entirely sluiced out already.

When we got back to Chalton Street, Douglas parked, facing the right way, and said, 'Let's have a coffee, shall we?' Did he think he was fooling me? He detests instant and knows that's all I have. He was worried, guilt-ridden maybe, and needed to assure himself I was in a better condition than he thought me before he departed – conceivably for good.

'What about them?' The clustered youths had barely left their posts (it is extraordinary how home-loving our local hoodlums are). 'Aren't you afraid your car'll be nicked or vandalised?'

'Oh, don't worry,' he said airily. 'It's wired. If anyone touches it after I've switched it on they'll get a nasty shock.' It's a measure of my discomposure that I was taken in and rose to the bait, allowing him to crow, 'Wind-up, Aunty. Wind-up.' None the less, he glared pointedly at them in order, so he explained, to be able to identify them if they so much as laid a finger on a bumper. 'Unlike you, Aunty,' he said, 'I don't have the slightest sympathy for teenage thugs, no matter how deprived.'

The flat was stuffy because I'd closed the windows before leaving so I busied myself with opening them again. 'Do you really want a coffee? Or another delicacy to remember me by? I would say a Hobnob, but they've all gone.' I put on the kettle although I thought it unlikely that either of us would actually drink anything.

Douglas said, 'I'm just going to look at her room. Remember her. OK?' What could his memories be? Aunty Pam, whom he had rarely seen since his childhood, would be imprinted in his mind – if at all – only as someone no doubt excessively old, who had objected to pieces of Lego left lying under the table. 'Hey, Aunty,' he called through the wall. 'What's all this clobber on the floor?'

Knowing Douglas, he would immediately be on his knees beginning to clear it up for me, which I did not want. Aunty Pam's letter to Harry Pollitt might be the first thing he picked up, and being a soul of the greatest indiscretion he would be bound to read it. I shot into her room with a mug of coffee in each hand and growled at him. Positively growled. 'Leave it, Douglas,' I said. 'I'll see to that lot later. Now come and sit down with me.'

'Why?' he asked. 'Is it something special?'

'Not in the least,' I said. 'It's a collection of old copies of the *Daily Worker* that Aunty Pam decided to keep for reasons of her own. Why those particular ones we have no idea.'

'We?'

'Your father and I. We were sorting them out just yesterday.'

'Dad came yesterday? Was he here long?'

I looked at him for a moment because I realised I had no

idea. 'D'you know,' I said, shrugging it off, 'I haven't a clue. I fell asleep but I don't know when. Must be getting old.' I pulled the requisite face and took a slurp of my coffee which, having an asbestos mouth, I have always liked hotter than anyone else can drink it. Then got down on my knees by the bed. 'Actually,' I said, 'we might as well pack it away now. Why not, after all?'

We began folding the newspapers back into the box, Douglas with great neatness and dexterity. Then he said, evidently needing to be on his way, 'Aunty, is there anything else I can do for you while I'm here, that can't wait a couple of weeks. 'Cos that's all I'll be away for this time, I promise.' So I replied, for something to say, 'Well, you could help me turn this mattress.'

It was merely a mind- and nephew-occupying ruse. As a matter of fact, turning mattresses is not something I ever do, although I read that one should. Doubles are beyond me. Too big and too heavy. This particular one could do with replacing altogether now I think how long Aunty Pam must have had it. Actually, now I *am* thinking about it, it's probably made up entirely of mites and particles of shed skin, nothing mattressy left in it at all. If I'd had any sense I'd have asked Douglas to help me carry it down and leave it outside. But I would have had to have contacted the council about coming to collect it, and, since I hadn't, lugging it down would be tantamount to flytipping.

Even between the pair of us just getting a grip on it was a tussle. Both of us on the short side, neither of us long in the arm, no convenient fabric handles on the sides to grab hold of. We huffed and we puffed and eventually slid the thing off the bed-frame and onto its side on the floor, and then saw that slap bang in the middle of the bed base was a small package wrapped in a plastic bag. Douglas hooted. 'Your aunt stashed her dosh under the mattress, did she?' He assumed an exaggerated northern brogue, 'Can't be doing with them banks, don't trust 'em now and never did, lad!'

But other thoughts were coming to my mind, although I can't swear that this is the order they arrived in. One: this package had been there since my parents' time – no, it can't have been because there weren't any plastic bags in the 1940s. Aunty Pam must have put it there because she was hiding it, which meant she hadn't wanted Roy and me to see it. Not like the old *Workers*, where she'd secreted her letter to Harry Pollitt. She'd wanted to have those with her but not this package; if she had wanted us not to see it, something had prevented her from throwing it away. Two: if she'd put it there on her own, how had she done it, given the palaver Douglas and I had just been through? Perhaps she'd levered up the edge of the mattress, shoved the package between it and the bed-base and then poked it into the middle with something like a broom handle.

Douglas reached across for the wrapped thing and passed it over to me. The plastic was sticky and cracked, and the elastic band holding it all together had so crumbled that it snapped as soon as I touched it. A smell of old paper and old glue came from the bundle – not old only in the sense that it had been under the mattress for decades but old in the sense of paper from another age.

'Aunty?' Douglas was hovering by the door. He needed to get off. Perhaps he still had to pack. I could see that although he had no curiosity about the crumbly old package itself he was intrigued by my interest in it.

I said, 'Two weeks. That *is* all you said, isn't it? Two weeks this time and not more?'

'And if the Green Card doesn't stand a chance,' he said, 'then that'll be it.'

'In that case,' I said, 'I put my faith in the certainty of the INS and its barriers. Will you ring?' He said he would, which means he will, and I hugged him.

'Don't you want that mattress back on the bed?' he asked. I said it wasn't worth it; I'd have to get someone in to take it away. So he hurried out and I listened to him shouting dire warnings at the lads on the street as he ran across the courtyard. I listened to the plutocratic thwump of his car door and the revving of his engine, listened to the expletives and cat-calling. But then I turned back to the package that I had laid on the upper edge of the mattress we had, between us, propped against the wall.

It was the size of a Penguin paperback, and no fatter than a volume of new poetry. On the top was a blank brown envelope; inside was a letter from the Infantry Records Office. It read simply:

> I am directed to inform you that a report has been received from the War Office to the effect that No: 7198 Private Jack Miller 1st (S) Bn. York and Lancaster Regt. was sentenced after being tried by Court Martial to suffer death by being shot, and his sentence was duly executed on 15th July 1915.

I did the thing you see people do in films – pointlessly: I turned the letter over and over as if that would somehow reveal something more. Then I took the package out into the living room and sat down with it in my lap. I couldn't understand why Aunty Pam should have kept, and so carefully hidden, a letter from the Infantry Records Office referring to a private called Jack Miller. I picked up the slender book, which had been wrapped in paper to protect it, I assumed. It had the dimensions of a passport – one of the old ones, not the flimsy bus-pass things they give you now. It turned out to be Private Miller's soldiers' 'Small Book'.

Inside the flap of the front cover was a white crocheted cross, like a pressed flower. I lifted it out as if it were indeed a pressed flower whose ancient petals might come to pieces in my hands, and set it to one side. Then I saw there was a photograph, browned by age. It showed a young soldier in uniform, his hat a size too large, standing formally by a high-backed and rather ornate dining chair, one hand resting on its frame, the other dangling but tense at his side. He was gazing steadily out at the camera and looked like a boy togged up in his father's military garb. Behind this picture was another, of a young woman wearing some sort of close-fitting cap and smiling very slightly over her shoulder. There was an inappropriate serenity about her, poor girl, and she seemed older than her young husband, or boyfriend, or brother at the front. I laid both pictures by the crocheted cross so that I could look at what was written. Some loose pages slipped out, the ink so faded that I couldn't make out all the words and had to get up and stand directly under the ceiling light.

No one these days has the curlicued handwriting of that generation – in so far as anyone has handwriting at all – and those faint loops and swirls spoke of the passing of time as did nothing else. There was a letter from Jack Miller to his wife, and one from his wife to him. His was dated 2 July 1915, two weeks before his execution and presumably some days before he was charged and tried.

> To my dear Wife.
> I am doing as well here as can be expected though we have had some rough times, some days we get forward a little but many days we are stuck without moving. It has been raining a good deal which makes it the harder for us which you wouldn't expect in the middle of summer, there's a lot of mud and we slip over in it from time to time. Frank Daley who came out with me sends you his good wishes and says to tell you that he hopes you all think of us when you are at home at night. I hope you and the little lass are well. I am expecting to hear that my leave will come up shortly so that I may be back with you before the next baby comes. Perhaps this time we shall have a boy but if we do I would never suggest soldiering to him. Give our lass a kiss from her father.
> Your loving husband
> Jack

Mrs Miller's letter must have crossed with his.

> My dear Jack
> I have been worried that my letters to you are not arriving because I have had none from you for ever such a long time. I hope you are well as I am the weather here is warm and the roses in their second blooming just as you like them in the Johnsons garden. Mrs Johnsons husband was killed you know which makes me so worried for you Jack so I hope you will take care I am growing very big now and I think the baby will be a grand size and helthy I hope but you are not to worry about us we

will be all right. Mary Louisa will be with me when my time has come.

Your loving wife

I opened the Small Book itself. Inside was Private Miller's name, his number, 7198, his regiment, the York and Lancasters, the date he'd attested, 12 September 1914. Then there were two pages for his service record, both with nothing entered into them. He was apparently so unremarkable as a soldier that no one had been able to think of any comments to make about him at all. He'd written his will and dated it 7 December 1914. His property and effects were too few to be worth itemising. It was a sad and uninformative little document if ever there was one. All it said was, 'In the event of my death I give the whole of my property and effects to my wife, Mrs Edith Miller of 48 Melba Street, Openshaw, Lancashire.'

What?

I turned the page. It told me he'd been employed as a grocer's assistant, that he was married to one Edith Miller, and that he had a child, a daughter . . . named Pamela.

Well, of course.

I thought of ringing Roy immediately, but it was late – not too late to ring because Roy is a night owl, but too late to ring with news of this sort. Besides, the facts needed checking. If I was going to tell him what I thought I was going to tell him, it had better be true. I went to bed to work out a plan of action, but although I counselled myself caution I couldn't still my mind, couldn't prevent it turning on what I appeared to have learned. When eventually I slept it was with that uneasy sleep of just-below-the-surface images shifting over one another, close enough to consciousness to reach out and touch: Private Miller's boyish face under his huge hat, Roy's face next to mine as we read Aunty Pam's letter, his face then Douglas's.

In the morning, I stumbled down into Chalton Street for breakfast. It was Friday and they were setting up the market – the stalls with the bolts of bright, thin cloth, the cheap saris folded on coathangers dangling from overhead rails, the cheap handbags hanging like bats and below them the wallets and purses, the stacks of nesting saucepans, the big knickers laid out in alternating pink and white along with what a friend once described as cantilevered bras – and already the elderly Bangladeshi men were out with their shopping bags, comparing the prices of the vegetables and the plastic washing-up bowls.

While I finished my tea and lit my cigarette I tried to re-create what this market had been like when we were children. Barrows of food principally, or at least I think so, pushed into place on huge wagon wheels, no vans or lorries. And of course in those days everyone was white. And it had been noisier because all the stallholders were out-shouting each other. Today's lot are much more restrained – the only sound was the clatter of the poles as the awnings went up, a certain amount of comradely chatter and some shrill warbling from one of the vans, Bollywood style. Later in the day I expect it would be more hectic but I've never been around during the day on a Friday to observe, and today wasn't going to be different.

I looked at my watch and decided that if I set off now I should arrive at the Family Records Centre in Myddleton Street soon after opening time – as indeed I did. I knew the year I was looking for: 1912. I knew the month: November – Aunty Pam had always tried to play down her birthday but every year had been pinkly pleased, and a little flustered, when Roy and I fussed over her with a bought-in cake. But the Index of Births didn't have a certificate for any Pamela Hoskins born that year, which didn't greatly surprise me. To be thorough I looked in 1915 for my father, Bill (William) Hoskins. And again drew a blank. There was, of course, only one thing left to do. I looked again, this time under Miller – and found them both.

I sat for a long time at the table with the huge register open in front of me until the dates and names that filled its pages blurred into a haze of navy blue, while inside my chest I could feel the heavy thumping of my disturbed heart. If I closed my eyes what I remembered most about Granddad was his smell, and warmth – physical warmth from his cradling arms, and the sound of his voice, not the words themselves, but the sound, deep, even, unhurried. Was he now not Granddad because he was not Bill's and Pam's actual, biological father? He had behaved like our grandfather. He was Nana's husband. He had loved us. Above all, he had loved Roy. He had doted on Roy, who had adored him then – and ever after. How do I tell Roy, I thought. And who was Private Jack Miller, really?

Everything we had been brought up with, all the stories that made our family-creating myth, had been a lie, and Aunty Pam had known and perpetuated it. But why? Clearly she had wanted to keep the truth from us, but she hadn't been able to bring herself to destroy the evidence of it. Without the little package under her mattress we would have gone on as before, and nothing would have made me suspect that Ken Hoskins was not who I was told he had been.

Perhaps he had formally adopted Pamela and Bill, and in time I would be able to find that out too. But how had he met Edie Miller, and when? Everything Aunty Pam had ever said, if I could trust a word of it now, suggested Ken Hoskins had, as it were, always been there, doing the fatherly thing, only ever away when the politics were hot. He was in London during the Hands Off Russia campaign, I'm sure – or I think I am – among the crowds of activists blocking the shipments of armaments to Poland. But once that was over he was back in Lancashire, with his young family. So much so that as a local Party member he'd been able to introduce his 'daughter' to a visiting Harry Pollitt in 1929, seen her employed as stenographer at King Street, and whisked away to the metropolis.

And what of *my* father, Bill? Had he known too, and kept it quiet, from us of course, but from Annie too? Or maybe he hadn't known, because he wasn't yet born when Jack Miller was charged with desertion, tried, blindfolded and shot, and at some stage in her life – when? – Aunty Pam had found out, or been told, and decided to protect her younger brother. But protect him from what? From the knowledge itself, or from a lingering sense of inherited ignominy? Activist Ken Hoskins was a father well worth having. But how, in those days, would you grow up in the shadow of a man most people of his generation, and hers, dubbed a coward?

And then I thought about Douglas, preparing to check out

real estate in Manhattan or the suburbs of New York and making appointments with INS lawyers, while I was poring over fading ledgers – as behoves a historian (surely you mean *an* historian, Aunty?). If he had not taken me out to dinner, had not seen me up to my flat to assuage his dismay at my despair, I should not have been able to shift the old mattress at all. Arguably, it might have stayed mouldering on the iron bedstead until *my* death, and Aunty Pam's little package would have gone the way of all apparently meaningless rubbish. That could not have been Aunty Pam's intention, to keep it so long only to have it lost. She must have kept it for it to be found; she must have wanted us to find it and understand it, but all in good time – and who was to be the judge of when that should be?

And then I have to say this. I asked myself how could I, who have spent my entire professional life interrogating information before I will accept its validity, have swallowed the family story without a single, sceptical qualm? It embarrasses me, does that one.

Roy

'You have to come round,' Mig said. 'It's important.'

I said, 'Why? What's up?' She said she couldn't say, not on the phone. She said she had to see me. I thought, shit. Is this to do with last time? But Gina was in the room so I couldn't ask. Poor Gina. She cuts up rough when there's too much family stuff going on – any sort. She thinks it all belongs in the past and ought to bloody well stay there. The trouble is she was an only child – and loved it – one of the reasons why we never had more than Dougie, so she just doesn't get the brother–sister thing. Can't. Not *our* brother–sister thing anyway. And she grew up like people should, with her Mum and Dad in the house they'd lived in since they were married. No evacuation from Surrey, no Mummy disappearing or Daddy dying or politics-mad aunty, never mind the Comrades. She had a really happy, ordinary childhood and hoped she could make it happen all over again here, and I'd say she has – give or take.

But we all have history, don't we? And Mig's and mine is so much ours you couldn't fit anybody else in if you tried. And we never wanted to try. Gina hates that. *Hates* it. And who wouldn't? She'd hate it even more if she knew how much Mig means to me and always has. Don't go there, as Dougie would say. And I don't. Stick to the fucking present, what's now.

Well, what's now is Gina throwing a fit, up and down, up and down in front of the windows, pulling at her blouse, her face all screwed up. 'Not again! Not your fucking sister again!' Gina doesn't swear; that's my bag. 'I thought you'd done everything. Done the cremation, cleared the stuff. So what is it now? I told you she'd be hanging round all the time, and I'm not having it, Roy. I'm just not having it. You ring her back and say you're not going. If it's so important, whatever it is, she can . . . I don't know, she can write you a letter about it or something. Writing's what she used to do, isn't it, when she had something useful to do, so let her bloody write you a letter. But I tell you, Roy, if you go over there now I'll . . . I'll . . .'

199

She was upset. 'Course she was. Dougie'd only just hopped across the pond and mothers, proper mothers like Gina, they don't want their kids swanning off. Your kids are your kids no matter how old they are. But I'd heard Mig's voice and Gina hadn't. 'Look,' I said, calm and reasonable, 'it sounds like something's up and I'm going to have to go over. But if it makes you feel better, why don't you come with me?' 'I don't want to come with you,' she screeched. 'Can't you get that into your thick head? I don't want to come with you to see your sister. Not now and not again. Not ever again, if I had the choice, frankly. Bloody hell, Roy. You must have understood that by now, haven't you?' 'Sure.' I said. 'Sure I understand, but I'm going. And you can come with me or sit here and scream at the mirror. I heard Mig and she didn't sound right.' And I went. But it wasn't easy. Like I said, how the fuck did those pashas do it! But nobody tells me what to do. Nobody puts threats over on me.

She had it all laid out in the kitchen, in the light – that 'Small Book', the little scrap of that cross, the photos.

What am I supposed to say? I don't know what you say. You could see Nana in that Edith Miller's face, just about. But this little guy in the big hat . . . I stood with him by the window and thought, this stranger is my grandfather. But he wasn't a stranger. I recognised him just like Mig must've. He was the one with the Hoskins face . . . no, that's wrong. He wasn't Hoskins. *We're* the ones with the *Miller* face – Bill and Pam and Mig and me – and Dougie. For fuck's sake.

Poor little blighter. Not much more than a kid really, like I was when I had my call-up. Like Ali MacDonald from Deptford, him and his face gone green when I turned my rifle on him. But dropped the rifle when Granddad came into my head. I remembered thinking how I'd be letting him down, and how I didn't ever want to let him down because he loved me so much and I loved him so much, and they'd made him stand in a line and turn his gun on one of his own in the name of the imperialist war. Made him. But Granddad – real Granddad – Jack Miller Granddad – some firing squad had shot him. He'd been the one standing there shitting his pants and crying, like Ali McDonald did, like I would've. Like anyone would.

When we were kids, Mig and me, they'd taunt us that Bill was a coward because he'd started out as a conchie. But it was Jack Miller who was the coward – official. I dropped his picture and went out to the bathroom and puked my guts up. But I couldn't say who for.

Mig was still sat where I'd left her, like she hadn't moved at all. She had some papers in front of her on the table. 'Have a look at this,' she said. 'I spent half the night trying to find it because I knew I had it somewhere, from when I was doing my doctorate. It was in one of the boxes under my bed. You'd think beds in this flat had given us enough surprises, wouldn't you?'

So I sat down and pulled the papers over. They were in her handwriting. 'Sorry,' she said. 'I had to copy it out. Photocopying was too expensive in those prehistoric days.' 'What is it?' I said. She said, 'You'll see soon enough.'

Reading's never been my thing. P used to say Nana had problems with it so maybe it's in the genes. Hoskins, Miller – no, whatever Nana's maiden name was. No fun in it when it's such tough going, and so fucking slow. 'No hurry,' said Mig, 'take your time.' But you never get used to it, struggling with words, never mind they're in handwriting, when you're sat opposite someone who's fucking made of them.

It looked like it was a diary. Or a bit of one, by some MO from that war. I began to get the shivers. 'Know what?' I said. 'Read it to me, Mig. Let me listen. I'd rather listen.'

So she began, pacing it, so's I wouldn't miss a word. '"This has been a wretched business. They have made a murderer out of me and all of us who were present. If that unfortunate man, Private Miller, was innocent of the charge . . ."' She looked up at me. 'I had it all this time, Roy,' she said. 'All this time! "If that unfortunate man, Private Miller, was innocent of the charge, and indeed even if he was not . . ."'

God! What can it have been like standing there in a blindfold, all alone, but knowing there was this line of men with their rifles trained on you, your skin prickling with it. Who knows, perhaps this was the first time in his life he'd had so many people all looking at him at the same time, all that attention, but only because they wanted to kill him. And the waiting. The fear of it. The fear of the pain. Throat full of tears. What would he have been thinking about in that last moment? Edie and their baby daughter? Or himself and how unfair it was? Or nothing? Couldn't think at all? And then having to be finished off with a bullet to the head because the squad had fired wide. I feel so fucking lucky. But so . . . far away too. Another world, wasn't it?

When she'd read it all through and put the papers down, shuffling them together like she was getting things under control, she said, 'Did you notice? Did you notice what he wrote? He said he was told Private Miller was teetotal.' I said, 'So he had to be stone cold sober when he was stood out there?' 'Yes that,' she said. 'But not only. How did they know – whoever it was who told the MO? How did they know he was teetotal? It's as he says. It means the people in the firing squad came from the same company, doesn't it? It means they knew him personally. Can you imagine? And then there's this bit . . .' She messed up her papers again till she found it. 'He says, "He was a small man – one of those many that I have seen who are undersized because they are undernourished, and who should not, in my opinion, have been found fit for service." Well, that's as may be, but look at us, Roy. All of us. We've not been undernourished, have we? We're just tiddlers by nature, us Hos—
. . . Millers. Unless of course they executed more than one Private Miller. And somehow I don't think that's hugely likely, do you? But I'll go and check on Monday.'

I didn't ask her how. She knows where to go and when she's found out she'll let me have it. I said, 'I'd best get back and tell Gina – if she's still there.' I got up and she got up and I put my arms round my sister and it was just the two of us, alone, like it used to be.

On the way home I thought, well, at least I *have* got a picture of my grandfather now, so I could edit him in and do the four generations after all. But then I thought, don't be so fucking stupid. It would be like kicking Granddad out. Jack Miller was my grandfather, poor little sod, but Granddad was Granddad.

Margaret

The more I look at the solemn young man in that purplish-brown picture, the more I want to weep for him. The more I wish there could be a way of making amends. Whatever he thought he was going to have to face – and there's no way of knowing how imaginative he was, or how much he knew before he set off for the front – I can't believe that a blindfold and a firing squad can have crossed his mind. What could he know of any of that? He was so young. He had a tiny daughter and a pregnant wife. His last letter to her assumes he'll soon be home – in time, he hopes, for the birth of their new baby.

And there was something more I was thinking last night after Roy had gone. I was thinking I wished we could hear Jack Miller's voice. I can't remember any more how many photographs of Great War canon fodder I pored over when I was researching my PhD, how many reels of silent film I sat through – the jerky men, and trotting horses pulling gun batteries, the crowded bumping vehicles, all moving faster and more hectically than is natural. But other than the rare recordings of their leaders, and the reminiscences of the few remaining survivors who are now in their nineties and more, I haven't come across anything with the voices of the ordinary soldiers . . . when they were still young men. Whatever they might have had to say wasn't important enough for posterity. Expendable, even as voices. Granddad was absolutely right when he banged on at Aunty Pam about class.

I hold Grandfather Miller between finger and thumb and I long to hear him speak. My father never heard him speak, but Auntie Pam must have, except that she wasn't yet three at the end of 1914 when he left, and the received wisdom is that memories as distant as that are out of reach. Was his accent like Auntie Pam's? Or was hers ironed out by the years of living in London? Would he have sounded entirely alien to my metropolitan ears? I am frustrated that I'll never know. I cannot bear not being able to know!

But there is at least one service I can render him, a belated family service, something I can learn now that I could not have when I was a student. I shall go to the Public Records Office and order up the transcript of the trial that convicted him. When I was young the records of the Field General Courts Martial were still closed, and I was told they would remain so until 2019. But times change, rules are tugged at, pushed, tweaked out of existence. With enough pressure, barriers give way. All those transcripts, once locked away in the vaults of the Ministry of Defence, are now there for the reading, and I am nothing if not an inveterate reader.

Will it be like this when we collect Aunty Pam's ashes? Her entire person contained in something like a jumbo jar of Nescafé; her physical self a few scoops of sticky, gritty cinders, her many decades beside the point? At least we know she'll be inserted into Commies' Corner alongside the Comrades, as close to her beloved Harry as we can arrange. But this – this thing I have in my hands, this buff-coloured file of fewer than ten sheets of paper. Is this it? Is this, apart from his Small Book, all that remains of Jack Miller?

Half an hour ago it seemed easy enough. I climbed to the vast sunlit first floor reading-room with its lightwood tables and numbered seating where I was allocated 29D. On three sides picture windows look out over the surrounding lawns to the thick summer trees, and somewhere behind those must be the sweet Thames, running softly to the sea. Perhaps young mothers with their children, or pensioners with their dogs, are even now sauntering along the river path in the sunshine, throwing bread to flotillas of lingering swans: the gentle people, genteel people of Kew with lunch and holidays on their minds.

I came prepared and efficient. I brought a notebook and a pencil because pens are, sensibly, forbidden. I opened the file with the scholarly intention of reading it word by word, without getting ahead of myself, not hurrying, making no assumptions. No leaps of emotional interpretation.

The first page was formal – they must be much the same in all cases – printed on blue paper, with spaces for the names to be entered in ink:

Form for Assembly and Proceeding of Field General Court Martial

PROCEEDINGS

[If Troops are not on active service]

Whereas complaint has been made to me the undersigned, an officer in the above-named country, that the persons named in the annexed Schedule being subject to Military Law, and under my Command, have committed the offences in the said Schedule mentioned, being offences against the property or person of inhabitants or of residents in the above-mentioned country.

This first paragraph had been crossed through in a line of black ink.

[If Troops are on Active Service]

Whereas it appears to me, the undersigned, an officer in command of *20th Brigade*, on active service, that the persons named in the annexed schedule, and being subject to Military Law, have committed the offences in the said Schedule mentioned.

And I am of opinion that it is not practicable that such offences should be tried by an ordinary General Court Martial [and that it is not practicable to delay the trial for reference to a superior qualified officer]

This last paragraph had been crossed out as well.

I hereby convene a Field General Court Martial to try the said persons and to consist of –

	President	
Rank	Name	Regiment
Major	*P.W. Heart*	*York and Lancs*

Rank	*Members* Name	Regiment
Capt.	*M. Hill*	*York and Lancs*
Capt.	*S.L. Browne*	*York and Lancs*

G.H. Hapworth Cmdg XXth Brigade

I certify that the above Court assembled on the *6th* day of *July 1915* and duly tried the persons named in the said Schedule, and that the plea, finding and sentence in the case of each person were as stated in the third and fourth columns of that Schedule
Signed this *6th* day of *July 1915*

P.W. Heart
President of the Court Martial

I have dealt with the findings and sentences in the manner stated in the last column of the said Schedule and subject to what I have there stated, I hereby confirm the above findings and sentences.
[And I am of opinion that it is not practicable, having due regard to the public service, to delay the cases for confirmation by any superior qualified authority.]

The last paragraph had been crossed out and initialled by Brigadier-General Hapworth

Signed this *9th* day of *July 1915*

G.H. Hapworth   Brigadier-General
Cmdg XXth Brigade

Field [or, General] Officer in the Force [or Commanding]

I turned next to the 'Schedule'. It named 7198 Private Jack Miller of 1st York and Lancaster Regiment charged with desertion while on active service; plea – not guilty. 'Findings and sentence of the Court: Guilty. To suffer death by being shot'. The Court, it said, recommends the accused to mercy on the grounds of his previous service and good character.

Below, Brigadier-General Hapworth had written, 'I confirm the finding of the Court but reserve the sentence for confirmation by superior authority.'

In a bold, slanting hand, Sir John French – then the Commander-in-Chief of the British Expeditionary Force – had written, simply, 'confirmed'. It was what you might call the clincher.

To the right of Sir John's signature another, unnamed, person had added: 'Sentence promulgated and carried out on 15-7-15.'

I had yet to read the trial itself, but I had in front me its outcome, which sounded so matter-of-fact. 'Sentence promulgated and carried out' . . . Well, of course it sounded matter-of-fact. It was. This was due process recorded in the terms appropriate to the circumstances. And public promulgation was said to be good for discipline. I was perfectly well aware of this. It was not new to me as a student of the subject. But I felt myself shrinking from reading further. I knew the result – I had known it even before I ordered up the file, and yet I had butterflies of anxiety and my heartbeat seemed to be shaking me so violently that I wondered if it was visible to others.

I closed the file and looked around, self-conscious and squeamish. Of course, no one was paying me the slightest attention. I had come to read this file and read it I must. But still I resisted.

Pull yourself together, I thought. You don't know this man. You never met him. Even Aunty Pam would have been hard put to remember him. Surely the biological line on its own isn't enough to account for . . . what is this? Fear? Why? If it was Granddad in this file, it might be another matter, but it isn't. It's a stranger who happens to be genetically uncannily similar to – well, the three following generations. Something happened, as it happened to about three thousand soldiers, who were all convicted of desertion or whatever. But this man was unlucky enough to be among the three hundred and six who had the recommendation to mercy, where there was one, disregarded and quashed. Go on, I said to myself. Order up another file. Get one of those, any one, which won't have any connection to you at all. See how you feel then. Sort your head out. What precisely are you afraid of finding out?

No one has ever been better at castigating me than I am myself. I opened the file again.

There were still seven pages to go, the next few all handwritten, in pencil, some on lined paper, others on plain sheets. I pictured a hearing convened in a Nissan hut or even a dugout, with a hurricane lamp for the court recorder to see by, or perhaps candles. It was July, but according to the MO's diary the weather had been bad for the time of year, so it could have been quite murky in there as they gathered round a small table with a blanket laid over it, the officers seated on upturned boxes, the witnesses waiting in line outside, brought in one by one to give their statements, still wearing their tin hats.

FCGM

No. 7198 Pte Jack Miller, 1st Btn, York and Lancs.
The Court satisfy themselves as provided by R.P. 22 and 23.
The names of the President and Members are read over in the hearing of the accused. The accused does not object to the President or Members. The President and Members are duly sworn.

In the case of 7198 Pte Miller of 1st York and Lancaster Regt.

1. The Commanding Officer states that the man came out with the Battalion late in 1914. That his conduct up to the time of his desertion was that of an average soldier.
2. The discipline of the Battalion is now good,

except that there is too much drunkenness in it. At the time Pte Miller absented himself such crime was prevalent, but was checked by a notice in brigade orders dated January 12th that cases would for the future be tried as cowardice.

3. The Commanding Officer states that in his opinion the man deliberately stayed away to avoid the [illegible] duty of the trenches.

Prosecution
1st Witness. No 5421 Sgt. L Penny 1st York and Lancs Regt stated: At about 4.30 p.m. on 30th June 1915 I called the roll of my platoon when I found the accused, Pte J. Miller, was absent. I warned the platoon at about 3 p.m. on 30th June that they would parade to march to the trenches at 4.30 p.m.

The accused refuses to cross examine the witness.

2nd Witness. No 8722 Lce Corpl. F Fisher 1st York and Lancs Regt stated: On 30th June 1915 at 4.30 p.m. I was present when Sgt Penny called the roll when the platoon was parading to go into the trenches and the accused Pte (J.) Miller was absent. The Company had been warned earlier in the day that they were to parade at 4.30 p.m. to march to the trenches. I do not know if Pte Miller was present when the warning was given.

The accused refuses to cross examine the witness.

3rd Witness. No 3136 Corpl. P.Baker MMP stated: On 3rd July 1915 I was on the road to Houplines when I saw the accused No. 7198 Pte (J.) Miller coming down the road in the opposite direction. Knowing he should have been with his battalion I asked him what he was doing there. He stated that he had become separated from his company a few days earlier and had lost his way, but had met a military policeman who had told him which way he should go and he was now returning to his company. I doubted the truth of his words and ordered Lce.-Corpl. Dearlove to take the accused into arrest. The accused was properly dressed in uniform at the time I arrested him.

The accused refuses to cross examine the witness.

Defence: Accused hands in a written defence because when asked whether he wished to give evidence or hand in a written statement he stated that he did not think he would feel able to make a statement before a court.

> In reference to the charge professed against me I wish to say I seemed to have lost my head and sincerely regret what has happened, I lost my company and not knowing what to do I took the course which has led to the charge professed against me. When I had lost my way I met a Military Policeman who told me where to go so I went in the direction he told me. I trust to you Gentlemen and officers of my Battalion, to look at this side of the affair, I have formerly proved myself a true soldier and have shared all hardships with my Battalion since coming into active service which you Gentlemen of my Battalion know what we have suffered in the past six months. On that day I was lost I felt queer but did not go to the doctor because I had had no satisfaction from him when I reported sick a week before and he only gave me some pills. Gentlemen I appeal to you to treat me as leinent as law and nature will allow as I leave two innocent lives behind a wife and child who will also share and suffer my punishment which is the most striking feeling in nature. Now I see the gravity of my offence

and I also feel the shame of it to the bottom of
my heart. I trust to your leinecy in the above
case and know you will give me a fair trial in
the case professed against me.

  I remain your obeidient servant
  (7198) Pte J. Miller

My grandfather stood near that table in his tin hat or, now
that he was a prisoner, bare-headed as he listened while others
recounted his actions, or lack of them. His knees were perhaps
buckling under his uniform. He kept swallowing. Maybe they
gave him a seat, maybe they looked at him – but again, maybe
not. Had they even read his statement all the way through
or only glanced at it, taking in (with contempt?) the poor
punctuation and his varied efforts to spell the word he most
wanted them to exercise?

Someone, perhaps the chaplain, might have intended to help
him and suggested he use it. 'Try and throw yourself on the mercy
of the court,' he might have said. 'Tell them you trust to their
leniency.' But he'd never heard the word before and the chaplain
hadn't written it down for him, so it stands out from the rest of
his statement, drawing attention to itself as the promptings of
another man.

> *Prosecutor states:* The APM 7th division stated he
> could not find the military policeman.

> Capt. B.L. Taylor 1st York and Lancs, being duly
> sworn, states that the accused has 7/12 year's
> service. Character very good. He has been out
> with the battalion since December 1914 and served
> continuously with it.

The trial papers must then have been sent back behind the lines
because the remaining sheets were partially typed, and stamped:
'Head Quarters IV Army Corps and Adjutant General's Branch of the
Staff. No. Case 1031, Date 9-7-15.'

Herewith proceedings of a Field General Court Martial held at La Maraine on the 6th July 1915,

For the trial of the undermentioned
No. 7198 Pte. J. Miller 1st Btn. York and Lancs Regt.

I forward herewith proceedings of Field General Courts Martial for transmission to G.O.C.-in-C., in accordance with Circular A.G. b/80, dated 4/10/14, and R.P. 120 (D) M.M.L., held on the undermentioned:

No 7198 Private Jack Miller, 1st York and Lancaster Regiment.

Information required by Confidential letter, No: 1st Army c/18, 4th Corps 1379 (a):
1. Private Miller has been with the Expeditionary Force since December 1914.
2. His general character is recorded as 'very good', but he does not bear a good character as a fighting man.
3. The Battalion is in an excellent state of discipline.
4. The Commanding Officer is of opinion that the crime was deliberately committed.
5. The General Officer Commanding, 20th Infantry Brigade, does not recommend that the extreme penalty should be inflicted on account of the excellent state of discipline in the Battalion and the fact that this is about the only case of desertion that has occurred in it.

Handwritten comments follow:

The case presents no extenuating circumstances and I recommend that the sentence be carried out, not because it is necessary to make an example but because there is no excuse for the man.

Rawlinson, Lieut.-General, Commanding 4th Corps

In this case, the Btn was in excellent state of discipline. Prisoner's character has been recorded as 'very good' but he does not bear a good character as a fighting man.
L. Mercer Major-General Coms 7 Div.

Although the prisoner's character has been recorded as 'very good' he does not bear a good character as a fighting man. I can therefore see no reason why the sentence should not be carried out.
Brig.-Gen. Harold Weatherall

I concur in the opinions expressed and also note that the prisoner does not bear a good character as a fighting man.
J. French, Gen.

The trial papers must now have been returned to the front because the lined notepad paper is back, and the handwriting is the same as one of the earlier samples.

The G.O.C. directs that the man be informed of the sentence by an officer during tomorrow afternoon. A chaplain of Pte Miller's denomination and a Medical Officer will be present.

The sentence will be promulgated on parade tomorrow with the hour of execution, which will take place early on 15th July. The APM has been instructed to make the necessary arrangements with you or an Officer of your staff.

Finally, attached at the end, is a scrap of lined paper evidently torn from a pocket notebook. It says only:

I hereby certify that this man died by shooting at 7.05 a.m. on 15.7 and that death was practically instantaneous.

F. S. Mason, M.O. (York and Lancs)

I lingered on one of his two last words, my finger repeatedly rubbing it: 'practically'. If it hadn't been for Dr Mason's diary, how easily I might have passed over what it meant.

I closed up the file, left it at my reserved seat, went down to the café to buy a coffee that I didn't want. But I couldn't sit down, so I went out through the great round atrium and began to pace the gardens, clasping the hot paper cup in both hands as if it were a chalice. In the artificial pond a single coot was scudding back and forth, an outcast in this the breeding season.

It's been so many years since I struggled through the tiny print of the *King's Regulations* and the *Manual of Military Law* that I shall have to go back to them to bone up. But I think I remember certain provisions well enough. Something wasn't right about this trial – and therefore quite possibly about others as well. Where was the 'Judge Advocate' that I thought the law required? And where the 'prisoner's friend' the *Manual of Military Law* guaranteed? Jack Miller would have had to ask for one, but may not have known he could – or didn't know how or whom to choose – if choice there were. Perhaps, though, the 'friend' was Captain Taylor, and his three-line statement that Private Miller's character was 'very good' and that he had 'been in continuous service since December 1914' was the entire expression of that friendship. My grandfather's only defence was therefore the stuttering and deferential plea he had written himself.

He had said in this statement that he had felt queer, but there is no mention of any doctor examining him, nor was he asked any questions about what he meant by 'feeling queer', though the MO, Dr Mason, gave him an Aspro! And then, there was that oddly chosen word – 'refuses'. The accused 'refuses' to cross-examine the witness. How would that have been read by the GOC back at HQ? Refuses. The connotations imply obduracy, all opportunities given but turned down. Even 'declines' would have grated, but Jack Miller had already said he didn't think he could speak in front of a court, so how was he to find the courage and resources to start cross-examining his superiors? Especially as, since the beginning of that year – I did remember that much – an order had been issued from High Command that henceforth a soldier was to be considered guilty until sufficient evidence could be provided to prove his innocence. But what could have proved his innocence? Only, in this case, if the military policeman he said he had spoken to had turned up to corroborate his story. Otherwise, it all stood against him. He was not where he was supposed to be, and, by law, being absent equated desertion.

Did they try to understand how it might feel to be Private Jack Miller in that position at that moment? Not very likely; after all, that wasn't what they were there to do. And why should they, with their responsibilities, in a field of battle, when keeping the army together, imposing discipline for the sake of consistency was more important than the shaking knees of a single private? Everybody's knees were shaking. Everybody was frightened. That's what courage is about – continuing in the face of fear.

In the end, though, it would have been irrelevant. He was going to be sentenced and executed anyway, not because they wanted to make an example of him – and let's leave aside the question of whether that worked – since the discipline of his battalion had been described as excellent. No, what was bound to sink him was the conclusion that he simply wasn't soldierly enough.

What you want in a war are solid soldiers, not just anyone in a uniform, but proper soldiers, good fighting men, or at the very least men who show some potential. Jack Miller, according to the senior officers, didn't have the character of a fighting man. He was irredeemable, no great loss to the regiment, and in his behaviour, on that occasion at least, a danger to his company. In the thinking of the times, dispensing with him was the simplest and only logical thing to do, and I, as a professional, was supposed to be able to understand that. I was also supposed to understand how differently they did things then; to be aware of the pitfalls of anachronism, of using the mores of one era to castigate the failings of an earlier one when shell-shock wasn't yet understood, and the capital punishment that we have long since jettisoned went unquestioned.

Yet what I could not help seeing, when for a moment I leaned on the railing by the forlorn coot's pond and closed my eyes, was

Private Miller's company standing to attention – all present and correct bar one – while the sergeant read out the name of the missing man, the charge against him, and the sentence. What did they really think? There but for the grace of God? Or were they angered that one of theirs had brought shame on the entire unit? Did they each feel individually disgraced as a result, or determined not to do as he had done, but only now because of the sentence? Did they think that Jack Miller's absence had left a gap in the ranks that had put them all at risk, while they – suffering as much as he had – had stayed at their posts? And was their resolve stiffened as a result? I had no idea. I was not there. And I have never been a soldier, despite defence having been 'my subject' all these many years. Even Roy, with his two-year call-up, is better placed than I am.

At the same time, I thought, I am my grandfather's granddaughter and as that granddaughter I reach back across the eighty-plus years to that . . . child, we would now feel, and want to comfort him, protect him; warn him actually – although I wouldn't know how to do any of those things, except possibly the warning. And I feel an urge to redress what looks like injustice.

I've known about the campaign that's been trying to persuade the government to pardon all the servicemen who were executed in the First World War. I was aware of it when it began in 1992 – but didn't pay it much attention, partly because in that year Sarajevo had come under siege and I was head down in an assessment of the capacity of the Yugoslav army to wreak havoc on its breakaway regions. I wasn't much bothered by national news and only briefly registered the frustration of the campaigners as one British minister after another turned them down – on my military historian's grounds.

But there's another problem with the campaign, I thought. If the executed servicemen are to be pardoned, will the courts look at each case, one by one? And what will they do if one file is complete, another isn't and a third missing altogether? How will they come to a judgement after all this time, when there are no witnesses left alive, none of those presiding officers of eighty years ago available to swear the oath and take the stand?

Is my grandfather's file complete? Scrappy as it is, thin as it is, it looks like it to me – in the sense that none of its papers seem to have been lost. In which case the only approach a judicial review could take would be on the grounds that the Court Martial might not have been following the rules of procedure. But even if that were found to be so, and he was procured a posthumous pardon on a technicality, it still wouldn't prove him innocent – because they couldn't find the military policeman . . . although not being able to find the military policeman doesn't mean there was no such man; it simply means they couldn't locate him – or didn't look too hard.

But all this was related to the conviction, not the sentence. And I distinctly remember the law says that the night before his execution a soldier – presumably even one whose character was not that of a fighting man – was supposed to have had the right to petition the King for clemency, and he didn't. In a flicker of triumph I thumped my cup of cold coffee on the railing of the pond.

Then thought again. How do I know he didn't petition the King? Perhaps there wasn't time between the sentence and the execution . . . aha! So he was executed more quickly than the rules allowed. Or he may not have known he had the right because he wasn't told; or he knew and did plead for clemency – but was turned down. Or he knew and didn't exercise his right because . . . a lad like he was, without schooling, from a family like ours? The law wasn't there for the likes of him, our Margaret. It was all down to class. That's what Father always said.

That's what Father always said . . . her constant turn of phrase. Not 'my father', but 'Father'. I hadn't thought of that before. Father, always Father. That word: it was a name to Aunty Pam, not the designation of a relationship, because much as she respected and probably loved Ken Hoskins, and conceivably couldn't remember Jack Miller, she went on making the distinction – if only to herself. But it was Ken Hoskins who brought her up and instilled into her the beliefs she tried so hard to pass onto us. If ten working-class men were coerced into pumping bullets into one of their kind on the order of the officer class in a war the imperialists were waging for their own ends, there was only one way you could see it. That single outrage informed the rest of his life, and hers, and, supposedly, ours thereafter.

But actually I realised that in the papers I had read there

217

was no mention of any firing squad at all: 'the sentence will be promulgated and carried out'; 'the execution, which will take place . . .', 'to suffer death by being shot'; 'died by shooting'. The guns that killed Private Miller might just as well have been firing themselves, without any human agency: no physical fingers on triggers, no tear-blurred eyes trying to focus down the sights at their disgraced comrade, no young men to fall out afterwards and vomit into a ditch. The individuals who made up the execution squads hadn't so much been expunged from the record – they had been *worded* out of it by abstraction and the passive voice.

And Nelson Barkworth thought attention to language didn't matter!

I poured my untouched coffee down a drain, scrunched the cup in my fist and threw it away. So the Ministry of Defence had capitulated under pressure and allowed the files of the 'shot at dawn' to be opened ahead of time; the pardons campaign was the result, and I was glad – even if the historian in me remained queasy about its terms of reference. But if at some future date my grandfather was to be seen as another hapless victim of that war, then what about Granddad?

When I was a student I had tried to find out the names of the men press-ganged into the firing squads, but, just as the papers of the Courts Martial were closed, so this too was classified information – if indeed it was ever recorded, and as far as I can tell it is so still. Which makes me think that even at the time the authorities must have recognised, just as they do now, it was such a terrible thing to make someone do, to have to live with afterwards, those individuals had to be protected. You can't go around 'outing' the members of firing squads, and which of them later was going to put his hand up and say, 'Hey, it was me. I was one of the people who did that'?

I went back upstairs to the reading room and photocopied my grandfather's file for Roy. Prepared to leave but then thought, perhaps I should just double-check. *Was* there in fact only one Private Jack Miller shot at dawn?

Yes, there was.

Then was he also the only man in his battalion to be executed?

Yes, he was.

There was a final question left to ask, but I did so with a terrible reluctance. I went hunting for Private Ken Hoskins. And yes, he too was in the 1st York and Lancasters, and the only man of that name in the regiment. So, although I cannot know for certain, I have very strong reasons to suspect that the man we knew and loved so very much, the man we were brought up to believe was our grandfather, had arguably shot the man who really was.

Now I had to go home and tell Roy.

Part 6

1945

Ken Hoskins

My time is running out and I can't stop it. It's my own stupid fault and now I can't stop it. You're with somebody and you think, I'll not say a word. I'll keep my trap shut. I can do that, you say. But things come round, things happen to a man, and you say what you shouldn't – and then you pay the price.

It were Mary Louisa, Harry Pollitt's mother, brought us together. She'd had Edie under her wing at Mason's mill in Droylsden a good ten years, weavers both of them, working the same shifts but Mary Louisa leading them. She were like a mother to Edie, who'd lost hers when she was still a mite, and they lived, Edie and her father, not four doors down from the Pollitts. So Mary Louisa watched her grow and had her in the house some nights if her father had to be working and didn't like to leave a little girl on her own. When the Pollitts left Droylsden and moved to Openshaw it were Mary Louisa suggested they move across too. I've heard some say Mary Louisa had it in mind that Edie might make a good wife for Harry – there weren't two years of age between them – but good friends don't always make a marriage, do they, and they weren't interested, Harry and Edie, neither the one nor the other. Maybe they knew one another too well, who's to say, and people need a bit of mystery at the start.

When they sent me home to Lancashire, from France, not long before the war's end because of my lungs, I had it in mind to ask about Jack Miller's widow. I were doing it for all of us on that detail, as we'd agreed. He weren't one of my close pals, but one or two who'd known him well enough said he had a wife and a kid, with another on the way. So we made a pact the day after the firing squad: whoever got home first would try and find out how she was doing. We had her on our conscience, no matter it were an order. The idea was we'd get together, once the war were over – though we didn't know it ever would be – and if need be we'd have a whip-round and get the lass some money. We didn't know what else we could do, well you don't, do you, but we couldn't just leave it as if nothing had happened.

The day after that day, they gave us all two weeks' leave. It were the worst thing they could've done. We couldn't stand the sight of each other, not any of us, and we had nowhere to go and nothing to do but be brooding on it, thinking over what we'd done. What they'd made us do, but we'd done it all the same. I don't know about the others but I know about me. I were crying my eyes out all the way through so I couldn't have shot straight even if I'd wanted to. It were anger at them, at myself – at the whole bloody business. I dropped my rifle as soon as I'd fired it, threw it down is the truth – and that's a capital crime too, they say – but the sergeant, he pretended he hadn't seen.

I didn't shoot straight, and what I hear is no more did the others, so in the end we didn't kill Jack Miller. We mutilated him, and left him jerking and twitching on the ground until the CO stepped up and finished him off. It would have been bad enough if we'd fired true, but we didn't.

One of the other lads, he went back after the APM had covered the body over, and put wild flowers on the grave. But others said later they'd heard how the Brigadier had come by and kicked them all off. We were told it were a disgrace to the Battalion and to the Regiment, and that was right. It were. But not the way they meant. Because it made me remember the beginning, when we'd only arrived a week before in France and hadn't even seen a trench yet. They'd had us all stood on parade and they told us that now we were on a war footing, if any one of us was to desert, or leave the trenches without permission, or join a mutiny, or sleep on sentry duty or show any cowardice, we'd get a Court Martial and could be sentenced to death. And then they read out the names of twenty lads who'd had the sentence not long since, and the sentence was duly carried out, they said. It were meant to scare us, and it did. But then we forgot it because there were more things than that to think about.

I were like everyone – a volunteer, one of Kitchener's Army and proud of it. We were all together, all joined up together. One day it was an ordinary day, and the next – up went those posters, and the Territorials were tramping up and down the High Street in their boots, military bands playing by the recruitment offices, and us lads all stood round listening. You couldn't resist a thing like that, so off we all went together, and signed up, whole groups of us all at the same time. We swore to fight for King and country, and meant it. It were how we felt. We didn't know about Austria or Germany and not much about the assassinated Archduke, but we knew about England and the empire, and that were enough.

It were going to be an adventure, and you could feel good about it if you were a young man, in a foreign place when you'd never set foot abroad before. We thought it were beautiful. Everything were green, the sun shining on the trees and fields, and the villages all quiet with the farmers and their cattle, and old ladies sat out on their chairs in the evenings making lace.

We'd been trained to be soldiers, they'd given us guns and it were the most exciting thing we'd ever done, any of us. At least I thought so, and I weren't alone. I'd never felt so alive. Exhilaration is what it was. It were like a game, a kid's game of risk: kill or be killed. Like gambling: if your number weren't on the bullet it wouldn't find you, but if the bullet had you marked there weren't a thing you could do about it. And if you had a good company, and we did, you got to be so close it were like no friendship you'd ever had could compare. Nothing could compare.

Of course, we did notice how smart the officers were, while the rest of us had uniforms that didn't fit. Odd that. Not one man had a uniform that fitted him. You'd have thought at least some would, but it were like they'd been made not to. And we did notice that the officers didn't have to carry their kit either, the way we did. But we thought that were simply the way it had to be. We were volunteers. No one had made us sign up the way they made them later, and we were proud to be volunteers for our country. We thought the same way top brass did: they were there to give the orders and we were there to obey. It's how it is with armies, and how it has to be. Slavish obedience I call it now, but I didn't then. I hadn't heard of slavish obedience then, and it took Mary Louisa to explain it to me, to explain about how it were always working men sent to fight a bosses' war, and die in it, and kill other working men who'd been sent without choosing it. Or having the education to know about choosing it.

We didn't know we were in a 'world' war then, and we didn't know there was going to be two of them. All we did know, when we were on the front line, was our bit of trench, a hundred yards of it up and down, and every yard between us and the bloody

Germans on the other side of No Man's Land. We knew every bit of root sticking out of the wall, every place where that wall were falling in, where there were a hole in the duckboards, how far it were to the nearest dugout where you might try and get a bit of kip, which way the entrance into it faced – we could've drawn it down to the last inch with our eyes closed. But what they call the bigger picture, that weren't none of our business and it weren't all a bad thing either. Nobody told you what was going on, so you just went on from day to day till something happened. If you didn't know there were going to be a bloody great battle any minute you couldn't get yourself windy about it. If they said to go over the top, it were over the top. The only thing that mattered were if the officer in charge was a man worth following.

But who was to know, when we took the King's bloody shilling, that we'd do as much hating as we did. We hated the bastard Jerry when any of the lads in the company was hit by snipers; we hated them for the coal-boxes and whizz-bangs they lobbed over us; we hated them when we were up to the waist in water and mud; we hated them because we didn't have enough to eat and what we had were rotten anyway; we hated them for the lice in our clothes that we had to burn out with candles; we hated them for the boredom, and then the terror when we were waiting and not knowing what to expect and when; we hated them for the tunnels they dug under us set with mines, like the ones we dug under them, and you'd watch the earth bulging and rising like a loaf in the oven before it blew, and if you didn't get away you'd be blown right up with it or killed where you stood, buried by the falling clods; we hated the bastard Jerry because our officers were killed at our feet and most of our pals, but we never saw the generals except once or twice on their horses. We hated the Germans, hated their bloody guts because it were going on, year in year out, no matter what anybody did. At first we kept our hating to the mornings and the evenings, but later we hated all day long. It took some of us a long time to work out we were hating the wrong bloody people.

But *fighting*. Fighting were different. You felt better when you were fighting. It were the thing we'd come to do and it kept us, or it kept me going. It weren't until Jack Miller that I understood. Fighting isn't for everybody, but a man can't know that until he's there. When you hear the bands playing and the mood for war has took the whole country, how's a man to know if he's a fighter or he isn't? You can have a scrap outside the pub, you can be quick on your feet and good with your fists, but it don't tell you a thing about how you'll be in all that *noise*; it don't tell you if your nerves will stand up to it or won't. When you imagine being a soldier you think of marching and you think of firing your rifle, but not the shells, not the noise that goes on and on and never stops. I remember a day when it were that much, that deep, like it were coming from underneath as well from up top, rattling the ground like a giant had picked it up and were shaking it easy as a tin of peas, so that I forgot which way I were facing and found myself wandered off without an idea of where I was or what I were doing there. God knows where I'd have ended if I hadn't run into a pal – who might have noticed something were wrong or he might not, but he had me by the arm and took me back.

That night the lads were all round me and got me drinking till I couldn't hardly stand, so that next day I were all right again, and forgot about it until it came to Jack Miller, up on a charge of leaving the trenches without permission. And I remember thinking, he's a teetotaller, isn't he? What man can get through this without a drink?

They'd told me he came from Openshaw, and it made me all the angrier. I hadn't known that when the sergeant called me into his firing squad, and I like to think I'd have said it weren't human to ask a man to kill another, not just from his own unit, but from his own home town too, in cold blood when he hadn't done a thing we hadn't all been near to doing. 'Course, if I'd known, and if I'd been brave enough at the time to say that and then refuse to be part of it, they'd have had me in chains and up there next to Jack Miller in five minutes, likely as not. But I didn't know, and anyway I'll say it now, I reckon I weren't brave enough. The ones that might have been, they're all dead and forgotten, even though they should be the ones talked of as the real heroes. Get posthumous medals – the lot of it. But I went when I were called out. I stood in the line with the others. I put my rifle to my shoulder. I put my finger on the trigger, and when they said, 'Fire!', I fired.

People know each other in a place like Openshaw but back then, with the war and news of it, there couldn't be any secrets at all. So it were easy enough to find Jack Miller's family. I only had to say the name and you could see the faces change. She must have thought, when she got the letter from the War Office, that she'd maybe be able to keep it to herself. Could she heck! It were all out and over the town in a day, the first morning she went to get her widow's pension money from Post Office and they said, top of the voice so all the gossips should be sure to hear it, 'We don't give money to the widows of cowards!' That's the way they did it back then, punish the family twice.

If it hadn't been for Mary Louisa, Edie says she doesn't know how she'd have got by at all. Our Pam were only three year old then, our Bill weren't yet quite born, and Edie with hardly a penny and none more allowed by order of the government. She were completely on her own, with her dad passed on before the war started, and her sisters all with husbands still at the front not speaking to her. Wouldn't even be seen with her, as if it would bring bad luck.

So I knew the address in Melba Street, and that's where I went. And stood outside, walking up and down all afternoon, but couldn't bring myself round to knocking on the door. I'd been so troubled by what I'd done – what all ten of us had done, I should say – and by finding out where Edie lived, that I hadn't thought out in my mind what I was to say to her when I *did* find her. But there in the road by number 48 it suddenly came to me, what do I do if she opens the door, face to face, with her kiddies at her skirt? How do I say what I've come all this way to tell her? So I took scared and I left that day. But along the road I passed a young woman, with a little 'un clinging onto her back and holding another by the hand, walking so slow you'd think she were asleep on her feet, and once she'd gone by I turned myself round and saw her going into number 48. And I thought, that lass has the loveliest face on her I ever did see, though she looks as tired as a soldier. But there were nothing behind the eyes. That's how it seemed to me on the first day.

I were back the next day and the next, early enough to watch them leave and later in the afternoon when they all come back, and then I started following them out, with a scarf round my face like a spy or a detective, to see where they went. I still didn't think what I'd say if she noticed and then stopped by me and asked what did I think I were doing, nor why, and I didn't ask myself that question either. It didn't seem to me, as maybe it should have, that it were a strange thing to be doing, tailing up and down the road after a young lassie with my face hidden like a common thief. All I knew was that I couldn't leave that place, like I were fixed to it by a chain, or a magnet.

It were the same every day, Edie taking her kids to a house down the road to leave them there while she went on to Buckley's Mill for her shift. And every day I saw her I tried to get a look into her eyes, but although they were open they were closed too, so I made myself a promise, one that I swore to myself with my hand on the Bible, like an oath in a courtroom. I swore that the day would come when because of me there would be a sparkle in those eyes again, just as there must have been some time in the past, before the war came and snuffed it out. But the day I made that promise – and every day following that I repeated it – took me one day further away from having the courage to tell her the truth, or even having the courage to speak to her at all. So that's why I say that if it hadn't been for Mary Louisa I still might be on patrol outside number 48.

It were raining cats and dogs and I'd taken up my usual position, waiting for Edie and her kids to come walking home, and a woman come up to me from nowhere, so it seemed, and tapped me on the shoulder, not gentle but with a finger like a bayonet. 'Young man,' she said. 'I've been watching you these past ten days, lurking outside our Edie's. You'd best step inside with me out of the rain and explain yourself.' It weren't unkind, the way she spoke, but it were meant to be obeyed. She said, 'You can have a cup of tea to help you once it's made.' Well, I wanted to get out of the rain, which were like France all over again, and this woman didn't look the type to let a man escape, so I followed her into her house. And she took off her coat and shook it out and I did the same, and then stood there while she put the kettle on the range, and all the while it took for the damned thing to come to the boil she didn't say a word, so neither did I. It were only once she had the cups filled, had given me mine and sat herself on one side of the range and said for me to sit the other, that she took her first sip, put her cup down and said, 'Well? What's your story? Where do you know our Edie from? And why aren't you at your job, wherever that is?'

She didn't say, 'Why aren't you at the front?' as most would have, and I took to her for that. So I told her about having been in France and invalided out, and I told her that I didn't have a job but was looking for one, and no problem with that because it weren't a lie. But when it came to Edie, and me trying to make out I'd happened to be passing when I'd seen this lovely lassie with her kids and couldn't wait to see her again, I knew I were in trouble because for the first time I found I couldn't look this woman in the eye. But she just sat there with her cup of tea, drinking it, and said, 'Oh yes?' Then she reached for the pot and topped me up.

Then it were one question after another: how much attention had I paid to my books in school? How much did I think people should be responsible for each other, and what was my understanding of socialism? Well, at the time, not much, and I said so. She just shrugged her shoulders and put more water in the pot and cut me a slice of bread and put a touch of jam on it, and gave me a lecture, you could call it. Worth a week of night school, I can tell you. By the time she'd done, it weren't raining any more, and she got up and folded my coat over my arm. 'Stop by tomorrow, when you're passing,' she said (not *if* you're passing), 'and we can talk some more.' I hadn't done any of the talking, but I went back the next evening and the next. And later, what I came to think was that it were like the fairy tales where the young man wanting the hand of the princess has to prove himself to the king, or the witch or the wizard before he wins her, and Mary Louisa were all those in one.

But I still waited outside number 48 in the mornings, not where I'd be seen, but where I could see.

The days were getting shorter and soon enough it would be dark come five or six, but something suddenly made Mary Louisa decide I'd do. She said, out of the blue, 'Perhaps you'd like to meet our Edie now, would you? Properly, I mean, not stamping about in the road for all to gawp at, the way you have been.'

It were everything I wanted and I nearly ran away. I'd got

myself past Mary Louisa but it didn't mean I'd get a welcome from Edie. And even if I did, what was I to say to her? How much? I were back where I'd started.

Well, what I've come to think now is that while Mary Louisa was grilling me in the evenings, she were doing her bit for me, arguing my case is the way you could put it, with Edie while they were working. I came recommended, as people say, and by now everybody knows that she accepted me, even if it took over a year of trying. But by that time our Pam were almost seven, old enough to have a memory of her real father, and to have her own things to think about having a new one. Spitting image she was of him, of Jack, and as he got older little Bill were the same. You'd have sworn he were Jack Miller come to life all over again as a child. I don't know what it is makes some people take after their mothers and some after their fathers and some not seem to be from the same stock as either – and maybe that's because there's been some hanky-panky – but with those two you weren't in any doubt. It worried me, did that, when they'd be old enough to pick up on what people were bound to say. And still I hadn't come clean. Hours and hours I'd talked to Mary Louisa, and told her all about the firing squad, but never who we'd killed, and I don't know what she said to Edie, how she prepared her for the half she knew, but I think she made it all sound political and historical, and of course it was. But that wasn't all it was.

It's still as clear as if it were this morning, the day Mary Louisa must have let some of the truth out, because Edie pulled herself back. Until that moment I'd get a smile when we met that always made me think of daisies. I know that sounds daft but I think daisies in a field of grass that hasn't been churned and trampled by boots and hooves, tanks and trucks are the most beautiful thing anywhere in the world. Then came that evening and I suppose Mary Louisa might have had a private talk with our Edie while they were on shift, and when we met it wasn't exactly that she turned away from me, but things had changed and when we got to Edie's there was something about the way she stopped on the doorstep that meant she didn't want me to come in. She stepped in, give Pam and Bill a little shove to hurry them along and the door closed, ever so quietly in my face as I were standing there.

I remember reminding myself over and over how gently she closed that door, not banged it, so perhaps I could take that as a good sign. But I didn't know whether to stay there and wait and hope she'd open up again, or go back to my room in the lodgings. I waited a while but then Mary Louisa came up the road and she called out to me and I went to her, and she said to be patient. She said, put yourself in her shoes. And that's what I did. I tried to imagine how it would be if I were a young woman who had loved her husband as I know Edie loved Jack, and he's killed the way Jack were, and another man comes courting, and a bit of time has passed and you think, well, this fellow's not so bad after all, I'll maybe give it a try.

But then you hear that while he were at war he were in a party that killed a man the way they killed your husband, you wouldn't want him touching you, would you? You wouldn't want to let him anywhere near you, or your kids, no matter that he could become a good friend to them and play games with them, and help you round the house and dig your bit of garden.

Putting myself in our Edie's shoes were a terrible thing to do because it made me realise she'd likely never have me. And why should she? I suppose when a soldier comes home to his wife and she knows he's fired on the other side and lobbed the odd minnie and maybe killed more people than he'll ever know he has, or tried to, she can accept that because it's what he were sent there to do. Unless she's one of the pacifists, she can maybe put that out of her mind. But if he lined up with his comrades and aimed his rifle at one of his own, a man like himself who spoke the same language and lived in the same sort of house and ate the same food for his tea, how can you take that? You'd be disgusted, I think, wouldn't you? Anyone would. But then, if your own husband had actually been killed in that way . . .

I were in despair – there's no other word for it that I know. I understood that I should have told her right off, from the start, all of it, even though that would have meant never having those days and weeks we did have. But Mary Louisa were right – even though even *she* still didn't know the full story. She said I could do something to atone for what I'd done. Funny thing, her using a religious word. She said I should become a socialist, like her and her Harry, join the ILP, and it would go some way to make up for being a part of that firing squad, never mind I didn't have the choice. And she said it would take my mind off our Edie, so I joined Harry Pollitt and the others at the blockade of the docks to stop shipments to Poland. It were the best thing Mary Louisa could have suggested and I found comradeship there nearly as good as we'd had at the front. And the same year, joining the Party when it started up, were like finding a new family, that kept growing and growing, even if I never was sure I believed in everything they said.

Harry were just like his mother: one of the world's great listeners when there's trouble. He said he hadn't known so much about the executions until I told him, and he kept asking more. I know that what I told him made an impression because he tried to have executions for deserters stopped in the Brigades in Spain – but it seems that top brass is top brass wherever you are.

When he were home, visiting Mary Louisa – he were always that close to her, he came up from London whenever he could – he stopped by Edie's and once the kids were safely asleep in their beds he talked to her for hours, like brother to sister. Hours, she said. He helped her understand better than ever I could what it were like for us poor sods in the firing squads who never asked to be in them. But he couldn't help her with all the information, because he didn't have it himself. Nobody but me knew I'd put a bullet somewhere in Jack Miller's body, and what I wouldn't give to be able to take it out again.

I owe it to Harry that he talked our Edie round, but I can't get out of my head one thing. Did she finally agree to stick with me because she didn't have the choice? With two kids, and a generation of young men missing, did she *have* to stick with me for fear there wouldn't be another man coming by and because she couldn't afford not to? Is that maybe even one of the things Mary Louisa said to her? Pointed out to her?

But it's the way a man's mind goes, I believe: when there's awkward thoughts that get in the way of the better ones, you put the awkward ones away. And there were real happiness in Edie's face the day she said she'd marry me, there were that light in her eyes I'd sworn to put back there, and she were the one, after a time, said it would be the best thing all round if our Pam and Bill took my name. It could have been that being called

Hoskins instead of Miller were a safer bet, but I don't think so. I think it were that Edie had come to the notion we were a true family, the four of us, and it doesn't do for families to go about with different names. So we did all the business with the official papers, but the most important thing was knowing that I were a father to her kiddies, a good one, I hope, and that that's how they took it. And I'd say in time people round about pretty well forgot it had ever been any different – or if they did remember they kept their mouths shut, which'll do as well as if they'd forgot.

The years went by, we worked, Edie and me, for our wage but for the Party too. And then came the day Harry took our Pam down to London with him to Headquarters – and her only seventeen. He knew what he were doing right enough because she were always a hard worker, and organised. One of those a man knows he can rely on. So it were an honour but a loss as well. We didn't know whether to celebrate or shed a tear, and I reckon in the end it were a bit of both. You might say the same when it came to our Bill getting wed – except there was no honour. Edie were troubled by it, by the look she said she sometimes saw in our Annie's lovely face. There's something not right with that lass, I'm sure, she said, more than once. She's like an egg with its shell too thin. But I had it in my head, foolish man that I am, that what really got at her were losing her son to another woman. Besides, I could see how much in love our Bill was. I recognised it. But now I ask myself how it might have all turned out if I'd seen what Edie saw, if I'd gone along with her when she tried to persuade our Bill to wait a while. Would things have been different if he had, and then maybe married another lass? If only, if only. It seems to me most of us can pass half a lifetime saying that, and the other half saying, what if? But it's what was, and what is, we have to live with.

When the second war got itself going and all the bombing in London, and we had the letter from our Bill about needing to evacuate Roy and Margaret, the only thing Edie said was, 'Why's it our Bill writing to us about Pam bringing them up on the train? It should be Annie writing to *her* people, taking the kiddies to her own mother and father to safety, shouldn't it?' She didn't say one word more than that because she didn't need to – it were all in there, everything she thought. And we were looking forward to having children in the house again.

But when they came! Oh, when they came. Baby Margaret went straight into Edie's arms, not able to walk yet, and got herself a real mothering. But that Roy. His thin little face, his hair and the way it stood up in a brush . . . I know I've said our Pam and Bill were both the image of Jack, which were bad enough when I first laid eyes on 'em. But somehow this time round it were worse. It felt deliberate, a reminder, like a message: did you think you'd get away from this, did you? Well, did you? When I looked at that little lad I wished we hadn't agreed to them coming, but of course there were no going back. And then, as it happened, he took to me, so sudden and so strong, and I were touched.

He'd be waiting for me when I came home from work and we'd go out for a stroll, the two of us, his hand went into mine before we were out the door, and if there were still enough light we'd go up and look down over the houses and just sit there side by side, like we'd been together for years. In the summer the grass were all daisies and buttercups, and we made daisy chains for the lasses. That were when it were hardest. The closer I felt to him the more he made me think of Jack Miller, and I came to love that lad so very much – more than I ever even tried to explain to Edie. I couldn't have explained if had tried, I think, because I couldn't find the words for it myself. It were just an overwhelming thing.

Then he turned five and started at the school where all the young lads were running round pretending to be soldiers, and then carrying on with their games out on the street in the evenings, and all you read about in the papers and listened to on the wireless were about war. Margaret were walking – talking now too, and going by the name of Mig which she gave herself when Margaret was too much for a baby's tongue. So she'd be out there on the street toddling round after the lads, and it brought tears to my eyes to see how careful our Roy were that she was never left out, never left behind. And I thought, though I tried not to think it, maybe if a lad takes so closely after his grandfather in the way he looks, maybe he takes after him in the way he is as well. I never knew Jack Miller properly, just the odd word, the odd nod – the way it goes. But I began to think I were getting to know him now, and every day the pain and the guilt were harder to bear. I tried to run from it. I started putting off coming home but stopping by the pub instead, trying to making out it were Party work.

The old nightmares had come back as if it had all been the week before, so I had the idea that if I could only drink enough, I'd get to fall into my bed and not see a thing all night. But it didn't work. I saw everything I'd seen near on thirty years before, only this time it were our Roy stood tied to the execution post, blindfold, but the blindfold fell away and he were looking at me, staring at me, puzzled. What are you doing, Granddad, he kept asking. And I'd be saying, I don't know, lad. I don't know, but I have to because it's orders. Do you see that? I've had my orders. But he just kept on. What are you doing, Granddad?

I'd wake sweating and crying, Edie shaking me to hush me because of the kiddies, but up on her elbow like she'd been awake a good while, watching and listening, and coming to her own conclusions. She's no fool, and although to me she's still the lass I courted twenty-five years ago, life's been hard on her, and after Mary Louisa died it seemed to me in some part of her Edie took over where she left off.

I remember the day exactly because it were 1943, February 3rd, when they announced the Germans had surrendered to the Red Army in Stalingrad and we were meant to be celebrating. It were a celebration twice over, one for the Allies and an extra one for us in the Party, for the USSR, but all I could think of were bullets and blood. And just the one falling body. I must have had such a long face on me, out of place among all the others, that Edie took me home and asked me straight out what she must have been waiting to ask for months.

Just at that moment I felt I couldn't bear to be alone with the full truth of it any more. I couldn't bear the truth of it but most of all I couldn't bear the pretending, the lying to my wife. So the only way to deal with it was to come clean and tell her it all. I were stupid enough to think our marriage could take it, and I were wrong. The night I confessed, she got up out of our bed without a word, put on her coat and went down to the front room and slept on the settee. In the morning she told me that, once it were safe enough for our Roy and Mig to be back with their parents in London, she would leave me – if I didn't have the decency to leave her first. Two year ago she said it. Two years of warning and two of dread. And this morning was the day our Pam came back up and took the kiddies away.

Roy were screaming, Granddad, Granddad. Mig were screaming too, for her Nana, but most because she were upset by Roy. Then the train went, and it were just Edie and me on the platform. Tomorrow it'll be just me. I could have maybe got through this with Edie, but without her I'm nothing. If only I'd kept my big trap shut and kept the truth to myself she need never have found out, because all it's done is break her heart a second time. There never was the need for so much truth and I'd have done better to put that bullet into my own chest at the time and get it over with then. When she shows me the door I'll not be able to bear it.

Acknowledgements

Thanks to Linden Stafford, as always, for her stringent editorial judgement. To Dave Edmonds, John Fielding, Rowena Garrod, Firdaus Kanga, David Malcolm, John Thorogood, Hana Rohan and Anne Theroux, who all read the manuscript at certain stages of its development, though never the one you have before you. Thanks also to Julian Putkowski, who patiently answered my pestering emails.

I am grateful for the extraordinary helpfulness of the staff at the National Archives and the Imperial War Museum, as well as the Camden Local Studies and Archive Centre.

If anyone wants to read further, I found the following books particularly useful:

On the First World War

Arthur, Max: *Forgotten Voices of the Great War* (Ebury, 2002)
Babington, Anthony: *For the Sake of Example* (Leo Cooper, 1983)
Brown, Malcolm: *Imperial War Museum Book of 1918*
Coppard, George: *With a Machine Gun to Cambrai* (HMSO, 1969)
Ferguson, Niall: *The Pity of War* (Allen Lane, 1998)
Holmes, Richard: *War of Words: The British Army and the Western Front* (CRF Prize Lecture, Edinburgh 2003)
Hughes-Wilson, John, and Corns, Cathryn: *Blindfold and Alone: British Military Executions* (Weidenfeld and Nicholson, 2001)
Putkowski, Julian, and Sykes, Julian: *Shot at Dawn* (Wharncliffe, 1989)
The Manual of Military Law 1914
The King's Regulations 1914

On the Communist Party of Great Britain

Beckett, Francis: *Enemy Within: The Rise and Fall of the British Communist Party* (John Murray, 1995)

Dutt, R. P: *Why This War?* (Communist Party Pamphlet, 1939)

Fryer, Peter: *Hungarian Tragedy* (Dobson Books, 1956)

Morgan, Kevin: *Harry Pollitt* (Manchester University Press, 1993)

Pollitt, Harry: *How to Win the War* (Communist Party Pamphlet, 1939)

Pollitt, Harry: *Serving My Time* (Lawrence and Wishart, 1940)

General period interest

Barnham, M., and Hillier, B.: *Tonic to the Nation, Festival of Britain 1951* (Thames and Hudson, 1976)

Broad, Roger: *Conscription in Britain* (Routledge, 2006)

Royle, Trevor: *The Best Years of their Lives* (John Murray, 1997)

Sissons, Michael, and French, Philip: *The Age of Austerity* (Hodder and Stoughton, 1963)

Zweig, F.: *Labour, Life and Poverty* (E.P. Publishing, 1948)

In 2006 the Pardons Campaign achieved a success of sorts: pardons were finally granted to all those servicemen who had been shot at dawn, so long as they had not been convicted of murder.

Lightning Source UK Ltd.
Milton Keynes UK
27 July 2010
157454UK00001B/44/P